BRICKING IT

OTHER TITLES BY NICK SPALDING

BRICKING IT
Nick Spalding

LAKE UNION
PUBLISHING

Published by Lake Union, Seattle

www.apub.com

Amazon, the Amazon logo, and Lake Union are trademarks of Amazon.com, Inc., or its affiliates.

ISBN-13: 9781503948426
ISBN-10: 1503948420

Cover design by Lisa Horton

To anyone who has ever tried to renovate a house.

You have my deepest sympathies.

CONTENTS

HAYLEY
April
£0.00 Spent

'What an absolute shit pile.'

I turn and give my brother a tight-lipped smile. 'It's not *that* bad, Danny.'

'Not that bad?' he replies in dismay. 'Half the bloody roof is gone!'

'It's certainly seen better days, I can't argue with you there.'

'When exactly were they? Before or after someone set fire to it?'

I peer over the vast thicket of overgrown brambles, and look at the large soot marks scorched across the left-hand corner of the house. 'I don't think the damage is too bad, actually.'

Danny gives me a look.

'I'm just trying to stay positive,' I tell him, through only slightly gritted teeth. 'This was Grandma's last gift to us.'

'Gift?' he replies incredulously.

'Yes. It was very generous of her to leave this place to me and you.'

'Really?' Danny rolls his eyes, crosses his arms and gently pushes the garden gate open with his foot. The gate, its hinges rusted completely through, falls over onto the cracked garden path with a loud clatter. Birds in the trees and bushes around us take flight, startled by such a loud noise in such a quiet place.

'Very generous of her,' he says drily. 'And what exactly did she leave Mum and Dad again?'

'£75,000. All her life savings,' I reply, as quietly as I can, so it doesn't sound so bad.

'And just remind me again, sister dearest. What are they doing with all that lovely cash?'

'You know what they're doing with it, Dan.'

'No, no. Come on. Say it again.' He jabs a finger at the derelict house in front of us. 'I want that thing to hear.'

'You're mental.'

Danny stares at me. He's not going to let this one go. 'They're going on a year-long cruise around the world.' I sigh.

Danny nods angrily. 'Yes, indeed. That's what our loving parents are doing with their part of Grandma's inheritance.' He waves a hand at the crumbling house. 'While we get to stare at this crap magnet and decide what the hell to do with it.'

'It could be very nice with some work,' I counter.

'Would said work involve several sticks of dynamite?'

'Oh, give it a rest. It's not that bad. Just try to see the potential.'

Danny opens his mouth to argue, but closes it again, noticing that my eyes have gone flinty and narrow. Instead of making yet another smart-arse comment he returns his gaze to the house. 'What did you say it was again?' he asks me, trying to sound more upbeat.

'A Victorian farmhouse. Built around 1890.'

'Right.' Danny stands and stares at the place a little longer. 'I like the windows.'

'They are nice.'

'And the place is quite . . . symmetrical I guess. That's good.'

'It is. Double-fronted, I think it's known as.'

'The walls haven't fallen in yet.'

'No, that's very true.'

'Chimney stacks are quite good as well. One on each end.'

'They are.'

A few moments of silence follow.

'I'm sure the front door was nice once. You know, when it wasn't quite so rotten.'

'You're reaching now.'

Danny throws his hands up. 'Oh, give me a break! I'm trying my hardest here.'

'Sorry.'

He rubs his face with both hands. 'And nobody knew Grandma owned this place?'

'Nope.'

'Not even Mum?'

'Nope.'

'Why the hell would she keep it quiet all these years?'

'I have no idea, Danny.'

'And why the hell would she leave it to us in her will?'

'I have no idea about that either, Danny.'

'And what is that brown pile in the middle of the doorstep?'

'Ah, I think I can help you there. That, Danny, is a big pile of cow shit.'

'I thought so.' He rubs his face again and groans. 'What a shit-hole.' Without saying more, Danny walks over the fallen garden gate, and starts to make his way down the cracked path, pushing the brambles out of the way as he does so.

I let him go.

Sometimes it's best to not talk to my brother when he's in one of these moods. He has a habit of dragging you down with him.

Instead, I look back up at the house and try to picture it in all its former glory.

This is a very hard thing to do, since that former glory was a good fifty years ago – if not far further back, considering the house's age. Since then, the place has been gently rotting into the picturesque Hampshire countryside, and is now what you would charitably describe as a 'fixer-upper'.

Victorian farmhouses are quite impressive when they're in decent condition, but the only thing impressive about this particular example is the fact it hasn't caved in completely after several decades of neglect.

'What the hell were you thinking, Grandma?' I say under my breath, as I follow Danny up the garden path towards the house.

We were both gobsmacked to be told that we'd inherited this place. My brother and I knew very little of Grandma's past before she married Granddad in the sixties, and moved into the vicarage with him. This must have been the house she left behind when she did. But how did she come to own it in the first place? And why did she keep it all these years without telling anyone?

These questions have been buzzing round my head for weeks. They will probably continue to do so, as I have no real way of getting any answers without the benefit of a medium or a Ouija board.

I join Danny, standing in front of the doorstep, looking down at the cowpat.

'It's still steaming,' he remarks.

I look around for the cow that left it, but none is immediately apparent.

Danny bites a fingernail. 'You know, I can't help but feel that this is a sign.'

'Shall we go inside?' I say, as I pinch two fingers over my nose.

Danny peers through the large crack in what's left of the oak front door. 'I'm not sure I want to. There could be anything in there. Rats . . . spiders . . . the Grim Reaper.'

'Well, I'm not standing out here smelling that thing for any longer,' I tell him, and step over the cowpat, being very careful not to let it get anywhere near my new Nikes. As I pull the front-door key from my jeans pocket, I am forced to reflect that I probably haven't dressed sensibly for this expedition into the unknown reaches of my grandmother's secret, derelict farmhouse. Brand-new trainers and £60 jeans you picked up in town a couple of days before are not ideal attire when entering a house thick with the detritus of fifty years' neglect. I should have taken a leaf out of Danny's book and worn ripped old jeans, battered motorcycle boots and a Call of Duty T-shirt. Mind you, this is what Danny wears *all of the time*, so I doubt he put much thought into it.

Nevertheless, into the dirty house I must go, so I'll just have to avoid brushing my crisp, white shirt up against anything as much as is humanly possible.

'If I hear any low, ominous laughter when you turn that key, I'll be back up that path and on the bike in a nanosecond,' Danny says, his eyes wide.

'Very funny,' I reply, trying not to wince too much as I turn the door key to the right. This does very little, other than dislodge some rust from the surface of both key and lock.

'Try the left,' Danny offers.

I do so, with no improvement.

'Wiggle it?'

'I am wiggling it.'

'Do it harder?'

'Shut up, Danny! I'm wiggling it as hard as I can!'

No matter what I do, the lock just will not budge. The whole mechanism feels like it's completely rusted shut.

'Let me have a go,' Danny says and pushes me gently out of the way. I let him take over, safe and secure in the knowledge that he won't have any more luck than I did.

Indeed, a couple of minutes go by that contain a great deal of swearing, but no real progress on the door opening. The smell from the cowpat is starting to get really bad, and I'm just about ready to give up and leave, when another thought occurs.

'Give it a kick, Dan,' I tell my brother.

'What?'

'Kick the door in.'

He looks horrified. 'I can't do that. That's breaking and entering.'

'It's our house, you goon!'

Danny looks nonplussed. 'Good point.'

'Well. Go on then. Give it a kicking.'

'Okay.' Danny steps back slightly – avoiding the cowpat by mere inches – and then lunges forward, giving the front door a solid kick with his thick black boot. This is easily the greatest trauma the door has suffered in years, so it immediately gives way with no resistance whatsoever. Danny shrieks in surprise and falls into the farmhouse, sending up a cloud of dust as he stumbles across the entrance hall, and nearly brains himself on the end of the large wooden bannister that runs up one side of an expansive staircase.

'Fuck me!' he shouts, as he veers off down the hallway towards the kitchen.

I take a deep breath and enter more carefully, fearing that any sudden movements may result in a severe case of tetanus. It is quite, quite disgusting. The floorboards beneath my feet are warped and rotten. The walls are covered in peeling wallpaper that gives off a deeply unpleasant aroma, and the ceiling is covered in spiderwebs full of dead or dying insects. There is some kind of unidentifiable brown substance smeared on the huge ornate cream lampshade above my head that doesn't bear thinking about. I'd still prefer to touch that than the thick black carpet of mould that runs along most of the skirting boards, though.

To my left is the dining room. At least I assume it's the dining room, given that there is a three-legged table leaning drunkenly against one wall. To my right is what could be a living room. There's certainly a fireplace in there. What horrors may lurk in that dark recess are anyone's guess.

Both rooms are bloody enormous, and continue the theme of peeling wallpaper, mouldy skirting boards and decades of old filth. Lovely.

On a more positive note, they also feature some rather ornate architraves and ceiling roses that once looked very grand, I'm sure.

I venture slowly down the hallway towards my brother, and what's left of the kitchen. As I do, I notice a doorway under the staircase and steps leading down into the darkness below, to what I can only assume is Stephen King's basement.

Suppressing a shudder, I enter the kitchen and walk over to where Danny is sat on a rickety chair, nursing his ankle.

'Are you alright?' I ask him.

'The bloody door gave way a lot quicker than I thought it would,' he replies darkly. 'I think I've sprained my ankle.'

'Can you walk?'

'Yeah. I'll be fine. No real damage done.' He looks around. 'Unlike this kitchen. It looks like somebody came through here with a machine gun.'

Danny is exaggerating, but only slightly. Cupboard doors hang off their hinges. The sink is full of holes, which is something of a pity as it means that the slow drip of rusty water seeping from the cold tap is going everywhere. Shattered pieces of tile are strewn across the floor. The cooker looks like it's managed to fuse itself into the floor, and the fridge is green.

I don't mean the fridge is the *colour* green, I just mean that the interior has *gone* green, for some horrible, horrible reason.

'The flies seem to be enjoying the place,' I point out, waving one hand in front of my face.

'At least somebody is.' Danny stands back up, testing his ankle. It seems to hold his weight okay. 'Shall we go upstairs? I haven't been grossed out quite enough yet.'

I nod and turn to leave the kitchen as quickly as my denim-clad legs will carry me.

At the bottom of the staircase, we pause.

'Do you think it's safe?' I ask Danny.

'I have no idea. Why don't you go first?'

'Why me?'

'Because I kicked the door in.'

I attempt to argue, but the sibling code dictates that I should suck it up and be the one to go up the staircase first. Chivalry simply does not exist when you're talking about the relationship between a brother and a sister. I know this. Danny knows this. I therefore take a deep breath and start my ascent, treading ever so lightly on every riser as I make my way to the first floor.

'Oh, come the fuck on, Hayley,' Danny remarks from behind me. 'If it was going to give out on you, it would have done it already.'

'Bollocks,' I respond. 'Every step is a new opportunity for me to fall screaming to my death.'

'You haven't put on *that* much weight recently. Get your arse up the stairs.' To underline his impatience with my slow progress, Danny pokes me in the ribs.

'Ow! You little shit!' I exclaim, and slap him hard on the shoulder. I do also increase my pace, however, given that he is still in close proximity to my ribcage and will no doubt give me a harder poke if I don't get a move on.

With a sigh of relief I reach the first-floor landing, and immediately wish I hadn't.

'It smells even worse up here,' I note, holding my nose.

Danny takes a deep breath. 'It's not that bad.'

I roll my eyes. 'I've been in your flat. I'm not surprised this place doesn't smell that bad to you.'

'Very funny. Which room do you want to catch a fatal disease in first?'

I look around the landing at the four closed doors leading off. I'm guessing three are the bedrooms, and the fourth is the bathroom. I think I'm going to need a bit of time to work up to the last room, given that it's the most likely to contain something nasty, so I elect for the nearest bedroom door and move towards it.

Danny can't help but draw a sharp intake of breath as I grasp the handle. 'That's really not helping, you know,' I tell him.

'Sorry, I've just watched one too many horror films over the years.'

'I know. I introduced you to them.'

Trying my hardest not to also draw in my breath – I've watched all those movies a few times myself – I twist the flaking door handle and push it open. It reveals . . . well, not much in particular, actually. There's a morbid part of my brain that finds this rather disappointing.

The bedroom is empty, save for a mustard-coloured carpet covered in unidentifiable stains, the same peeling wallpaper as is evident throughout the rest of the property, and yet another open fireplace, this one boarded up with a few hastily nailed-on planks of two-by-four. A large sash window dominates the front of the room, and here, unlike most of the windows downstairs, not one of the panes has been smashed.

'No murderous clowns then,' Danny remarks.

'Apparently not.'

'Big room again, though. They seemed to like their space back then.'

'Yeah. You could get two double beds in here easily.'

'I wonder if the other two are the same?'

And, by and large, they are. Each bedroom is large and very similar in terms of décor and disgusting mess. Estate agents would no doubt call them 'generous', but I'm not going to, given that the chances of finding a random pile of cash hidden in any of them is extremely small. I see nothing immediately terrifying in any of the three, though the floorboards do creak ominously in the one that sits in the front right-hand corner of the building. I try to tread as carefully as I possibly can, but Danny does the usual thing all men do when faced with a potentially hazardous floor surface – he jumps up and down on it several times to see whether it'll give way under his weight.

'Idiot,' I remark. 'If you go through that I'm not tying off any of your arteries, you know.'

So then we come to the final room on the first floor, and the one that a rather horrific smell is coming from – the bathroom.

'You can open this door,' I tell Danny. 'I've done all the others.'

Danny sniffs. 'That's entirely unfair you know. I would have cheerfully swapped door-opening tasks had I known that was the deal.'

'Three bedroom doors equals one bathroom door. It's a fact.'

'Is it really?'

'Yes. And I should know, I'm a teacher.'

'Yes, but you're very bad at your job, sis. Your pupils have all told me so.'

'I can well believe you've spoken to a bunch of eight-year-olds, given that you are on the same intellectual level. Open the chuffing door, you twat.'

This is a fine example of typical conversation between my brother and I, of a type that has been repeated ad nauseam over the years. These kinds of arguments are only possible between siblings.

If you tried to speak to anyone else in the same way, you'd probably get a punch in the mouth.

Danny doesn't continue the quarrel. He knows I've always been better at the clever put-downs than him. He pushes the bathroom door open and we both take in the sights beyond with more than a little revulsion. In fact, it's a wonder I don't upchuck all over the faded landing carpet.

'Well, that'd be where the smell is coming from then,' Danny says helpfully.

'Which one? The dead crow in the bathtub? Or the three decaying rat corpses on the floor?'

'Either/or. Take your pick.'

'Why the hell are there so many dead animals in here? They're not anywhere else in the house. Not that we've seen anyway.'

Danny pauses for a moment. 'I'm going to suggest a scenario here. It might seem a little far-fetched, but stick with me.'

'Go on,' I reply carefully.

Danny presses the fingers of both hands together under his chin. 'I believe a fight to the death has taken place here. Crow versus rat. From the looks of things, the crow has managed to vanquish his ratty opponents, but not without suffering terminal injuries himself. He has then tried to flap away, only to get as far as the bathtub before expiring. It truly was a hero's death.'

'Face down with your beak stuck in a plughole?'

'Exactly.'

'You're an idiot.'

'Very probably.'

I take a step back. 'At some point, I may have to go into that bathroom, but it will not be today, Danny. I guarantee you that.'

My brother nods. 'I agree. Let's just shut the door and not go back in until we're wearing breathing apparatus and plastic boiler suits.' Danny closes the door to the avian/rodent horror show and turns around.

'That's about it for upstairs, then,' I point out. 'Other than the bathroom, it's not too bad.'

Danny shakes his head. 'Haven't you forgotten something?'

'What do you mean?'

He slowly points upwards, a look of sheer terror crossing his face. I follow his finger up . . . and see the loft hatch above my head.

'No! No fucking way. I'm not going up there,' I state in a firm voice, folding my arms across my chest.

'Chicken.'

I flap my arms up and down a couple of times and make *buck buck* noises.

Danny stares up at the loft hatch for a moment. 'I'm going up there,' he tells me.

'Why?'

'Because there might be treasure.'

'Or a human corpse.'

Danny shrugs his shoulders. 'Either is fine by me.'

Men.

'How exactly do you plan on getting up there? I don't see a ladder lying around anywhere.'

'I can balance on the bannister and boost myself up.'

I give the wooden bannister a long, hard look. I can't see any immediate signs of woodworm, but am not taking that as an indication of its safety level. 'I don't think that's a very good idea,' I say, underestimating things just a tad.

Danny waves a hand. 'It'll be fine. Give me a shoulder.'

And with that he places one hand on my shoulder blade, boosts himself quickly up onto the bannister and leans across the landing, bracing himself with one hand as he pushes the loft hatch up with the other.

Danny pops his head into the open hatch. 'Dark up here,' he says. 'You don't say.'

'Hang on.' He produces his Zippo lighter from his front jeans pocket and lights it. 'Christ, it's big up here, too.'

'Any spiders?' I say with a catch in my voice. 'I can't stand the little buggers.'

'Loads. Webs everywhere – but there's not a lot else to see. Just some old wooden boxes full of shredded paper, a few bits of old cloth, a— *What the hell is that?*'

'What is it? What have you seen? Is it a *corpse?*'

'No corpses, just what looks like . . . well, I don't really know. It looks like some kind of harness from here.' Danny cranes his head a bit further into the loft. 'Yep. Must be for a horse or something. I think it's called a *tackle* . . . though I could be completely wrong. It's hanging up on one of the joists.'

I am incredulous. 'A horse's harness? You mean like the halter and reins? Why the hell would Grandma have that?'

'No idea. We are in the country. Maybe she owned one . . . I'm going to have a closer look.'

With that Danny puts his arms up through the hatch, sets himself and pushes off from the bannister and up into the loft in one swift movement.

For a few moments all I can hear is him clumping around. 'Can you see anything else?' I ask.

'Not much,' Danny replies, and I hear the clinking of metal as he picks up the harness. 'It's really odd. I don't see how a horse's head would fit over it. The leather is rotten through, and the metalwork is rusty. Must've been up here for ages. I wonder if— *AAAARRRGGHH!*'

There is a terrible cracking sound of rotten wood giving way, followed by a loud, high shriek.

'Danny!' I shout in dismay, and watch in absolute horror as my brother appears from above in the bedroom opposite where I'm standing, surrounded by a cloud of dust, plaster and wood.

DANNY

April

£0.00 spent

It takes a couple of seconds for me to realise that I'm not dead.

I see Hayley come running into the bedroom, where I'm now lying spread-eagled on the dirty yellow carpet.

I replay the last few moments of my life – and none of them are good. One minute I'm looking at something you'd sling over the nearest mare, the next I'm heading south at a rapid pace thanks to some rotted loft boards, with a load of debris flying around me.

Luckily for my continued existence, I don't fall through the ceiling instantly. The breaking ceiling plaster slows my progress. I just about have enough time to prepare myself for the shock of landing on the floor below, remembering to bend my legs on impact. This doesn't stop jarring pain from shooting up both my legs as I hit the bedroom floor. I'm saved a broken back when the carpet and floorboards give under my weight slightly, before springing back again. Thank Christ the wood isn't as rotten as in the loft I've just broken my way through.

I have never viewed myself as a lucky man in life, but after this I might have to re-evaluate.

'Danny! Danny!' Hayley screams at the top of her lungs. Always with the melodrama, my sister. 'Are you alright?!' She also has the knack of asking stupid questions during a crisis.

'Oh yeah,' I reply, coughing up plaster and dust. 'I'm great. There's nothing like falling through a loft to really help your cardio programme.'

Hayley bends down and takes one of my hands tightly in hers. 'Is anything broken?'

'My hand will be if you keep gripping it that hard.'

'Danny!'

'No! Nothing is broken. I didn't fall too fast, so I had time to prepare myself for the shock. All those years of jumping off garage roofs as a kid have finally paid off.' I roll over with a groan and slowly get to my feet. I keep expecting to feel sharp and hideous pain rocket through my body as I do so, but am amazed to bring myself upright with only the merest twinge. 'Bloody hell. I think I'm okay.'

'Really?' my sister exclaims in a disbelieving voice.

'Yep, everything seems to be where it should be,' I tell her, brushing the dust off my jeans.

'You lucky bastard,' she mutters.

'Oh no . . . wait. It looks like I have a splinter.' I hold my left hand out to her, showing her the half-inch long splinter of wood buried in my thumb.

Hayley looks up at the large hole I've created in our new house, and then back down at me. 'You mean to tell me the only injury you appear to have suffered after having fallen several feet through a ceiling is a small splinter?'

'Oi! That's not small,' I argue, waggling the thumb in her general direction. 'It's quite big. And painful, as it happens.'

'If that had been me, I'd have broken every bone in my body,' Hayley tells me, shaking her head.

'Oh, well, try not to sound so disappointed that I'm not crippled, sis. I can always jump back up there and have another go, if you like.'

'Don't be ridiculous.'

'It's going to be bloody expensive to get that fixed,' I point out.

Hayley gives me an exasperated look. 'Danny, there are dead animals in the bath, somebody has attacked the kitchen with heavy artillery, the garden looks like a jungle and the staircase could give way at any moment. I'd say an extra hole in the ceiling isn't much to worry about at this stage.'

I have to agree. So far this tour around Grandma's past hasn't exactly been a barrel of laughs – unless you call narrowly avoiding serious injury a fun pastime.

Hayley looks me up and down again. 'Are you sure you don't want some kind of medical attention?'

I hold my hands out, palms up. 'Nope. I'm fine. Keen to get back down the stairs again though, before this floor gives way underneath me as well.' I give the carpet a concerned look.

'Alright,' Hayley agrees. 'Let's get out of here. I want to go look out the back anyway to see how much land this thing comes with.'

And with that, the Daley siblings make their careful way back downstairs, one of them worrying at the splinter caught in his thumb, the other watching for spiders and dead human bodies.

Sadly, to get to the back garden, we have to go through the fly-infested kitchen. At least, I assume most of them are flies. If there are any mosquitoes in the cloud of small black bodies flying around the green fridge, we'll both be scratching ourselves into insensibility for the next couple of days.

The back door is a lot harder to open than the front.

'Are you going to kick this one too?' Hayley asks, as I push against the solid door with my shoulder.

I peer through one of the opaque windows in the door, and spy a large heavy object against it on the outside. 'I don't think so, not this time. There's something stopping the door from opening. Something heavy.' I pause for a second. '. . . And no, Hayley, it isn't a corpse.'

What it *is*, is a tyre. Not one from a small family hatchback, either. This thing came off a tractor. It takes a lot of pushing and shoving on my part – with a little help from my feeble, weak sister – before the tyre has shifted enough to allow us to get out of the door.

By the time we squeeze through the gap, I've got a real sweat on thanks to my efforts and the unseasonably mild spring weather.

'Christ,' I say, wiping my brow with one hand. 'I hope that was worth it.'

'Well, it was the only way to get out here,' Hayley comments and looks off to one side, making a face. 'Oh . . . apart from the fact we could have just come out of the front door and walked round.'

'What? And get ripped to pieces by the brambles? No thanks. I've already nearly broken both my ankle and my back today. Adding severe lacerations to the litany of injuries this place has caused me in the last half an hour is something I'm happy to avoid.'

'Fair enough. Let's see how the garden looks.'

It's not really a garden, though. What we're talking about here is a bloody huge field covered in a thick, tall layer of plant life that will need way more than a strimmer from B&Q to get rid of.

'Great. I wonder if there are any Triffids out here?' I say, knowing full well the reference will probably be lost on my sister.

'What's a Triffid?'

See what I mean?

'Never mind,' I tell her. 'Not something we have to worry about.' I look out over the vast sea of green. 'Probably.'

'This hasn't been cut in a while,' Hayley remarks.

'In a *while*? More like never.' And that's no exaggeration. The grass is easily a foot and a half high at its shortest length, even now in April. This grass obviously hasn't been cut in years. The only places where it isn't that long are where some kind of creature has forced its way through, trampling the grass flat. I'm resolutely not going to think about what that creature might be at the moment, in case it is just about to leap out of the grass and take my throat out.

There are more of the massive overgrown bramble bushes dotted around the large patch of land laid out in front of us. At least four gnarled apple trees are in evidence towards what I can only assume is the back of the land this house comes with, and I swear I can see a Christmas tree growing way off in one corner, proving that Mother Nature doesn't give a monkey's about human customs.

'Exactly how big is the land?' I ask Hayley, as I peer down the left side of the field at the remains of a barbed-wire fence that marches its way for several hundred feet down towards a large wall of trees right at the end. Over the fence is pastureland.

Standing here in this quiet vegetative expanse, it's hard to believe that we're only a minute's drive from the village centre down the rough, pot-holed road that runs right up to the broken garden gate.

Hayley pulls a piece of paper out of her pocket and reads. 'Apparently it's one point one acres.'

'Wow. That sounds like . . . a lot?'

I'm hazarding a guess here. I actually have no idea how big an acre is. Nor does anyone who grew up within walking distance of a metropolitan town centre. I know it's supposed to be quite a large unit of measurement, but quite how large, I have no clue.

What I do know is that the overgrown land in front of me is *bastard* big – and in dire need of someone with a bulldozer and some imagination.

'Not really much of an improvement on the inside is it?' Hayley says, a little deflated.

'Oh, I don't know. At least out here we can get a nice suntan.'

'Where does it end?' Hayley ponders.

I indicate the barbed-wire fence. 'I think that's where the left-hand side ends. I guess the back is where those trees are, but as for the right . . .' I tail off. There appears to be no clear indication of where the land ends on that side. It slopes down into a shallow valley, and I can't see any signs of a boundary marker. Where the land starts to rise again is a neat cornfield, so that's obviously not ours.

'Look! There's a patio set.'

Hayley points over to where a wrought-iron set of chairs are stacked against the back wall of the house. The table that comes with them must be a relative of the one in the dining room, as it too only has three legs.

I sigh. 'Well, let's see if they'll take our weight. I need a sit down. All this exploring and near-death calamity has knackered me out.'

I tramp over to the chairs and yank a couple of them from their long-term resting place. I plonk one down for me, and gratefully sit down on it. Hayley is less keen on planting her backside on the chair I've moved out for her.

'What's the matter?'

'My jeans will get ruined,' she complains.

I shrug my shoulders. 'Well, you always were one for dressing inappropriately, sis. Remember Clacton?'

Hayley shudders. When we were kids, Mum and Dad took us on holiday to Clacton-on-Sea at the height of what you could laughably refer to as summer. Seventeen-year-old Hayley obviously thought we were going somewhere where the temperature would be up in the twenties, and only packed light summer dresses and bikini tops. Eleven-year-old Danny knew full well what the weather would actually be like, and packed a duffle coat.

The doctor was very gentle when he broke the news that she had come down with a mild case of hypothermia. Dad was not happy about having his holiday cut short by four days.

As Hayley doesn't want the chair, I prop my legs up on it and heave a grateful sigh. I then link my hands behind my head and yawn.

'So then, what the hell are we going to do with this place now we've got it?' I ask, tipping the chair onto its back legs.

Hayley's brow wrinkles. 'We've only got two choices, according to the research I've done.'

'And they are?'

'We can sell the place as it is.'

I groan. This doesn't sound like much of a choice. The house is an absolute state, and the huge garden is no better. Who the hell would want to buy it?

'It's not going to be worth all that much then?' I say to Hayley despondently.

'No. Only about one hundred and sixty thousand, I'd say.'

'What?!' I exclaim, nearly tumbling backwards out of the garden chair as the shock hits me.

'One hundred and sixty grand,' she repeats. 'The house would probably have to be knocked down, and there could be planning issues with a new build, so it keeps the price down a bit.'

I am speechless. No, more than that – I am virtually incapable of movement. For a moment, all I can do is stare, dumbfounded, at Hayley.

'Are you alright?' she asks. 'Is it the fall? Are you having a delayed reaction?'

'Did you . . . did you just say *one hundred and sixty thousand pounds?*'

'Yep. That's how much Grant at the estate agents said he could probably get for it, if we sold it as is.'

I leap out of the chair. 'Then what the fuck are we still doing here?' I cry in excitement. 'Let's get down there and get your mate Grant to put it on the market today!' Another thought occurs. 'In fact, why did you insist I come up here with you to see the place at all? You should have just told me how much it was worth, and I would have agreed to sell it without all the bother!'

Hayley scowls. 'Hold your bloody horses. There's a very good reason why I brought us both up here to see the place. I wanted to get a good look at how much work is needed.'

'To do what? Bulldoze the place?'

'No. Renovate it.'

'Renovate it? Are you *mental*? You did see me fall through the ceiling, didn't you?'

'I did. But Grant didn't just quote me on how much the place would sell for as it is. He also gave me a figure for how much we could get for the house if it was completely renovated.'

Now I'm curious again. 'How much?'

'Here.' She hands me the piece of paper she's been clutching.

I give it a read, and have to sit back down again very quickly.

'Six hundred thousand?' I say in a faraway voice.

'Yep.'

'Six hundred thousand quid,' I repeat.

'That's right.'

'*Six hundred thousand.*'

Hayley sighs. 'Yes, Danny. That's how much this place would be worth.'

'Why?'

She throws a hand out. 'Are you kidding? You can see how glorious the view is, can't you? And the place is a massive, three-bedroom, detached Victorian farmhouse. Properties like this go for a premium, especially out here in the country.'

'But we'd have to fix it up, though, yeah?'

22

'Yes. That's the problem. It's not a small job.'

Understatement of the century there, I think. 'How much would that cost?'

'I don't know. Not until we've had people in to look at it. But it's going to be expensive. Probably as much again as what it's worth now. At least a hundred and sixty grand.'

My shoulders slump. 'Well, that's us fucked then. You're a teacher, I'm a caretaker, we're both single, and we both rent the places we live in. Neither of us can stump up anything like that kind of cash.'

'We can if we re-mortgage the house.'

It sounds like Hayley has put a lot more research into this than I thought. 'But would a bank give us a mortgage? I mean, neither of us are the best of bets, are we? I live in what could charitably be called a shoebox on the worst council estate in the area, thanks to the fact I earn such a shitty wage, and after what happened with you and Simon . . .' I trail off as I see the look of hurt in Hayley's eyes. That bastard really screwed her over in the divorce. It's a miracle she can even afford somewhere to rent on her teacher's salary.

'I know,' she replies. 'But there's still a chance. If we can just prove to the bank that we can make the money back when we sell the place.'

I lean back in my chair again, mulling both options over.

On the one hand, six hundred thousand quid is a huge amount of money – but with it comes a *huge* amount of work. It might just be better to take the one sixty and run.

I say as much to Hayley. She doesn't look happy about it.

'I thought that'd be how you'd feel,' she says and kicks an inoffensive stone into the long grass. There's a look of deep disappointment in her eyes.

'Did you really?' There's an edge to my voice. This sounds like the beginning of the same conversation we've had many times.

'Yep. It's the easy way, and we all know how you like the easy way, Danny.'

I throw my hands up. 'Oh, for fuck's sake! Not this again.'

Hayley folds her arms and looks daggers at me. 'Yes! This *again*, Danny. Anytime something comes along that requires you to put some effort in, you run a bloody mile. Look at the job with Halifax . . . or helping Dad with the boat . . . or Kelly.'

'God! You just love trotting all of those out every time you bring this bloody subject up, don't you?' I shout.

'That's because you keep doing the same fucking thing, Dan!'

'For the last time: the Halifax job was hideously boring, Dad was never going to get that stupid boat back in the water anyway, and Kelly was a control freak!'

Hayley stamps her foot. 'She just asked you to wear a pair of trousers when you met her parents, you maniac!'

'Exactly! I don't like to be told what to wear.' I'm in danger of stamping my feet. 'She did it more than once!'

'She was also beautiful, caring and the best chance you've ever had for a proper relationship, you bloody tool!'

'Oh, and I should be taking advice from you about relationships, should I?'

This, I fear, is an insult too far. I instantly regret it the second it comes out of my mouth.

Hayley's break-up with Simon wasn't her fault. Not in the least. He was the one who cheated on her with *two* women, after five years of what looked like married bliss – at least from the outside. Five years that came to a sudden halt when one of the women turned up at Hayley's doorstep, trying to assuage her guilty conscience by confessing everything.

No, the only mistake Hayley ever made was marrying Simon in the first place.

'I'm sorry, sis,' I say to her, squirming at the look of dismay on her face. 'I shouldn't have said that. It's just you brought up Kelly, and I got angry, and . . . and . . .'

Hayley turns away from me for a second, and looks at the dilapidated house that started this argument. I can see she's trying to compose herself. I hope she does a good job of it. My sister is slow to lose her temper, but when it arrives, it's time to batten down the hatches – and possibly update your life insurance.

'I think we should leave,' she eventually says, in a calm, tight voice.

'That might be for the best,' I agree. When Hayley and I start to argue, it's invariably a good idea for us to be split up as quickly as possible. Our parents learned this early on in our lives, and were quick to pull us apart before any serious injury could be done.

They weren't always quick enough. I still have a small scar on my shoulder from when Hayley whipped a plastic necklace across it when I pulled the left leg off her favourite Sindy.

'But I want you to have a long think about this place, Danny,' Hayley continues, her voice taking on what I like to call the 'teacher's tone'. 'Don't just dismiss the idea of renovating it so you can avoid doing any work.'

I start to open my mouth to protest, but the daggers in her eyes are even sharper now, so I think better of it.

'Just think about it overnight, *okay*?'

'Alright, alright. I will,' I agree, despite myself.

'Good.' She looks at her watch. 'I'm babysitting for a friend in half an hour, so I'm going back to the car.'

'Through the house?' I say with mock horror, trying to lift the atmosphere a bit.

Hayley's having none of it. 'Yes, Dan. Through the bloody house.'

And with that, she walks back through into the kitchen, and towards the front of the property.

I heave a sigh. One of these days, I'll learn to think before I speak. Probably on my deathbed.

Hayley's car is already gone by the time I get back to the motorbike.

I shouldn't be that surprised really. My sister is one of those people who take a long time to come back off the boil once you get them riled up.

I can only hope she's forgiven me, and is in a better mood the next time I see her.

The twenty-minute ride back to town through the leafy country lanes gives me time to think about what my sister had just said. Pretty much all of my family are of the opinion that I am a lazy slacker, based on the last five or six years of my life since I left university. But I can't help it if the jobs I get are dull, or the girlfriends I have are too controlling, can I?

And as for this house . . . I don't think Hayley realises just what she'd be getting us into if we do try to renovate it. I've seen enough episodes of *Great Locations* to know that it's never easy, never cheap, and is back-breaking work for the most part. Do I really want to spend the summer painting that shithole?

But then I see that look of disappointment in Hayley's eyes again – swiftly followed by the hurt at the mention of Simon's name.

Christ.

When I get back to the flat, my head is still buzzing. Usually a nice ride clears it, but not today.

I don't really taste my hastily thrown together beans on toast, nor do I enjoy the cigarette I have after them. I just keep seeing Hayley's disappointed face floating in front of my mind's eye.

Fuck it.

I'm going to have to learn how to lay bricks, aren't I?

I pick up my phone and dial my sister's number. She doesn't answer, and it goes to her voicemail. Hayley always answers her phone. She's obviously still angry with me.

'Hi, sis,' I say after the beep, 'I just wanted to say sorry again for bringing Simon up like that. It wasn't fair of me.' I pause for a moment. 'And, if you want to renovate that house, then I'm in . . . I guess. Give me a call when . . . when you want to. See you later.'

It only takes her ten minutes to call back, so she can't have been that mad after all.

'You really want to do this?' she asks warily.

'Yeah, yeah. I do,' I reply, trying to sound convincing. 'Six hundred thousand is a lot of money.'

'It'll be hard,' she cautions. 'All our time will be taken up with it.'

'I know.'

'And you'll need to help me with all the admin stuff like calling people, filing documents, paying bills.'

Shit. I'd forgotten about the admin. Trying to build a brick wall is one thing, but admin work is quite another. It's the main reason I quit that job with the Halifax. I've committed myself now, though, haven't I?

'Yes, yes. I know,' I say through gritted teeth. 'I'm up for it.'

'Great! Then we'll get together tomorrow morning to chat about it a bit more. Ten o'clock at the Long Café?' Hayley's voice is lighter and brighter again – and all it took was for me to agree to months of back-breaking labour.

'Yep. Sounds good to me. See you tomorrow.'

I end the call and throw the phone onto the couch.

So that's that, then.

I've just passed up an easy payday to keep my older sister happy. I must be mad.

Having said that: *six hundred thousand pounds* . . .

. . . Less the money we spend renovating Grandma's farmhouse, and the cut the taxman will take, of course.

I'd get fifty per cent of more than £300,000, give or take. That buys an awful lot of Xbox games and new tyres for the Kawasaki. I could also afford to rent a much better flat. Hell, I could afford to *buy* a bloody flat. Maybe one of those posh ones down by the quay. Lovely stuff.

Maybe, just maybe, the effort *will* be worth it . . .

I flick on the TV and start to channel surf. By startling coincidence, an episode of *Great Locations* is on BBC Three. I settle myself down to watch it. Previously, this show just used to be on in the background while I was doing something else, but now it has my undivided attention. I'm about to get into the property renovation game myself, so I figure it's vital to pick up a few tips.

An hour later I am as white as a sheet and reconsidering the whole bloody idea.

I've just watched two people descend into madness while trying to renovate a barn in the Lincolnshire countryside. By the end of the show, he'd lost half his hair and she'd piled on three stone.

What the fuck am I letting myself in for?

HAYLEY

May

£500.00 spent

Of course, neither my brother nor I have the first clue how to renovate a property. You might as well hand us both a scalpel and ask us to perform brain surgery. On each other.

But while I don't know how to refurbish a house, I do know how to use Google.

And the first thing I learn during a constructive couple of hours of research is that we need to enlist the help of two very important people if we're going to have any chance of getting this project off the ground: an architect and a builder.

I hand the task of finding the builder to Danny, while I search for an architect in our local area that doesn't cost an arm and a leg. I could go national, but if something goes wrong with the build, I want to be able to physically get hold of people, so hiring someone in the Outer Hebrides just isn't practical. A local architect is a must.

Sadly, there are surprisingly few of them – and all of them appear to be astronomically expensive. If I ever do decide that I want to risk getting into another relationship with a man, I will make it my goal in life to find the nearest architect. If nothing else, my financial stability will be assured.

I wish I'd chosen it as my field of study at university, rather than teaching. There would have probably been less job satisfaction – but a lot more soft-top convertibles and holidays to the tropics.

A lot of advice online indicates that the best way to find an architect is by word of mouth and through the local council. So I look at various property renovation forums, and write an email to the relevant council offices, asking for help. Over the course of the next two weeks I arrive at a shortlist of architects that we can probably afford if I've done my sums right on the budget, who work within a twenty-mile radius of the house. The list is very, *very* short: just *three* names in total. I am dismayed to realise that all of them are men. Maybe I should have studied to be an architect, after all.

Of the three names, I have to discount two almost immediately. One is busy for the next two years with a variety of projects, and the other requires a hefty fee up front before completing any work – a fee that we simply don't have. This means we don't have to bother with the tedious process of putting the job out to tender and waiting for quotes to come back. A saving grace, I guess.

The only local architect I can find who will take a minimal up-front fee, and has a schedule that's not fully booked up, is a gentleman called Mitchell Hollingsbrooke.

From his website it appears that Mr Hollingsbrooke is in his late twenties, and is a wanker. There's only one picture of him, and he's wearing a trilby hat in it. A white one with a paisley band. He also has a moustache. One that tapers to a point at either end. Given that it's not Movember, I can only assume that this is a permanent piece of facial furniture. I think the expression he is trying to achieve in the picture is one of considered intellect. Sadly, he's failing, and it just looks like someone's recently inserted a set square into his rectum.

Nevertheless, all the reviews and opinions that I can find of Mitchell Hollingsbrooke say the same two things over and over again: he is good at his job, and even more importantly, he is *cheap*.

With more than a slight degree of trepidation I call his office and book an appointment to meet with him, through his exotic-sounding assistant, Mischa.

Danny is initially reluctant to attend the meeting as it's at 8.45 in the morning, but I sweeten the deal by offering to buy him breakfast afterwards.

'Alright, I'll come in that case,' he says, proving that any man can be pretty much told to do anything, providing you reward them with something covered in sugar that they can shove in their mouths. 'Please don't expect me to do much of the talking, though,' he adds. 'I haven't the slightest idea what to say.'

I snort. 'And you think I have? Basically I'm going to show him a few photos of the farmhouse along with a floor plan, and hope he doesn't throw us both out of the door with a sneer on his face.'

Mitchell Hollingsbrooke doesn't have an office in the strictest sense of the word. You might think somebody in the architectural world would secrete himself away in some ultra-modern, high-class office space, full of interesting and valuable pieces of art that inexplicably look cheap and nasty when you actually get up close and give them a good hard look. Everywhere is lit with long strip-lighting, and the furniture is the optical illusion type that looks comfortable from a distance, but the minute you park your backside on it, you discover that you're sitting on something even Torquemada would have found a bit excessive.

None of this for Mitchell Hollingsbrooke, though. He chose to set up shop on a houseboat. A very large, blue houseboat. And not one of the new ones either. This thing looks like it just sailed straight out of an episode of *Howard's Way*.

When Mischa told me the address was 13 The River's Edge, I thought it would be a road *next* to the river, but no, here we are, standing right *on* the riverbank, and there is the sign for Hollingsbrooke's architectural practice, nailed to a pole next to a long gangplank that leads down to the deck of the aforementioned gigantic old houseboat.

'This guy designs houses?' Danny asks, as we study the sign, double-checking that we haven't got the wrong end of the stick completely.

'Yep. This is it,' I reply, consulting the email Mischa sent me.

'Fantastic. Well, we're fine then, providing you want the place to have a nautical theme,' Danny says, and takes himself off down the gangplank.

This is a somewhat worrying development, it has to be said. What kind of architect would keep office hours on a houseboat?

The stark raving mad kind, that's who.

When I join Danny on the deck outside the – the what? Front door? Cabin door? I know as much about boats as I do about brain surgery – I can't help but feel we may be on a hiding to nothing here. The front windows on the houseboat are tinted so you can't see in. A small plaque on the door features Hollingsbrooke's name again, as well as the entreaty to knock politely and wait. I feel less like I'm about to meet an architect, and more like I'm about to meet a lower-ranking member of the royal family.

'Oh yes, this is going to be fun,' Danny intones.

'We don't have any other choice. I took the morning off work for this, so we're going in. Besides, the only other guy available wanted at least five grand up front.'

'Really?' Danny's eyebrows shoot upwards. 'Captain Pugwash it is then!' He raps smartly on the door a couple of times. 'If he answers in waders, carrying a harpoon, I'll get a bank loan out to pay for the other guy.'

Mitchell Hollingsbrooke does not answer the door dressed that way. In fact, Mitchell Hollingsbrooke does not answer the door at all. Rather, we are greeted by a smiling young dark-haired girl, who is probably far too pretty to be stuck on a houseboat with an architectural reject from *Pirates of the Caribbean*.

'Good morning,' she says to us. 'You are here to see Mitchell, yes?' The accent is Eastern European, but her English is extremely good.

'Yes, that's us,' I reply. 'Hayley and Danny Daley.'

'Yes. That's us. Hayley and Danny Daley,' my brother parrots from beside me. His voice has taken on an odd robotic tone. I turn to look at him and instantly realise he will be very little use to me in the coming conversation. If we were in a cartoon from the 1930s, there would now be birds circling around Danny's head, tweeting musically, and two bright pink hearts would have replaced his eyeballs.

As stated, this girl is *very* pretty, and the accent is *very* exotic. Her tits look rather fabulous as well, I'm disgusted to say. I'm quite proud of the fact that mine continue to remain more or less upright as I enter my mid-thirties, but compared to the perky wonders underneath the tight shirt the girl is wearing, mine are like two spaniel's ears.

'Please come in,' she tells us, and opens the houseboat door wider to allow us entry. 'My name is Mischa,' she adds with another dazzling smile.

'My name is Danny,' my smitten brother tells her.

'Yes, I think she's got our names,' I inform him, resisting an eye roll as I do. 'In you go.'

I push Danny through the door, and into the kind of room that anyone with a nautical persuasion would probably orgasm over in three seconds flat. There is polished oak in here – a great deal of it. And brass. Oh my lord, there is *so much brass*. Maps cover the walls, all of them the out-of-date, brown kind that probably cost a fortune, despite their inaccuracies. There's something that I believe is called a sextant stood in one corner on a giant tripod. Dominating the room, however, is a massive polished-oak console replete with buttons, knobs, old-fashioned electronic displays and a gleaming ship's wheel that is more highly polished that the surface of the Hubble Space Telescope. Frankly, the room should just have 'A Life on the Ocean Wave' piped in through speakers, just to set the whole thing off.

'Well, this is . . . this is nice,' I tell Mischa, not sounding convincing in the slightest.

'Boaty,' Danny adds. It seems that being in the presence of a beautiful girl has regressed my brother back to toddlerhood, when the only phrases that came out of his mouth were of the simple, one-word kind.

For the first time Mischa looks a little awkward. 'Yes. It is, er, nice, isn't it? Mr Hollingsbrooke is currently in a sea-faring frame of mind.'

'Currently?'

'Yes. He goes through creative phases such as this quite a lot. He says it informs and improves his work. Last year we were based on a farm because he was in a rustic period.' Mischa's perfect little nose wrinkles. 'I prefer this. It smells better.'

'Ah, I see,' I reply. 'Well, we're here about a farmhouse, so that might help us.'

'Our place doesn't smell, though,' Danny blurts out. 'Even with the cow shit on the doorstep.'

Mischa looks taken aback. I look thoroughly disgusted. Put my brother in front of perky tits and a nice smile and this is what you get. A man with the social skills of Jeremy Clarkson.

'That is . . . that is very nice,' Mischa tells Danny, stepping back slightly as she does so. 'Shall I take you through to meet Mr Hollingsbrooke?'

'Yes, please,' I say to the girl, hoping and praying that Danny doesn't say anything else to embarrass either one of us.

'Yes,' is all he manages to come out with. We're back to the monosyllabic toddler again.

Mischa bids us follow her across . . . I guess what you'd have to describe as the bridge of the boat, and through another door that leads down a long corridor with rooms off to either side. One is a kitchen, one a bathroom, and the other two must have been bedrooms at some point. I say that because now they are stuffed to the rafters with paperwork of all shapes and sizes. I see a lot of house blueprints, mixed in with Ordnance Survey maps and the occasional copy of *Sailing Today*.

At the end of the corridor is another door that Mischa knocks on. 'The Daleys are here to see you, Mr Hollingsbrooke,' she says through the door.

'Wait! Wait!' a strangled voice replies from within.

Oh God. He's masturbating.

We've arrived earlier than he was expecting and he's still cracking out his morning pick-me-up. Any moment now the door will be thrown open by a lunatic in a sailor suit, and I'm going to get covered in an unfortunate substance.

Mischa offers us both an apologetic smile. 'I'm sorry. Mr Hollingsbrooke is a unique man.'

There's nothing unique about spanking the monkey, sweetheart. They all do it.

'Very well! Come in!' the voice from beyond the door says. 'I am now ready.'

Ready for what exactly? A court case involving indecent exposure?

Mischa opens the door to reveal Mitchell Hollingsbrooke – not holding his penis, thankfully, but holding something even stranger.

'What do you think?' he asks, looking directly at me for some reason.

'What do I think?' I reply, completely confused.

'Yes! What do you think?'

I don't really know how to respond, but I give it my best shot. 'Is it a tuba?'

Hollingsbrooke's brow furrows. 'Well, yes. Of course it's a tuba! But what do you think?'

'Er . . . it's a nice tuba. Very shiny.'

He tuts loudly. 'I mean, what do you think of the shape?'

'Which bit?'

'Curvy,' Danny remarks. I *think* he's talking about the tuba and not Mischa.

Hollingsbrooke literally jumps up and down. 'Exactly! *Exactly!* It's perfect, isn't it?'

'Perfect for what?' I ask.

'The roof of the swimming pool.'

Okay, this conversation has now officially gone so far off the beaten path I'm going to need a satnav and survival rations.

'What I think Mr Hollingsbrooke is trying to say,' Mischa jumps in, 'is that the curve of the tuba is just right for the shape of the new roof he is designing for the nearby community centre. It is a very prestigious job.'

Wow. She's handled that magnificently. You get the distinct impression that this isn't the first time she's had to explain the rather odd behaviour of her employer to a potential client. I hope he's paying her well.

'I see.' I look back at Hollingsbrooke, who has now discarded the tuba and is sat on a large chrome-and-glass desk, which looks completely incongruous in this old-fashioned nautical setting. 'It's a nice shape for a roof,' I say to him.

'We'll see,' he replies, nibbling a fingernail. 'Do you want to sit down then, or what?' he adds.

Now he's got rid of the tuba, let's discuss what he's wearing, shall we? It shouldn't be possible for a fully grown man to pull off a tweed jacket, purple corduroy trousers, a paisley shirt, a bow tie and a white sailor hat.

It sure as hell isn't possible for Mitchell Hollingsbrooke. He looks like someone has thrown the contents of an Oxfam shop at him. There's every chance that I'm currently in the presence of the worst dressed man in England. If we hire this maniac, and his architectural skills are on a par with his dress sense, our farmhouse will end up painted bright orange and thatched with pubic hair.

'Please take a seat,' Mischa says. What I feel she should be saying is: 'Please run a fucking mile.'

Danny, bless him, is so enamoured with the girl that he automatically sits down in front of Hollingsbrooke's desk without a word of protest. This forces me to join him, despite every fibre in my being telling me to leave.

Hollingsbrooke instantly sits bolt upright and gives us both a steely look. 'A farmhouse then!' he exclaims loudly, and looks up at his assistant before we have a chance to say anything in return. 'Tea, Mischa! Tea and biscuits for our guests!' he orders. Then a firm finger is held up. 'Not the garibaldis, though! You know how I feel about them!'

Mischa nods, smiles and backs away calmly, as if she hasn't just been treated like a lowly servant by a man in a sailor hat with a tuba parked next to him. She must be used to this kind of behaviour as well.

'A farmhouse then!' Hollingsbrooke repeats loudly.

'That's right,' I say.

'It's a big place,' Danny adds. 'It'll be a big job.'

Miracle of miracles. Without a hot woman in the room, my brother has returned to his senses. Let's just hope it takes Mischa a good ten minutes to sift out all the garibaldis.

Hollingsbrooke puts his elbows on the glass desk and steeples his fingers. 'A big job, you say?'

'Yes. Danny's right. It needs a lot of work,' I say.

'What year was it built?'

'1890,' I reply.

'Where is it?'

'About ten miles north of town.'

'A good location?'

'Yes. Very pretty.'

'Is it on loam?'

'What?'

'Is it on loam?'

'No, chalk, I think.'

'Architraves still present?'

'Some of them.'

'Plumbing still working?'

'No idea!'

'Is it iridescent at sunset?'

'What?'

'Iridescent at sunset!'

'We haven't been there at bloody sunset!' This quick-fire inter-rogation is making my blood boil.

'The garden's massive,' Danny pipes up.

Hollingsbrooke looks horrified. 'I care nothing for gardens!' he shrieks.

'I don't think we should—' I start, but I am again interrupted by the upraised finger.

'Wait! Wait! Look at this please!' the architect snaps, and reaches behind him for a large leather-bound photo album on the shelf behind his head. He throws it onto the glass desk and sits back, a look of triumph on his face.

Danny opens the album and we both peer at its contents.

There are page after page of pictures of some of the loveliest-looking houses and rooms I have ever seen. All of them are in the style of an English country cottage, and all of them are marvellous. There are images of pristine kitchens with butler sinks and Shaker style cupboards; gorgeous bedrooms that look so comfortable I have to stifle a yawn; lounges decorated and designed with such ruthless attention to rustic detail that I am quite taken aback; and lush, shiny bathrooms with roll-tops that I would happily stay in until my entire body had turned into a prune.

I look up from the album to Hollingsbrooke, who has raised eyebrows and an expectant expression. 'Thoughts?' he demands.

'Is this your work?' Danny asks, earning him a sharp and derisory exhalation of breath.

'Of course!' the architect says. 'All projects similar to yours that I have completed. Four in all, I believe. Each one better than the last.'

Wow. I can't tell which is worse, the purple trousers or the ego.

. . . Actually, it's the purple trousers. They are truly dreadful.

What quite clearly isn't dreadful is Hollingsbrooke's talent as an architect – and it turns out, as an interior designer as well. If this is an example of how good he is at planning renovations on properties like ours, then I want to hire him – horrible cords and inflated ego notwithstanding.

'These are very good, Mr Hollingsbrooke,' I tell him. 'I didn't realise you designed interiors as well.'

'Of course! The work is only half finished if all you build is the shell!' He points a finger at his own face. 'I am a completist! I cannot walk away from a project until I know every element of the house is *in situ*!'

'Well, that does sound very thorough, Mr Hollingsbrooke.'

He quickly sits back again in his chair. This bugger is twitchier than a man whose pants are made of ants. 'Please! Call me Mitchell,' he tells me with a smile. Then he looks up and his eyes widen with pure happiness. 'Aha! Tea! And biscuits!' The brow instantly furrows. 'No garibaldis, though?'

'No garibaldis, Mr Hollingsbrooke,' Mischa assures him as she steps back into the office, holding a tray of cups and an assortment of biscuits. I spot a Jammie Dodger, which pleases me no end.

'Aha! There are Jammie Dodgers!' Hollingsbrooke virtually shouts. Oh great . . . now I have competition for my favourite biscuit.

'Jammy,' says Danny from beside me, giving Mischa an awkward smile.

Mischa departs, to presumably go and feed all the garibaldis to the seagulls, so we have Hollingsbrooke's undivided attention once more. I nibble on a Jammie Dodger while leafing through the pictures of his work for a second time.

'What would you need us to provide?' I ask him. 'You know, about the house?'

He waves a hand around in the air. 'Oh, as much as you can possibly give me. Your email gave me a good idea of the project, but there is some paperwork I will need. A floor plan of the property, information about the deeds, the local services, etcetera, etcetera. Mischa and I will undertake the necessary research, and then we will start to draw up plans.' He springs forward in his chair again, giving both Danny and I quite a start. 'Do you iPad?'

'What?' we both reply at the same time.

'Do you, or do you not, iPad?'

I wasn't aware iPad was now a verb. 'Er, I have an iPad, yes,' I say to him.

'Excellent! We have recently discovered a rather wonderful app on iPad that can create a three-dimensional interpretation of a planned renovation. I am finding it invaluable for giving my clients an accurate representation of what I have planned for their property.'

I'm slightly taken aback. If the shiny glass desk plonked in the middle of a rustic houseboat is incongruous, then a man who wears tweed and corduroy, likes a tuba and has a moustache from the 1920s knowing all about iPad apps is doubly incongruous, with a side order of highly unlikely. I am forced to remember that Mitchell Hollingsbrooke is only in his late twenties, despite all sartorial evidence to the contrary.

'What about money?' Danny asks, seeking to make up for his uselessness in the presence of Mischa with a question that cuts right to the heart of the matter.

This earns him a raised eyebrow from Hollingsbrooke. 'I'll need a small retainer to begin with,' he tells us. 'Five hundred pounds should do it. My standard rate is ten per cent of whatever the total build and design cost may be.' He gives us an indulgent smile. 'I'm sure we can work everything out once I have a better idea of the job at hand.'

Ten per cent of the cost is quite a lot of money once we've borrowed it, but then £500 up front isn't. The only other option open to us would cost far, far more before any work had actually started. Hollingsbrooke represents the best deal we're going to get. He probably knows this as much as we do. Without architect's plans, we can't work out a budget, and without a budget we can't mortgage the property. We're just going to have to throw our lot in with this eccentric, or risk not being able to move forward on the project at all.

I look round at Danny, to see what he's thinking. He catches the look I give him, understanding it in an instant. In silent reply he shrugs his shoulders and nods his head. *What other choice do we have?*

I look back to the architect, safe in the knowledge that my brother and I are on the same page. 'Fair enough,' I tell him. 'I'll bring all the information about the house to you tomorrow.'

Hollingsbrooke's eyes light up. 'So does that mean we have a deal?'

I smile. 'Yes, Mitchell, it does.'

He stands bolt upright. 'Excellent!' One arm goes out, with hand extended and palm open. 'High-five me then!'

'You what?'

'High-five me! I can never say I have started a job until I high-five my client!' He points at us with his other hand. 'Do not, as the common vernacular holds, leave me hanging!'

So let's reflect: I am about to enter into a business relationship with a man who works on a houseboat, wears a headache-inducing combination of clothes, despises garibaldi biscuits and insists on a high-five instead of a handshake; all because I like the way he positions a roll-top bath.

Reluctantly – oh so very reluctantly – I slap Hollingsbrooke's hand.

Danny is far more enthusiastic about the whole thing, and delivers a right palm stinger. This doesn't seem to bother Mitchell in the slightest. 'Fabulous! I'm so excited that you're going to be working for me.'

Eh? Aren't *we* the clients?

'You just wait,' he adds, waggling a finger in our general direction. 'I will transform your farmhouse into something fit for a king!'

I admire his conviction, but I've seen the place up close and personal – he hasn't yet. I just hope Mitchell Hollingsbrooke's rock hard self-confidence is enough to withstand the horrors that await him at the Daley farmhouse.

'Thank you, Mitchell, we look forward to working *with* you too,' I say, emphasising the word *with* for all I am worth.

'Yes . . . you and Mischa,' Danny adds with a dumb smile. Mitchell's eyebrow goes up once again. Purple-corduroy-wearing lunatic he may be, but there's evidently a shrewd mind underneath all that bombast.

'Indeed,' he says, a sly smile crossing his face. There's obviously nothing going on between architect and assistant then, judging from his reaction. 'I'm sure she is looking forward to working with you as much as I am.' He breathes in deeply and picks the tuba up again. 'Now please get out.'

'I'm *sorry*?'

'Please pop off. I have to ruminate on my tuba.' He cranes his neck. 'MISCHA!!!'

'Good grief!' I exclaim loudly, deafened by my new architect's shrieking command.

Poor old Mischa re-enters the room calmly. 'Yes, Mr Hollings-brooke?'

'Show my two new valued clients out please. Feel free to issue them with garibaldis on their way out.'

'Yes, Mr Hollingsbrooke.'

Mischa holds out a hand towards the door. I quickly take it before Mitchell has the chance to destroy any more of my five senses.

'Bye,' Danny says, and gives Mitchell a little wave.

I suppress a sigh of exasperation, and make my way back to the front of the boat, leaving Mitchell to gaze lovingly at his tuba and twiddle his moustache.

'If you could email me all of your contact details,' Mischa asks at the main door, 'I will draw up the preliminary contract and get it to you for signing. If you like, I can come and pick up the paperwork for the house from you later today, if that is convenient.'

'Thank you, Mischa, that's very kind of you.' I regard the young girl for a moment, before continuing. 'Can I ask you something personal?'

She looks a bit startled. 'Um, okay?'

'Why do you work for him?'

Mischa smiles. Not the first time somebody has asked her this, I believe. 'He isn't as bad as he appears. I want to be an architectural designer, and I want to learn from the best. Mr Hollingsbrooke is the most talented artist I have ever met.'

'But he treats you like a servant.'

'No . . . no, he really doesn't. I have worked for other architects and interior designers, and he is the only one who values my opinion, and lets me contribute to the projects he takes on. All the others just see a silly little girl from Slovenia. He sees a fellow architect and designer. Everything else does not matter.'

Interesting. I'd completely misjudged their relationship.

'Slovenia,' Danny remarks helpfully.

Mischa smiles. 'Yes. I am from Novo Mesto, Mr Daley. Have you heard of it?'

Have you ever seen a small defenceless mammal trapped in the glare of your headlights on your way home from a late-night party?

Mischa stares at my brother's blank expression for a few moments, trying to figure out what is wrong with him. 'Would you like a garibaldi?' she ventures, holding up the packet.

Danny fumbles a biscuit out of it. 'Thanks,' he says, taking a bite.

I grab his arm. 'Come on, Danny, let's leave Mischa here in peace and go see if we can find a builder who can work with Mitchell.'

'Okay,' my brother says around a mouthful of crumbs.

I lead us back up onto the deck and along the gangplank to the safety of dry land. 'Well, that was quite an experience,' I say as we walk back to my car.

'You think he's actually going to do a good job?' Danny asks me.

'Oh! Hello, Danny! Come back to us, have you?' I mutter sarcastically. 'For a while there, I thought you'd been replaced by one of the pod people. Was she really that pretty?'

He blushes furiously. 'I've just never seen a girl like that before. Did you hear her accent?'

'Yes, Danny, I did hear her accent. It was very musical.' I stop and place my hands on my hips. 'Look, are you going to be able to function while she's around? It sounds like Mitchell works quite closely with her. I'm sure she'll be on site at the house quite a lot.'

'I'll be fine!' he replies, not sounding convincing in the slightest.

I'll have to take Mischa to one side and ask her to wear an unsightly boiler suit and no make-up if she comes within a mile of the Daley farmhouse. Smearing herself with cow shit may be a good idea too. 'You didn't answer my question. Do you think he'll do a good job?'

I look back down the river at the houseboat and draw in a breath. 'I don't know, Dan. I really don't. But he's cheap up front, comes highly recommended . . . and doesn't seem to doubt his own abilities one bit. I guess we're just going to have to take the plunge and hope he's everything he's cracked up to be.'

Danny looks dismayed. 'It's risky.'

'No arguments here.'

'Do you think this entire project is going to be like this? *Risky*, I mean?'

'Probably. We're going to have to take a chance on everyone we work with.'

Danny looks doubly dismayed. 'Great.'

'Speaking of which, have you come up with any good ideas for a builder yet?'

He opens the car door. 'Well, there is one guy I've found, but we need to have a chat about him . . .' Danny tails off mysteriously.

'What the hell is that supposed to mean?'

'Well, let's just say that Mitchell Hollingsbrooke might not be the only slightly odd character we could have involved in the renovation.'

'Wonderful. It sounds like Daley Farmhouse is attracting all sorts of weird people already – possibly including us.'

Danny laughs. 'What did you just call it?'

'Sorry?'

'You just called that tumble-down shit pile *Daley Farmhouse*.' He laughs again. 'You're not getting attached to it, are you?'

My turn to go flame-faced. 'Of course not! But we have to call it something, don't we?' I throw open my car door and climb inside. The key is in the ignition before Danny has got his seatbelt on. This is not a conversation I wish to pursue any further.

Possibly because Danny is right.

Have I started to get attached to the old wreck already? Is it, like the mould along the skirting board, growing on me? And if it is, what effect will it have on my approach to this renovation?

A lot of questions start revolving in my head as I drive away from Mitchell Hollingsbrooke and his purple cords. Not least of which is, why would anyone want to swim in a building shaped like a tuba?

DANNY
May
£514.58 spent

When you hear the name Fred Babidge, what kind of person is conjured up in your mind

Is there a flat cap involved?

Wellington boots?

A rolled-up cigarette permanently parked on one side of the mouth?

A grizzled, stubbly chin, and a hoarse, echoing laugh that sounds like it's at least thirty-two per cent gravel?

Congratulations.

Meet our new builder.

Now, I'm going to be honest here and say that I found Fred Babidge thanks to a conversation I had down the pub. I am fully and comprehensively aware that you should never enter into any kind of business relationship based on a conversation you had down the pub, but researching and finding a builder is bloody hard work. So hard in fact that up until the pub chat, I had spent four frustrating days trying to nail down (no pun intended) a builder who was cheap enough, and *competent* enough, to take a load of complicated architectural plans and make a half-million-pound house out of them.

Unlike Hayley and her search for an architect, I had plenty of options to choose from. Too bloody many, as it happens. How exactly are you supposed to decide which building firm you want to hire when you know nothing of the industry, and only have the reviews of others to go by? It's all very well Find a Trade giving you a comprehensive listing of customer reviews on every builder in the local area, but if at least eighty of those builders rank ninety-five per cent or above, it doesn't really narrow the playing field much, does it?

I've spent more time on the phone in the last few days than I have in my entire life, speaking with a series of men who all sounded exactly the same, and said much the same thing too – all of it mildly baffling.

At the end of the four days I had successfully narrowed the one hundred and sixty-three builders in our area down to just seventy-eight. If I kept going that way, I would have arrived at a final choice around the same time Daley Farmhouse finally collapsed into dust, which would have rendered the whole search completely bloody moot.

In disgust, I threw down my phone and buggered off down to the pub, to see if a little light refreshment with some friends would help me with my problem.

A solution arrives when Fat Bob suggests Fred Babidge.

'Who's Fred Babidge?' I ask him, sipping my pint of John Smith's.

'He did my nan's conservatory. He's brilliant.'

'Is he?'

'Yep!' Long Johnson pipes up from where he's standing at the nearby fruit machine. 'He rebuilt my cousin Jeff's house after that water main burst and the whole left-hand side sunk two feet into the ground. Did it in half the time any other builder could, and at a fraction of the price.'

'Babidge is a local legend,' Fat Bob continues. 'You ask around this pub, or any other of the locals, and I'll bet you'll hear loads of people recommend him.'

'Is he on Find a Trade?'

'Fuck no. Fred Babidge doesn't need any of that nonsense.'

This one fact endears Mr Babidge to me more than anything else. 'How do I get hold of him? Have you got his phone number?'

Fat Bob picks up a beer mat and peels it apart. 'You write your number down on this, and I'll see if I can get it to Fred. No guarantees, mind. He's dead popular in these parts.'

Fred Babidge is starting to sound like some kind of folk hero, rather than an inexpensive builder. Still, this is the clearest direction I've had yet on where to go to find someone to fix up Daley Farmhouse, so I'm not going to look a potential gift horse in the mouth, until it tries to bite my nose off.

And yes . . . I'm fully aware that I am now referring to the place as 'Daley Farmhouse'. Blame my bloody sister for that one.

The next day I am sat enjoying a Pot Noodle in my broom closet at work when my phone rings.

'Hello?'

'You alright there, mate?' a man asks me with the thickest cockney accent I've heard outside a Danny Dyer film.

'Um. Yes? Who is this?'

'The name's Fred Babidge, chief. I hear you're looking for a builder?'

'Um. Yes. We are.'

'What's the gaff?'

'Pardon?'

'The gaff, son. The place you want crowbarring. What's the job?'

'Er, it's a farmhouse.'

'Nice country pile, then?'

'It's a pile alright.'

I'm treated to my first dose of the Babidge gravel-filled laugh. 'Blinding. Shall I come have a look at the gaff?'

'Um. Okay?'

'Smashing. I'll bring a few of the lads. They can have a crawl over it and see what's what. When are you free, captain?'

I'm not a captain, but I can't pretend I mind being referred to as such. 'We've got a meeting with an architect tomorrow, so maybe the day after?'

'Got an archy lined up already then? Hit the ground running, have you?'

'Yes.'

'Good for you, china. Alright, Friday it is then. Email me over the address and your details, and I'll see you there at ten.'

'Okay, Mr Babidge.'

'Call me Fred, teacup. The only person who ever called me Mr Babidge was my old parole officer, and he was a twat.'

Hayley is going to kill me. 'Okay, *Fred*. See you Friday then?'

'Smashing! See you then, champ.'

And with that, the phone line goes dead. A few seconds later a text comes through with Babidge's email address. I was half expecting it to be cockneystereotype@hotmail.com, but it is in fact fred@babidgeandco.com. I fire off the email as requested and sit back, wondering how the hell I'm going to break it to Hayley that I may well have hired half the cast of *EastEnders* to rebuild our house for us.

'So, you have no recommendation for this man other than the one you got from somebody called Fat Bob in your local boozer?' Hayley asks me, the look of barely concealed contempt growing on her face with every syllable spoken.

'More or less,' I reply, trying to prop the garden gate back up. I look at my watch. It's 10.40. Babidge is late.

'There was nobody else, Danny? No other builder within a thirty-square-mile radius who would have been a better option?'

'Not really,' I lie through my teeth.

Hayley folds her arms. 'Just because our surname is Daley, it doesn't mean I want *Arthur* Daley anywhere near this build.'

'He's not that bad.'

'Oh no? The only recommendations the man has is from half-drunk locals. And he called you *china*?'

'And captain.'

'Yes. And *captain*. These facts do not fill me with a huge amount of confidence.'

We both hear the sound of an engine and look down the road. 'And neither does that,' Hayley adds, pointing at the vehicle now coming into view.

Yes, it's a bloody Ford Transit. Yes, it's white. And *yes*, it's half covered in rust. I'm sure there's every chance it cut up fifty or sixty others cars on its way here.

Down the side of the transit is the legend: *Fred Babidge – The Builder You Can Rely On.*

'Rely on to do what, exactly?' Hayley says out of the corner of her mouth. 'Insult you in rhyming slang and steal your back tyres?'

'Just let's give him a chance, shall we?' I implore, knowing full well that if this goes as pear-shaped as it looks like it might, I will have all decision-making responsibilities on this project taken away from me.

The van comes screeching to a halt in front of us, and out jumps Fred Babidge – along with two heavily tattooed lumps of muscle that are no strangers to a nice casual glassing in the pub, I have no doubt.

'Oh good fucking grief,' Hayley whispers.

Babidge strides over, removing his flat cap as he does so. This reveals a gleaming bald pate that he must wax to get it so lovely and shiny. 'Morning,' he says with a big smile.

'Hello, Fred,' I say.

'Good morning, Mr Babidge,' Hayley says. She's using her teacher voice. This does not bode well.

Babidge smiles even more broadly. 'Please, call me Fred,' he tells her. 'I'm an old-fashioned sort, Miss Daley, so might I take your hand and give it a gentle kiss?'

What the fuck is this? Fred Babidge has gone from East End barrow boy to Shakespearean lover in the space of two heartbeats.

'Er . . . I guess so?' Hayley replies, hesitantly offering out her hand.

Babidge takes it and plants a gentle smacker on it. 'It's lovely to meet you, Miss Daley.'

Hayley actually *blushes*. My sister *never* blushes.

'Call me Hayley,' she tells Babidge.

'Very musical,' he says.

'What is?'

'Your name. *Hayley Daley*. I like it.'

Hayley's face clouds for a moment. 'I don't. Blame it on my parents. There were a lot of drugs going around in the early eighties.'

'Don't you worry about it,' Babidge tells her. 'I was called Babidge the Cabbage right up until I left school, and now look at me.' He holds his arms out expansively.

I don't know what to do with that, I truly don't.

'Would you like to look over the farmhouse, Fred?' I ask him, changing the subject for all I am worth.

'Why the hell not, chief!' he gestures to his two tattooed colleagues. 'These are my two boys, Baz and Spider. They'll be my right-hand men on the build if you hire us.'

Baz smiles a lot more pleasantly than should be possible with teeth like that. 'Nice to meet you,' he says. Spider looks even happier to see us. 'Alright,' he says, beaming for all he is worth. It's a shame about the spider web tattoo running down the whole left-hand side of his neck and half his face. It turns what I'm sure is intended to be a welcoming grin into something that you'd usually see plastered across the face of the nearest child killer. The strange tribal symbol that snakes its way around his right eye and temple doesn't help matters either. Both of them look positively terrifying, beaming smiles notwithstanding.

You get the impression that Fred has taken a great deal of effort and time to ensure his men are polite and courteous to his clients. Possibly employing a cattle prod to do so.

Babidge stands back and puts his hands on his hips. 'So this is it, is it?' he says, looking at the farmhouse.

'What's left of it,' I reply, only half joking.

Babidge pulls out a rolled-up cigarette from behind his ear. 'Ah, it probably looks a lot worse than it is.'

'You think so?' Hayley says, with a sardonic laugh.

'Yeah. I've done tons of these jobs. It won't have anything I ain't seen before, little lady.'

Hayley's eyebrow shoots up. She holds out a hand, indicating the way over the broken gate and down the path. 'Then by all means, Fred, go have a look and tell us what you think.'

Babidge laughs and gives my sister a florid bow. 'It'd be my pleasure, Hayley!' He regards his two boys. 'Let's go crawl over the place, lads.'

And with that he steps forward. Before he can go two paces though, Babidge stops and laughs once more. 'Almost forgot! Can I have the key to get in?'

'You won't need one,' I tell him.

'Oh . . . that bad, is it?'

'Pretty much.'

Babidge laughs again and sets off down the path. 'Any chance of some tea and biscuits?' he calls over his shoulder. 'I think I saw a nice little café in the village back there! Three builders, please! And some garibaldis if they've got any!'

I look at Hayley. She looks right back at me.

'I'll be back in a bit,' I say with a sigh, and trudge off down the road, the good little errand boy that I am.

Twenty minutes later I'm back to discover that Hayley has made it back into the house. 'I hope he *is* good,' I tell her as I enter the front room. 'This little lot cost me nearly fifteen quid.'

Fred Babidge's head appears from around the doorframe. 'Is that tea and biscuits?' he says cheerfully. It doesn't take much to keep a builder happy. Tea, biscuits, the opportunity to slap on a seventy-five per cent markup.

'Yep,' I tell him, carrying the cardboard tray over. Babidge and his two looming associates take their drinks.

'What's this?' Spider remarks, picking up his biscuit.

'It's a flapjack,' I reply, a little uncertainly. 'It's all they had.'

'It's got bits in it,' he remarks, examining the oat-based snack with a furrowed brow.

'Just eat the thing,' Babidge tells him. 'It'll be good for your dicky digestive system.'

Who'd have thought it? A man with a spider web tattoo down one side of his neck has irritable bowel syndrome.

'So, what do you think of the place then, Fred?' I ask the builder as he dunks his own flapjack into the tea.

Wait for it . . .

Wait for it . . .

Here comes the sucking in of the air through the teeth!

'*Sssscchhhhhwwwww* . . . Well, it's not a bloody show house, is it?' Fred intones, and takes a large mouthful of flapjack.

'No.'

Fred gravel laughs, and draws in a deep breath. 'I'd say your

54

main problems are a touch of subsidence at the back on the right-hand side – probably done by the fact you're on loam. That'll need underpinning. The back wall is going to need ties put in, cos there's a fair bit of bowing going on. You got some lovely woodworm munching their way through the floor joists in here, the kitchen, the roof and at least two of the bedrooms, so they'll need killing. Your pipes need ripping out and replacing, cos they're copper and gone to shit. There'll be a good two or three blockages down to the main junction, you mark my words. There's rising damp in the kitchen and the basement too, so you'll need a course put in both. And there's penetrating damp upstairs, which means the gutters and flashing need ripping out and redoing. That's after the roof's been rebuilt and retiled, of course.'

I am slack-jawed in amazement. Horrified, knee-trembling amazement.

I look at Hayley, who resembles someone who's been sat down and shown an extensive slide show of dead puppies.

'And you worked all that out in the twenty minutes I was away getting tea?' I ask him, dumbfounded.

'Yep,' he replies, taking another bite of flapjack.

Hayley swallows hard. 'Is that everything?'

'Oh no!' Fred responds in ebullient fashion, spitting oats everywhere. 'That's the structural stuff. We haven't even got on to the renovation yet! That'll need a new kitchen. A new bathroom, and an en suite putting in off the main bedroom. Complete strip of all the walls and a re-plaster. You'll want the whole of the electrics and water re-done. Don't fret! I got boys that can do that, no problem. Then there's repointing the walls outside – all of 'em. Painting everything. New floors.' He drains the last of his tea. 'And that's all the stuff you'd do to get it back to square one. If your architect bloke wants any changes put in, then that's all extra too, cos you'll need RSJ supporting beams and new brickwork if there are any room configuration changes . . . after you've got all the planning permissions of course.'

I feel light-headed. All of that sounds like it'll take a thousand years and cost a hundred million pounds. We should just bulldoze the place and be done.

'That sounds like an awful lot,' the ghost of my sister says from my side.

Fred Babidge gives us both a sympathetic look. One only slightly ruined by the bits of flapjack clinging to the edges of his mouth. 'It sounds like a lot, but that's what happens when you take on these old places. To tell you the truth, it could be worse.'

'Could be *worse?*' I say, highly unconvinced.

'Oh, Christ yes. We did a place down by the river a few years back that was leaning over like the bleedin' Leaning Tower of Pizza. It was only held together by spit and sawdust. Half the job was just clearing out all the rat corpses and bat shit.' Fred looks at Spider. 'Are you gonna eat that flapjack or not, my son?'

Spider hands the baked biscuit over and starts investigating one earhole with an enormous index finger.

'How much do you think this will cost?' Hayley asks Babidge.

The amount of air he sucks in through his teeth could have filled up the Hindenburg. 'Most builders, it'd be about two hundred grand.' He lets that sink in for a moment, like a hot coal into a tub of margarine. 'Me? I can probably do it for what? Hundred and fifty, tops? But probably more like one hundred and forty. I'll have to sit down and work out the numbers in more detail, but that's a pretty good guesstimate for now.' He looks at his two companions for confirmation. They both look around the room and nod expansively. 'There you go. If the boys say that's about right, then that's good with me.' Fred beams.

Hayley looks suspicious. 'And you can tell all of that in just a twenty-minute cursory look around the place?'

Fred finishes Spider's flapjack, chewing it slowly as he gives Hayley a thoughtful look. 'Hayley, I've been in this business for forty-five years,' he says, 'ever since I was old enough to pick up my first trowel with my dad at the tender age of ten. I've built more houses that I can remember, and done up twice as many wrecks like this in that time too. When you've been around as long as I have, you can tell what needs doing and where, don't you fret.'

I don't know about my sister, but I'm bloody convinced – especially if he can do the job for fifty grand cheaper than anyone else.

'There is one thing I can't do much about, though,' Fred tells us.

'What's that?' I ask in disbelief. From this man's general persona and attitude, I'd be half convinced that if you asked him to cure cancer, he'd tip you a wink, drain his tea and tell you he'd have it done by teatime.

'I can't do much about your cow.'

I take a couple of moments to digest this. Surely he didn't just say *cow*, did he? I must have misheard.

'Did you just say "cow"?' I ask, safe in the knowledge that Fred is going to laugh at me and tell me to clean my bleedin' ear'oles out.

'Yep. Your cow.'

'But we haven't got a cow,' I state, very sure of myself. At no point have Hayley or I purchased a cow. Of that I can be sure.

Fred grins. 'You have, you know.'

And it was all going so well. Here I was thinking that Fred was a sensible, down-to-earth sort of chap with a firm grip on the world and his own sanity, and yet here we are, discussing non-existent cows. Maybe Spider and Baz can cart him away before he starts seeing other farmyard animals where there are none.

He leans forward. 'Why don't you go have a look out the back door?'

'Okay.'

Giving Fred a concerned look, I edge around all three of them and walk down the hallway. I pass through the kitchen, and open the back door onto the garden.

Not that I can see much of the garden, because my view is now eighty-three per cent cow.

'Hayley!' I call back into the house. 'We have a cow!'

She appears in the hallway, Fred Babidge and the muscle twins in tow. All three have smirks on their faces. 'Are you sure?' she asks me.

I step to one side. 'Have a look for yourself,' I tell her.

Hayley draws closer and regards the cow – which is black and white, and something I believe is called a Friesian. The cow looks solemnly back at Hayley, chewing cud as it does so. It seems perfectly at ease standing here at our back door, as if this is the correct place for it to be in the world. Most cows seek open pastures. This one apparently prefers an overgrown patio.

'Well, at least we know where the cowpat on the front doorstep came from,' Hayley remarks.

'How the hell did it get into the garden?' I wonder. 'The fences are still up.'

'Maybe it jumped over them,' Spider offers helpfully.

'Yeah,' Baz agrees. 'I saw a cow jump once.'

Fred rolls his eyes. 'It wasn't jumping, Baz. You was in Afghanistan and an IED went off under it. What that cow was doing, my boy, was exploding.'

Baz shrugs his massive shoulders. 'It looked like it was jumping.'

I look back at the cow. It doesn't show any signs of leaping into the air. In fact, I'm pretty sure the only way it could leap into the air would indeed be if somebody set explosives off underneath it. I think Baz's theory may be wholly inaccurate.

'We'll have to get rid of it,' I say.

'Nah, leave it there for now,' Fred tells me. 'She's doing a nice job cropping your grass for you.'

My heart sinks. 'Oh crap. I'd forgotten about the garden. That'll need fixing as well, won't it?'

Fred nods. 'Yep. Not one for us though, captain. We don't do gardens.'

My heart sinks further. Fred grins. 'But don't you worry!'

'You know a man who does?' Hayley interrupts.

Fred claps his hands together. 'That's right, Hayley! Now you're getting it!'

'So what do you think?' I ask my sister, as I watch Fred Babidge's white Transit van speed away off down the road.

'I think he could charm the hind legs off a donkey, and our new pet cow, in three seconds flat.'

'Yes, but do you think we should hire him?'

Hayley scratches the end of her nose thoughtfully. 'He does seem to know what he's on about. And he seems very confident about getting the job done.'

'And he's cheap, which in our case is always the magic word.'

Hayley gives me a long look. 'Well, I found Mitchell Hollings-brooke and we've gone for him. Maybe we should go with your choice for a builder?'

I wave my hands. 'Oh no. Don't put this all on me. Joint decision, remember?'

'Fair enough.' Hayley considers the idea a little more, before her eyes narrow slightly. 'Alright. We'll give him a go.'

'Yeah. Why the hell not?'

I have been completely convinced by Fred Babidge's forceful personality. This is probably a poor reflection on my character, but I'm too relieved at the moment to realise it. Hiring a builder and an architect are the two biggest jobs you need to accomplish up front, and we appear to have done it without too much fuss and bother. If the rest of the build goes as smoothly as the past few days, we'll be laughing!

I'm sure most home renovators make the mistake of thinking much the same way when they start out on a project. It's only when their hair starts falling out that they realise the error of their ways.

What they don't have to worry about, though, is the removal of a half-ton cow from the back doorstep. Not unless they're converting an old dairy farm, I'd imagine.

'How do you shoo a cow away?' I ponder, standing back at the rear exit to the house. The cow has not budged an inch.

'I have no idea. Maybe poke it with something?' Hayley says.

'No chance. Cows are deadly,' I point out.

This earns me a look of derision and a short bray of laughter. '*Cows*, Danny? Cows are bloody harmless!'

'No they're not! I've heard stories.'

'*Stories?* What kind of stories?'

I cross my arms. 'People walking through fields, not paying the cows any attention . . . and *wham!*'

'George Michael appears?'

'Very funny. No. Trampled underfoot they are.'

'Rubbish,' Hayley insists.

'It's true!' I doubly insist. 'Herds of cows trample people to death. It's a well-known fact.'

'Well, this is just one cow. I think we're safe. I don't see any doe-eyed calves in the vicinity for it to protect. Poke it with something.'

'Don't be so cruel.'

Hayley tuts. 'You're such a softie,' she tells me, before stepping forward and pointing a finger at the cow. 'You!' she snaps at it. 'Fuck off!' Her finger quickly points away from the house.

'Oh yeah, that'll do it,' I say in a flat tone. 'Nothing like a bit of insulting language to get a cow to do what you want. Why not call her a fat bitch while you're at it?'

'Shut up, Danny! *You!* Cow! Sod off right now!'

As you might imagine, this has little effect on the cow. I doubt it bothers you too much to be told to fuck off when you weigh half a ton. These are the benefits of girth.

Hayley tries another tactic.

'If you don't go away,' she tells the cow, pointing her finger right between its big liquid eyes, 'I will eat a hamburger right in front of you.'

'Really?' I say, rather contemptuously. 'You think threatening to munch one of its relatives will get it to take to the hills, do you?'

'It'll get what I mean.'

'Will it? I bloody don't.'

'It's a threat, isn't it?' Hayley maintains. 'Either you go away, or I'll eat you the same way I'm eating this burger.' To underline her point, Hayley mimes taking a bite out of an imaginary Big Mac.

'I think you might be overestimating the cow's brain capacity on that one,' I say, in a withering tone.

Hayley steps back. 'Oh well, genius. You think of something then!'

This presents something of a problem.

I have no idea how to get rid of a cow any more than she does. Perhaps I'll go for a more polite tone.

I look down at the cow, which continues to chew slowly, and regards us both with blank-eyed disinterest. 'Erm, excuse me, cow. Would you mind leaving our garden please?' I entreat.

'Oh yes! That'll do it!' Hayley roars. 'There's nothing more guaranteed to get a cow to move than – *I don't fucking believe it!*'

The cow is turning around. I am as stunned as Hayley. Who knew the bovine species responded so well to a polite request? Or is this a special cow? If I tried the same tactic with a different member of her species, would I get the same result? I'll have to try it one day, when I'm completely alone, and possibly drunk.

'There you go,' I say to Hayley in a very self-satisfied tone. 'Sometimes you just have to be nice.'

'Oh, sod off. Where's the bloody thing going to go now, though?' Hayley comments, as the cow saunters off into the long grass.

'Not a clue. But I'm sure if it found a way in, it'll find a way out.'

We both watch the cow disappear from view as the rolling garden field dips down towards the trees at the back of the property. 'So that's that then,' I say, once I can no longer see the cow's backside. 'We've hired a builder and an architect.'

'Yep. All we need to do now is re-mortgage the place once Mitchell and Fred provide us with a rundown of costs.'

'How long is that likely to take?'

Hayley shrugs. 'Depends on how fast they work, I suppose. A month, maybe?'

I sigh. I had hoped work could start quicker than that, but there's no rushing these things – especially when you have other people involved, who work to their own schedules. I sniff the air. 'I think the cow has left us another present,' I remark.

'Smells like it. Why don't you chase after her and ask her not to do it again?' Hayley takes on a simpering expression and grasps her hands together. '*Excuse me, cow. Would you mind awfully not shitting in our garden again? Thank you so, so much.*'

'Fuck off.'

'That won't work on me any better than it did the cow.'

'Shall we get out of here and start on that mortgage application?' I suggest. 'I think we've accomplished about as much as we're likely to today.'

'Yeah, alright,' Hayley agrees. 'We've bonded with a cockney in a flat cap, and you've discovered a talent for cow whispering. I'd call that a productive day.'

And with that we leave the house, before the smell of cow shit has a chance to permeate our clothes.

As I ride away on the bike, I swear I catch sight of a black-and-white hide between the brambles, down the left-hand side of the farmhouse. That cow is going to be a problem, I just know it.

Do they have pest exterminators that can deal with cows?

Is that even a thing?

I'll have to ask Fred Babidge. I'm sure he'll know someone.

HAYLEY

May

£12,826.16 spent

These wellington boots really don't suit me. Green has never been my colour, and I simply don't have long-enough legs to look like anything other than a bandy-legged gnome, when forced into a pair of rubber wellies.

Still, better that than ruin another pair of expensive trainers wandering around this place. Especially now that work has started, and vast sections of the overgrown garden have been transformed into a building site.

I'll give Fred Babidge his due, once he gets the green light to start on a job, he doesn't hang about. A mere forty-eight hours after I rang to tell him that we'd had the mortgage approved and now had the cash in our bank account, he was on site and conducting a symphony of clanking metal that would be guaranteed to give anyone a headache who wasn't foresighted enough to stick in a pair of ear plugs.

I knock back two paracetamol as I watch the concrete start to be poured underneath the right-hand side of the house.

This was the first job Fred and his crew of five lads insisted we

get done. 'Ain't much point doing anything before those foundations are sorted,' he told us. 'You don't want the gaff toppling over,
do you?'

And who could argue with that?

So here I stand, watching several tons of concrete being poured
into the vast hole underneath the house. It looks like enough to
support St Paul's Cathedral, so I'm assuming it'll render the farmhouse safe from further subsidence with no problems at all.

It had better, given that it's costing twelve bloody grand to get it
done. When we started on this renovation I had visions of the cash
being spent on roll-top baths and new kitchen cabinets, not on filling a big hole under the ground. I hate to spend money on things
I can't see, and it's rapidly becoming evident that when it comes to
house building, most of the money gets spent on stuff that will end
up being invisible.

Still, at least I'm not being called upon to actually help pump
the concrete into the hole. I'm all for equality between men and
women, but when it comes to standing in a wet muddy hole for
hours while heavy machinery turns you deaf, I'm quite happy to
live in the 1950s.

No such luck for Danny, of course. There he stands, looking as
miserable as sin, trying to help Fred and his boys, but failing *magnificently*. It's like watching a small boy around his dad and uncles.
Any minute now they're going to ask him to go make them a nice
cuppa, just to get him out of the way.

Still, bless him for wanting to be helpful, and actually getting
off his arse to make the effort. It's a good job he only works part-
time at the museum, otherwise he'd have no time to come down
here and be emasculated by large men covered in tattoos.

I've had to take an unpaid sabbatical from the school. I just
couldn't stand the idea of all this work going on without me here to
supervise. And by supervise, I mean stand at the back in ill-fitting

wellies and worry about all the money disappearing down the nearest hole. I asked for nine months off, and was amazed to get it with relatively little fuss. I don't know whether I should be pleased that they capitulated so easily, or worried that they think I'm dispensable enough to get rid off for three-quarters of a year. What I *do* know is that this house had better sell for the money it's supposed to; otherwise I'm going to be eating dry pasta out of a hubcap for the rest of my life.

Taking so long off work is a *massive* risk. Probably an extremely stupid one, given that I still have to pay rent every month and do annoying things like eat and drink. Luckily, I had these old wedding and engagement rings lying around that I no longer have any use for, so I pawned the bloody things for a few thousand quid, which should keep me going for quite a while.

I'm betting that the farmhouse will sell for a considerable profit – and that's far more likely to happen with me on site every day, rather than dividing my time between here and the school.

I guess I've always got the credit cards to fall back on if things get really tight.

Speaking of tight, these wellies are quite, quite uncomfortable. I can feel a nice big blister forming on my right heel already. It's probably just as well that I'm stood still a good twenty feet away from all the action . . . *supervising*.

Ah, here comes Danny. His face is like thunder.

'Off to the shop are we?' I ask as he tramps towards me.

'They want crisps with the tea this time. Spider likes Monster Munch.'

'I'm sure he does.' I try very hard not to smirk. 'We'll have to get a kettle on site before you walk through the soles of your shoes.'

Danny looks past me, ignoring my comment. 'Who's that?'

I turn and see a car approaching. It's a beige Citroën 2CV.

There's only one person in this world I know who would drive such a bizarre car in this day and age.

'What the hell is Mitchell doing here?' I wonder out loud. 'He's not supposed to be on site for another week.'

Danny shakes his head. 'No idea. Perhaps he's come to see how the work is going.'

'But we haven't even started on his designs yet. Not even for the roof. Fred says that's a few days away at the absolute earliest.'

'Well, tell him that.'

The 2CV shudders to a halt just behind one of Fred's Transits, and out jumps Mitchell Hollingsbrooke. I'm pleased to see the sailor's hat has gone. Sadly, it's been replaced by a bowler. The purple trousers are still in evidence as well, unfortunately.

Out of the passenger seat climbs another person. One I seem to recognise, though I can't quite put my finger on why.

Danny recognises him as well, and has no doubt who he is. 'Fuck me! That's Gerard O'Keefe!'

'Who?'

Danny rolls his eyes. 'Come on, Hayley! Gerard O'Keefe? He hosts *Great Locations!*'

'What? That stupid daytime show on BBC One? The one they sling on before the lunchtime news?'

'Yes!'

'Why the hell is he here?'

Danny shrugs. 'I have no clue. Shall we go and find out?' Without waiting for me, he marches off in the direction of the 2CV. I look back over at Fred and his team, who are still pumping in the concrete. I hope Danny doesn't get too distracted by our new visitor. Spider looks like he could do a lot of damage to my brother's spinal cord if he doesn't get his Monster Munch.

'Hayley! Hayley!' Mitchell shouts at me over the sounds of heavy machinery. 'Come over here! Over here, *now!*'

I grit my teeth. Some might find Mitchell's aggressive approach to social interaction to be endearing. I resolutely do *not*. But I have to say, Danny's excitement has piqued my curiosity about why Gerard O'Keefe would be here, so I gingerly raise one blistered, wellington-boot-clad foot, and slowly make my way over to them through the mud.

'Morning, Mitchell,' I greet our architect.

'Good morning, Hayley! Wow! Those are nice wellies. Very flattering on you!'

Mad. Completely mad.

It's a bloody good job I fell in love with his design for the en suite bathroom the second I laid eyes on it.

'Thank you, Mitchell,' I reply. I give the other man an expectant look. Now I'm up close I recognise him properly. I've never watched more than two or three episodes of *Great Locations*, but Gerard O'Keefe is quite hard to miss, given that he is a good six foot three, has floppy brown hair that is only slightly greying at the temples, and is prone to wearing army surplus clothing that must give the BBC wardrobe department nightmares every time he steps on set. 'It's nice to meet you, Mr O'Keefe,' I say. 'My brother enjoys your show a lot.'

'I do!' Danny agrees enthusiastically. 'That one last week? The Georgian townhouse with the dry rot and fungus everywhere? That was great!'

Only home improvement shows can make a rational human being that excited about fungus.

'Thank you, Danny,' O'Keefe replies with a smooth smile, before turning back to me. 'And I'm very pleased to meet you too, Hayley. Mitchell has told me a lot about you . . . and your farmhouse here.'

'Has he?'

'Oh yes!' Mitchell interjects, all eyeballs. 'I've known Gerard since university. He used to come in and give guest lectures back before the TV show started. I like to keep him up to date with my projects. He seemed very keen on finding out more about yours, so I brought him down so he could see it!'

I give Gerard O'Keefe a rather disbelieving look, which he picks up on instantly. 'I have a soft spot for these old Victorian piles,' he confides. 'I was brought up in one until the age of fourteen.' He looks at Daley Farmhouse with a wistful expression. 'This place looks just like it.'

'With less people covered in tattoos pumping concrete, I'd imagine,' I say, as I watch Spider guide the spout coming from the concrete mixer to another part of the hole. They must be nearly finished now, surely?

Gerard O'Keefe laughs. 'It does rather ruin the picturesque quality of the place doesn't it?' He gives me a dazzling smile. 'Do you mind if I look around? Mitchell has been telling me all about it. I'm keen to see some of the original features.'

I almost ask if those original features include the dead animals in the bathroom and the nuclear green fridge, but manage to bite my tongue at the last moment. 'Yes, that's fine. Just to warn you, though,' I tell O'Keefe, 'we've not cleared anything out of the place yet. It's pretty much still the way we found it. Fred said it wouldn't be worth doing any of that stuff until the foundations were secure.'

'Fantastic!' O'Keefe responds. 'The less work you've done the better.'

What's that supposed to mean?

A suspicion begins to form in my mind – one that probably should have started to take shape the second I clapped eyes on the presenter of a daytime TV series about house renovations . . .

I decide to hold my counsel for the time being. I don't want to look like an idiot in front of this impressively put together individual. It must be all that camouflage. 'After you,' I tell him.

O'Keefe marches off down the cracked garden path with the three of us in tow right behind him. He veers off to the right to walk down the side of the house, giving Fred and the boys a wave as he does so. 'I'd like a chat with you at some point, Mr Babidge!' he calls to the flat-cap-wearing cockney, who gives him a doubtful look before replying.

'No problem, Mr O'Keefe. I'd be delighted to make your acquaintance!'

It seems Fred Babidge is a fan of *Great Locations*. It's not that surprising, to be honest.

'Excellent!' O'Keefe exclaims, and re-joins us at the front of the house. 'Shall we have a little explore, then?' he says, rubbing his hands together.

'By all means,' I reply. 'You may want to hold your nose.'

O'Keefe does so, in very theatrical fashion, and strides into the hallway, a look of real purpose in his eyes.

What follows is half an hour of Gerard O'Keefe studying every single nook and cranny of the building. His studiousness puts our first visit to the house completely to shame. He takes time to examine each and every architrave, cornice and skirting board, even going so far as to sketch the ceiling rose in the living room in a small notebook he carries around in one large front pocket of his green ex-army jacket. Nothing about the house seems to faze him. The dead rats and crow in the bathroom are virtually ignored in favour of commenting on how wonderful the taps must have been when they were new. The hole Danny put in the ceiling is laughed off as a minor issue. The overpowering smell of cow shit and old plumbing in the kitchen barely registers on the man's face as he examines the fireplace, commenting on how marvellous it is that the thing wasn't filled in decades ago.

My main thoughts on Daley Farmhouse have largely been that it is currently Hell on Earth, and doubts as to whether thousands of pounds can possibly make it any better. Gerard O'Keefe seems to be able to see beauty and charm in the place, even in its dilapidated condition. I don't know whether this is an admirable trait, or the first signs of an incipient slip into senility. O'Keefe only looks to be in his mid-forties, but these things can come on early if you're unlucky enough.

'What's the basement like?' he asks, having crawled over every other inch of the place.

'No idea,' I tell him.

'No idea?'

'Yep. Haven't been down there. Nobody has except Fred, and he wasn't divulging much.'

'He did say it was large,' Danny points out. 'That was about it, though.'

O'Keefe looks at Mitchell. 'What about you, Mitch? No plans for the basement?'

Mitchell looks awkward. 'I felt it best to wait until Mr Babidge's structural work was complete. Besides . . . *spiders*.' Mitchell's face contorts in a combination of loathing and terror.

'Ah, I see,' O'Keefe says, and pushes the under-stairs door open. 'Well, I'll have a look if you don't mind.'

'Be careful!' I warn him. 'It's very dark down there.'

'Not a problem, Hayley,' he tells me, and produces a torch from another one of his voluminous jacket pockets. There's something very James Bond about the smile he gives me before disappearing down into the depths.

Danny, Mitchell and I are all far more hesitant about going down there.

'One of us had better follow him,' I say, peering into the gloom.

'Yes, I suppose so,' Danny replies, giving me a meaningful look.

'Spiders as well?' I ask him in the tones of one resigned to her fate.

He shakes his head. 'Nope. Spiders are fine.' It's now Danny's turn to look horrified. 'But the moths can go fuck themselves.'

Ah yes, I'd forgotten my brother's completely irrational fear of moths. Blame it on a rather unfortunate incident when he was two, involving him, a family holiday to Morocco, and a midnight visit from one of the local hawk moths that took a liking to Danny's sleeping face.

'I don't think there are likely to be moths down there, Danny,' I try to reassure him.

He folds his arms. 'I'm not taking any chances.'

I resist the urge to knock their heads together and step through the dark doorway. Luckily, Gerard O'Keefe's torch is one of those ridiculously bright ones – one he probably purchased from the same army surplus store as his clothes – and casts more than enough light for me to see by as I make my tentative way down the steps to join him.

Fred wasn't lying. The basement is *enormous*. Composed of several areas bricked off from one another by crumbling masonry, it's a rabbit warren down here.

I find O'Keefe standing in one of the larger areas at the rear of the basement, examining a wall.

'You hear that?' he asks as I join him.

'The slurping sound?' I respond, craning to hear.

'Yep. That's the concrete going in to shore up the foundations. Lucky for you, the basement terminates before reaching the corner of the house. Otherwise we'd be knee deep in the stuff by now. Mr Babidge seems to know his stuff, especially where to pour his concrete.'

'I'm glad you think so.'

'It's a good space you have down here.'

I look around at the dingy basement. 'You have a talent for seeing potential where I can't, Mr O'Keefe.'

'Every house has potential, Hayley. You just have to see past the problems.'

'Your eyesight is better than mine.'

O'Keefe laughs and walks through into another area of the basement. 'Do you know much of the house's history?' he asks me.

I shrug. 'Not really. It was my grandma's. None of us knew she owned it. We all knew she was married before she met our granddad, but she never talked about it. The deeds say this place was bequeathed to her by her first husband when he died, but that's about as much as I know.'

'Aren't you curious to find out more?'

'I guess. But I've been up to my ears in just getting everything sorted out for the renovation. The history of this place will just have to wait. Probably until we're getting near completion – whenever that happens. I'll have the time and energy to devote myself to it then, but for now, it's on the back burner.'

'Were you close to your grandmother?'

I laugh ruefully. 'I thought so. We were certainly close when I was a little girl. I used to write her letters all the time about what I was up to. She'd always reply, telling me how her day was going. All slightly pointless to be honest, as we lived a twenty-minute drive away from her, and I saw her every week, but you know what children are like.'

'It sounds as if she was encouraging you to write, as much as anything.'

'Quite possibly.'

'Sounds like a lovely woman.'

My eyes light up. 'Oh, she was. Kind, considerate. The kind of grandma anyone would want. She always made me happy when I was around her. In fact, from what I remember, she was the type of person who could brighten anyone's day.'

'So she never mentioned the house in any of her letters to you?'

'Not once! She just talked about her life at the vicarage with my granddad. Before he died, that is. Then she went in to the nursing home . . . and the letters got a *lot* shorter. She never wrote anything about her life before marrying the local vicar, though. Certainly never anything about her first husband – or this place.'

'So, this is a quaint Victorian farmhouse set in idyllic country-side, with plenty of original features and a mysterious past?'

My eyes narrow. 'Yes. What are you getting at, Mr O'Keefe?'

'Please, it's Gerard.' His eyes light up. 'And I want this house, Hayley!'

I scowl. 'Well, you can't have it yet, it's not finished.'

He laughs. 'I mean I want it for *Great Locations!*'

I bloody *knew* it.

The last thing I want is for this project to be featured on the TV.

It'll just be a massive hassle from start to finish. Also, what if everything turns out shit? What if the renovation is a disaster? It's one thing to throw hundreds of thousands of pounds down the crapper when nobody is looking, but to do it on national TV is another thing entirely.

'I'm not sure that's a good idea,' I argue.

'No, no, no! It'll be marvellous!' Gerard replies with excite-ment, and starts to make his way back towards the stairs. 'A brother-and-sister team new to house renovating; a young exciting architect and interior designer working on his latest project; a farmhouse with a past shrouded in secrecy . . .'

'It's not really shrouded in secrecy, I just haven't bothered to Google any—'

'The producers will love it!' Gerard interrupts as he reaches the top of the steps with me just behind, still trying to lodge my objections.

I stumble on the last step as I try to keep up with the enthusias-tic TV presenter. He steadies me with one strong hand. 'They might love it, but I'm just not sure it'll be a good idea for us,' I say.

'What'll be a good idea for us?' Danny asks as I emerge in a cloud of basement dust.

'I want this house to be on *Great Locations*, Danny!' Gerard tells him.

Danny's expression instantly changes. The last time I saw that look he had just been told we were going to Disneyland.

'Brilliant!' he shouts excitedly.

My fate is bloody sealed, isn't it?

I can protest as much as I like, but I'm done for. Even if I sat down with my brother for an hour and showed him a convincing PowerPoint presentation of all the reasons we shouldn't invite the BBC onto our building site, there's no way I could convince him not to accept Gerard O'Keefe's offer.

'When would you want to start?' I ask Gerard, trying to ignore my brother bouncing up and down beside me.

'Tomorrow?'

'*Tomorrow?*' I repeat in utter shock. 'I thought you TV types needed ages to make a show!'

Gerard waves a hand. 'Oh, it'll take a while to get all the crew arranged and the financing sorted, you're absolutely right. But I can have a camera down here tomorrow morning to start filming, that's the most important bit. It won't cost much, and my favourite cameraman is available.'

'Oh good,' I reply in dismay. I thought I'd at least have a few days to prepare for this latest twist. If nothing else, we could have had some time to smarten the place up a bit before the cameras descended.

Mitchell holds up a hand. 'One thing, though . . . you'll have to get Mr Babidge to agree to it.'

Of course, Fred! How could I forget!

Surely he won't want a load of limp-wristed TV types getting in his way while he restores this building to its former glory, will he? Fred is *bound* to object!

* * *

'Fine by me,' the cockney git says when Gerard asks his permission a few minutes later.

You can't bloody rely on anyone these days, can you?

'The boys will love it, won't you, lads?' he asks his crew. Cue a chorus of uncertain nods. 'Think of how much the ladies will like seeing you on the telly, eh?' This is greeted with *far* more enthusiasm. Baz and Spider look positively delirious at the prospect of women dropping at their famous feet. Comically so, in fact. They actually hug each other in sheer, unbridled joy at the prospect.

'Excellent!' Gerard replies, sharing a firm handshake with Fred Babidge. There's a great deal of alpha maleness going on here that I clearly have no part of.

My mood can best be described as morose as we walk back up the garden path to the 2CV.

'You're not happy about this at all, are you?' Gerard O'Keefe says to me quietly as we walk behind Mitchell and Danny. The architect is waving his hands around in excitement, and my brother is practically vibrating with his own exhilaration about the prospect of being on TV. Neither share my misgivings, at all.

'Honestly? Not really,' I tell Gerard.

'Why do you feel that way?' His tone is soft and calm. I'm surprised. From a man who appears to thrive on being larger than life, the swift change in gears is rather difficult to deal with.

'Oh, I don't know. I've never done anything like this before, and if we're on the TV . . .' I trail off, unable to put into words what I'm thinking.

'You don't want to be seen as a failure by millions of people. You don't want to look stupid,' Gerard finishes for me.

I blink a couple of times. 'Yes, that's it. It's not so much about the cash we're spending, but I can't stand the idea of coming across as some kind of naïve idiot.'

'Completely understandable. You're not the first person I've met who feels that way at the start of a project. The whole thing is a learning curve. But . . . let me try and sell the concept to you by saying one thing.'

'What's that?'

'If the house is on our show, it'll sell for more money.'

'How would that work?' I ask, confused. 'You wouldn't broadcast it until after it's sold, would you?'

'That's not how *Great Locations* works. You're thinking of one of those other shows.'

'*Location Location Location*?'

'Yes,' Gerard agrees through instantly gritted teeth.

'And what's that one with Kevin Whatshisface?'

'*Grand Designs*,' Gerard says in a flat tone.

'Oh yes. That's right.' I cock my head innocently to one side. 'They're on in the evenings, aren't they?'

A wry smile crosses Gerard's face. 'Are you mocking me, Hayley?'

I press a hand to my chest. 'Whatever do you mean, Mr O'Keefe?' I drop the act. 'Why is your show different?'

'We film a house renovation as it goes along, and we come back several times as the build progresses. Daley Farmhouse will be on the TV for everyone to see on three or four programmes during the series. That should increase your chances of flogging it for a premium, don't you think?'

Damn it. He's got me. You can appeal to my brother, Mitchell Hollingsbrooke and Fred Babidge's men with the lure of fame, but Hayley Daley's ego doesn't not need such massaging. Her bank balance most certainly does, though.

We reach Mitchell's car and I look at Gerard O'Keefe with a strange combination of optimism and suspicion. When a man makes me a promise these days, my guard immediately goes up. I can thank my arsehole of an ex-husband for that. But this man isn't talking to me about relationships, he's discussing a business deal. There's no ulterior motive in his actions, other than to make us all as much money as possible.

'Alright Gerard, let's do it,' I tell him, trying to sound more confident that I really feel.

'That's brilliant! I wouldn't want to get going without you both completely on board.' He holds out a hand. 'I look forward to working with you, Hayley.'

'Me too,' I say, surprised that I now genuinely feel that way, and take his hand. It's quite calloused and rough, but his grip is gentle.

'Me too!' Danny pipes up from where he's appeared at my side, thrusting out his own hand, which Gerard takes and pumps up and down a couple of times.

Gerard then looks at his watch. 'Right. Back up to the city, then. I can make some calls on the way to get things moving. If I can get it all sorted out, I'll be back tomorrow morning with my camera guy to film a quick intro to the project. We'll get the paperwork out to you for signing in the next few days. How does all that sound?'

'*Fast*, Gerard,' I reply.

He smiles. 'No point in hanging around, Hayley. We don't want this place looking too good before we start, do we?'

I look back at the war zone that is Daley Farmhouse. 'Not much chance of that happening any time soon,' I say.

Gerard climbs into Mitchell's 2CV and within moments they are driving away from the house, leaving Danny and I alone – and not a little shell-shocked.

'That's brilliant,' Danny says breathlessly.

'Yes.'

'We're going to be on TV, sis.'

'Yes.'

'You seem less than enthused.'

'About the *house* being on the TV? No. I'm fine with that. My ugly mug, on the other hand?' I have to suppress a shudder.

'Oi! Danny!' Fred Babidge calls from behind us. 'Spider needs those Monster Munch. His blood sugar is dropping like a stone over here!'

Danny sighs. 'From errand boy to TV star and back again in the space of an hour.'

'Well, you don't want to have your ego too inflated, do you?' I suggest.

Danny gives me a look. 'I work as a caretaker in a public museum that has been on its last legs for thirty years, Hayley. I don't think my ego is in any danger of getting inflated any time soon.'

'Yeah, well, you just wait until the first show airs and that Mischa sees you in a whole different light.'

Oh crap.

I shouldn't have said that. I can see the light bulb going on behind Danny's eyes, and I instantly regret my choice of words.

'I hadn't even thought of that!' he declares.

'Just go get the Monster Munch before Spider has a hypo,' I order him.

My brother floats off down the road on wings I've just accidentally nailed to his back. He is officially now going to be a nightmare every time the cameras turn up to film.

Speaking of which, I hastily withdraw my phone from my pocket and Google the phone number for my hairdresser. I'd best be getting in this afternoon, if I can. The last thing the viewing public needs is the vision of Hayley Daley with hair like an epileptic-bird's nest. The wellington boots will be bad enough.

As the phone rings I look over at where Fred and the boys are finishing off the concrete pouring.

One job down, then. Seventy-five million to go.

. . . And now all of them are going to be recorded in HD for posterity.

God help us all.

DANNY

June

£37,745.82 spent

With a month already gone on the house renovation, I am starting to feel like I am completely surplus to requirements.

I suppose this shouldn't shock me. After all, I am to building what Ed Miliband is to male modelling.

Hayley's alright. She can do all the administration and money stuff in her sleep. Every time I so much as look at an Excel spreadsheet I come out in a cold sweat.

Given the fact that I work as a caretaker, you'd think I'd have more to offer on the labour front, but compared to Fred and the boys I am a total novice. Oh, I can screw in a light bulb and fix the ballcock in the toilet when called upon to do so, but I have no experience of the kind of big, sweaty tasks that Spider and his cronies are faced with each and every day on this build.

They've already shored the entire house up so it's now rock solid from below, and tied the walls back together with enormous steel screws so they're not bowing out all over the shop. Daley Farmhouse is now looking more stable than it has in decades, and I haven't contributed a single thing to the process, other than the purchasing of tea, biscuits and many, many variety packs of Monster Munch.

I said as much to Hayley.

'Well, don't feel too bad. You're not a builder.'

'No. But my job is one that's mostly manual labour. I should be able to do *something* of use here.'

'Maybe just wait until they move on to something that you're more familiar with, and offer to help out when it comes up.'

Sound advice.

Luckily for me, that day has now arrived!

About six months ago, we had woodworm in some of the roof joists at the museum. A roofer was called in to fix the problem, but he was a bit of a one-man band, and the job turned out to be bigger than initially thought, so I got drafted in to help him out. This gave me some experience of roof joist replacement, even if it was purely in the role of willing assistant.

And what do you know? Fred and the boys have moved on to the roof this week . . . and some of the joists need replacing.

This is my chance!

I sidle up to our cockney builder and his crew as they're drinking their morning tea, with an ingratiating smile plastered on my face. 'Er, Fred?'

'What's up, flapjack?'

Fred's nicknames for me are becoming progressively more and more surreal. I'm being optimistic by taking it as a sign of growing affection on his part.

'Well, I was just wondering . . . Can I give Trey a hand with the roof joists today?'

Trey, a gigantic black guy from Barbados, does his level best not to look horrified at the prospect of my assistance.

Fred's mouth goes tight. 'I don't know, chief. Don't you think it might be better for you to help out down here? You know, where it's easier for you to get back outside if you're needed?'

Needed to go and buy the bloody lunch is what he means.

'I know what I'm doing with a roof joist, Fred,' I assure him, and regale him with my story of woodworm repair at the museum.

Both Fred and Trey seem to visibly relax slightly when I start talking about construction adhesive and strut beams. I think I'm winning them round.

'It might help, boss,' Trey tells Fred in his lyrical Bajan accent. 'It will mean one of the others doesn't 'ave to do it with me. They can help you with the flashing outside.'

Fred nods carefully, obviously taking his time to think about my proposition. I can't really blame him. As far as he is concerned, the evidence shows that I am only good for the purchasing of pickled-onion-flavoured wheat snacks. But if I can help Trey out it would free another one of his men up, and would thus speed up the job just that tiny bit.

'Alright, my old muck spreader, you're on. You go help Trey today, and if that goes well, we'll see what else you can do around here.'

I have to resist the urge to jump up and down. I'm rather like a puppy that's just been given a treat for not shitting on the lounge carpet for the first time since it was born.

I try to contain my pleasure, not wanting to come across as a complete fool in front of all these burly men. Now that I'm officially on the workforce, I feel an immediate sense of kinship with all of them I haven't felt before. I even go so far as to pour myself a nice cup of tea from the flask Fred brought down to save me the trouble of going to the shop quite as often.

It's disgusting. There's so much sugar in it, it's a wonder any of these bastards still have a front row of teeth.

Still, I'm standing in the mud with a bunch of builders, and I belong, dammit!

Two hours later I don't want to belong any more. The entire thing has been a massive mistake. Why didn't I just accept my position as Monster Munch purchaser, and be happy with my lot? Why did I have to push things?

The loft is hotter than the surface of the sun. The June weather has taken a turn for the ridiculous, and it's a good twenty-five degrees outside. Yesterday it was nineteen and raining. The day before it was seventeen and hailing. It's been more up and down than a whore's drawers – to use a phrase that Fred loves to trot out whenever he gets the chance.

If you know your lofts, you'll know that if it's twenty-five outside, then it's *thirty*-five under the eaves. The three portable work lights that have been rigged up to provide us with illumination really aren't helping matters either. The only real ventilation we have up here is two small holes caused by slipped tiles and rotten roof lining. These give us a bird's-eye view of the front garden below, but the slight puffs of wind that occasionally blow through them are about as much use as a fart in a hurricane.

The sweat is pouring off me.

Worse, it's pouring off Trey, and Trey is not a man who sweats in a genteel fashion. You'd think a bloke from such a hot country would be used to these kinds of temperatures, but by the way he keeps wiping his brow and swearing, this is apparently not the case. With great sweat, must come great smell, and boy does Trey stink.

I'm no better. The supermarket-brand antiperspirant I'm currently using gave up the fight a good ninety minutes ago, and my T-shirt is now soaked with sweat. I can feel it dripping down into my butt crack, which, as you might imagine, is a deeply unpleasant sensation.

Still, we have managed to accomplish quite a lot in our two sweaty hours. Trey certainly knows his way around the supporting beams of a roof. We've changed three of the rotten beams already, and have started on the fourth and last one. There's more to do up here, but until the chimney breasts are sorted out at either end of the building, this is as much as we can do for now.

I have been a good little assistant, obeying Trey's every command as soon as he has given it, and I haven't once screwed anything up. I feel the big Barbadian and I have bonded over our thankless task.

'Nearly done now eh, Trey?' I say to him as he walks over to me carrying the last replacement joist. It's a testament to the height of Victorian roof spaces that Trey is able to do this without having to duck.

'Yep man, we'll be done in double-quick time. Which is just as well. I need to change my damn underwear!' Trey laughs in a big, Barbadian sort of way. I assume he means because they are sweaty, rather than that he's had an accident. Trey gives me a contemplative look. 'Actually, Danny, how do you feel about giving this last one a go on your own?'

'Really?'

'Yeah. You know what you're doing now. I think you can handle it, yeah?'

How proud am I right now?

I've gone from Monster Munch fetcher to valued and independent member of the construction team in the space of one morning!

'Sure!' I bark excitedly, 'I can do it, Trey. No worries!'

'Great!' He hands me the joist. 'Just remember to get those screws in nice and tight and make sure the adhesive is spread like I showed you.'

'Yep. I've got it, Trey. You go grab yourself a nice drink. I'll get this done in no time.'

Trey laughs, claps me on the back, and makes his way back over to the ladder poking through the loft hatch. As he starts to descend he looks back at me. 'And hey! If you do that okay, maybe we let you fix that hole you made over there, yeah?' Trey laughs again and is gone from sight.

I try to ignore his reference to my fall from grace the first time I looked around the house, and busy myself with the task at hand.

Said task is a lot more difficult when there isn't somebody standing over you, giving advice. What seemed like a relatively easy job with Trey by my side is most definitely *not* now that I am alone in the sweatbox. Manhandling a long, heavy length of wood around on your own is bloody hard, especially in thirty-five degree heat. It took Trey and I half an hour to do each of the other joists. I'm still at it on the fourth one a good *hour and a half* later. But I can't leave until the job is done. I simply cannot climb out of this loft space with my tail between my legs, and let Trey know I have failed him. It just *won't happen.*

Besides, as I peek out of the hole in the roof, I can see that the BBC camera crew have arrived for a day's filming. There's no Gerard O'Keefe with them today, but they'll no doubt want to crawl over the house again to get shots of all the work going on. If it gets caught on camera that I am unable to do something as simple as fixing a roof joist, I will have to kill myself. I won't be able to take the shame of it.

This leaves me in what you might call a sticky situation. I can't climb down to ask for help, because it might end with my unwanted suicide, but that leaves me up here in Sweatsville still struggling to finish a job I started four and a half hours ago. I am hot, thirsty, hungry and tired.

Unfortunately, there's something else I am as well – in dire need of the toilet.

Not for a pee, you understand. All the moisture has been leached from my body by the heat up here. No, I am in need of a number two. In a house with no working plumbing and no toilet, given that it was ripped out last week. We do have a Portaloo in the front garden, but the bloody thing is broken (Baz's fault I'm led to believe), so the nearest toilet that I can use to have a decent crap is now a good ten-minute walk away in the village.

It's a tricky problem, and no mistake.

I try not to think about my rolling bowels, and continue with the slow and painstaking task of hammering the joist into the correct position. The bloody thing just won't marry up with the ends of the old beam, no matter how hard I bang it with the hammer. The next twenty minutes are spent angrily tapping and whacking the wood this way and that to try and get it to fit properly. I'm only interrupted from the task when my bowels roll over a lot harder than they have previously, and I am forced to stand up, holding my belly and groaning in discomfort.

What the hell do I do now? Shuffle out of the house and hope I don't have an accident while walking down the road?

No bloody chance.

Think, Daley, *think*!

Wait a minute . . . Wait just a damn minute!

I look around the loft at the detritus surrounding me. There's not much up here apart from the work tools and lights Fred's team have brought with them. But over in one corner, pushed out of the way so they don't interfere with the workspace are all those empty wooden boxes I first spied on my initial – and disastrous – trip up here.

One of them is even about the same height as a toilet seat. *And* there's old shredded paper in it that if you squint hard enough, you could mistake for a load of discarded Andrex . . .

I am immediately disgusted by the idea. What kind of lunatic would rather have a poo into a loft box, than act like an adult and make a run for the toilet down in the village?

This kind of lunatic, unfortunately.

If I can just get this out of the way, I can cover it up with some more of the paper and tuck it away in one corner, get the joist fixed, and do away with the box later tonight when everyone else has left the building.

It's the perfect crime.

Oh, good Lord above.

I shuffle over to the most appropriate box for the task and peer into it. A closer look at the paper inside reveals that it is in fact a lot of torn up newspaper from the 1960s, yellowed with age. Some of the pieces are large enough for me to still just about be able to decipher the story. The newspaper must have been a local rag, as there are stories about places in the area I recognise. Somebody grew a prize-winning marrow in the village, another person narrowly avoided being run over by a man in a Wolseley Hornet on the High Street, and scandal rocked the community when a 'gentlemen's club' was discovered close by.

I start to wonder why anyone would want to run a knocking shop out here in the sticks, but am cut short by another roll from my bowels. I'm going to have to make my mind up right now over whether to put my disgusting plan into action or not.

Gritting my teeth and praying to whatever gods of home renovation might be listening, I unbuckle my jeans and perch myself over the box, lowering my backside gently down onto it.

Success! The thing takes my weight. Now to just relax and let nature take its course.

Nature does indeed take its course, very rapidly. I've always been a man blessed with a strong digestive system, unlike poor old Spider and his IBS.

Within moments I am finished and am just about to clean myself up with what remains of the letters page. All has gone well. I can now get back to work safe in the knowledge that—

I freeze. Voices are filtering up to me from below.

'Is anything going on in the loft today?' I hear someone ask. I have to think for a moment as to who it is, but then I remember – the voice belongs to Pete, the BBC cameraman. A chubby, balding fellow, who favours a black leather waistcoat and worn-out BBC T-shirt, Pete only transferred onto the *Great Locations* crew a few months ago, and is a man determined to prove his worth. To that end, he's spent two days with us here already, poking his lens into every nook and cranny. I'm led to believe that Daley Farmhouse will be featured in four half-hour shows across the renovation, but Pete seems to be recording enough material to fill a thirty-six-hour miniseries.

'Yep, Danny is up there doing the joists,' I hear Fred reply. 'Come to think of it, he should be done by now. Are you alright up there, captain?' he hollers.

Fuck.

What do I do? What do I do? What do I bloody *do*?

I elect to remain silent, hoping that both men will just go away and leave me be. My thighs grip the sides of the cardboard box as I try my hardest not to move a bloody muscle.

'He must have finished up and come back down again,' Fred says. 'Here, Hayley?' he calls downstairs.

I hear my sister's faint reply.

'Have you seen your brother? I thought he was doing the joists? Pete here could get a good shot of him at work!'

Oh yes, he can get a good shot of him at work, alright.

Hayley's reply drifts up the stairs, but is too mumbled for me to hear properly.

'He must have finished, I guess,' Fred says to Pete.

'Okay. Can I pop up there and get a shot of the new joists any-way? It might make a good cutaway.'

Say no, Fred. Say no, Fred. Say *NO*, Fred!

'Sure! Take as long as you like!'

Aaaarrghh!

I hear Pete's foot on the first rung of the ladder, and my heart rate shoots up. I have nowhere to hide. The loft is more or less empty, and the only thing big enough for me to hide behind is currently underneath me, and full of my effluence.

Pete continues to climb the ladder, and I see the camera lens poke into the loft.

In absolute terror I look around, searching for something that might help me. I could throw another box at Pete's head, or maybe dazzle him with one of the lights—

The lights!

That's it!

If I can put the lights out, Pete won't be able to see me!

I bend down and pick up the extension cable that the lights are all plugged into. With one swift movement I grab the end in my sweaty hand and hammer the cut-off switch.

The loft is instantly plunged into darkness, other than a few thin shafts of light from the various holes about the place. Luckily, I am not in one of them. Instead, I am now shrouded in complete darkness.

'Oh!' Pete exclaims, his head popping through the loft hatch. 'The lights have all gone out, Fred!'

'Must be a fuse gone, mate. Sorry, not much I can do from down here.'

'No worries,' Pete says. 'I can use the light on the camera to get around. Maybe I can see what the problem is using that.'

My blood runs cold again. Pete presses a button on the side of the camera, and a bright, white lamp flicks on at the top of the machine, bathing a large circle of the roof above his head in light.

'Maybe I'll do a bit of filming like this,' Pete adds. 'Get a bit of spooky atmospherics on the go!'

'You do whatever makes you happy, Pete,' Fred replies, trying not to sound patronising.

Pete laughs, climbs into the loft, and starts to wave his camera around the place.

As the beam of light goes over my head I hold my breath. He still hasn't seen me! If I stay very, very quiet, he might not shine the light over here again.

Then Pete starts to do something very strange: an unconvincing impression of David Attenborough.

'And up here, in the eaves of the house,' he says in a raspy voice, reminiscent of the legendary documentary presenter, 'what kinds of interesting specimens might we encounter?'

The impression isn't *that* bad, to be honest. It seems like Pete is the kind of BBC cameraman who wishes he were on location somewhere tropical, filming Sir David as he stands next to a rare species of bee, talking about its fascinating abdominal striping.

'The heat is stifling,' he continues, 'the humidity is high. Only certain creatures can survive in such a harsh climate.'

Okay now, Pete. You've had your fun. Why not fuck off back downstairs?'

Pete sniffs the air. 'Here, Fred?' he bellows back down the ladder, breaking character for the moment. 'It doesn't half stink up here!'

'Probably where the fuse has gone! See if you can spot the extension cable!'

'Okay, but it doesn't really smell of burning, more like something's taken a shit up here!'

The camera swings around again, tracking across the floor a mere few metres in front of me.

'The environment could not be more extreme,' Fake Attenborough says. 'The heat, the smell, the darkness. What kind of strange and bizarre creature could possibly want to make this place its hom— *JESUS CHRIST!*

My eyes close reflexively in the glare of the camera's light. One hand cups my genitals, while the other is thrown up to protect myself from Pete's prying electronic eye.

'Danny?' Pete exclaims in horror. 'What the hell are you doing?'

'Composing a bloody symphony, Pete! What does it look like?'

'It looks like you're pooing in a box!'

'Does it? Does it really? Well, that must be what I'm doing then!'

'Why?'

'*Why?*' I repeat, incredulous. 'Because there's nothing I like more than defecating in the pitch black where it's boiling hot. I would have climbed into the airing cupboard if it wasn't too small.'

'Really?'

'No, not fucking *really*! I got caught short and didn't have much of a choice!'

'But there's a Portaloo downstairs.'

I don't have an answer for that. Well I do, but it's a ridiculous one.

'What's going on up here, then?' Fred Babidge says, poking his head into the loft. 'I can hear a load of commotion—' Fred spots me in the corner. His eyes widen. '*Aha ha haha ha haha ahha ah.*'

Much as I hope and pray that the ladder gives way under Fred's shaking body, I fear that it probably won't.

'Oh, give it a bloody rest,' I tell him and point my finger back at Pete. 'Could you stop waving that thing in my face?' I notice that the little red light is on. 'Are you *recording* this?' I wail.

'What's happening?' I hear Hayley ask someone from below.

'Don't know. We only came here to ask the boss something,' Baz says.

'But we think he's having some kind of fit,' Spider adds.

I now have an audience, each no doubt lining up to stick their heads through the hatch to see the amazing Loft Poo Man in action.

I give Pete my best 'I will come over there and crap on you too if you don't do what I say' look. 'Turn the camera off Pete, and go away. See if you can calm Fred down before he has a hernia.'

'But I wanted to get a shot of the joists!' he complains.

The scowl deepens. 'Pete, if you don't sod off that camera's getting shoved where the sun doesn't shine.'

Pete grumbles something about being sick of people threatening him like that, but does switch the bloody machine off, once again plunging me into darkness. He climbs back down the ladder, leaving me gratefully alone, but with my untenable position more or less unchanged.

'Are you okay, Danny?' Hayley calls up.

'Yes! Just get everyone downstairs please!' I plead with her. 'I'll be down in a minute!'

I just about hear the shuffling of feet over Fred's continued hysterical laughter, and take a deep breath.

Now what?

I fumble around until I feel the head of the extension cable again and hit the switch. The glare of the lights blinking into existence is so bright I jerk my head backwards, bringing it into sharp contact with the roof beam behind me.

'Oh crap!' I screech and rock forward again.

The wooden box, which hasn't taken too well to all this abuse, having been left to its own devices in a damp loft for fifty years, gives way under me . . . and I find myself sitting in my own crap for the first time since I was a baby.

I don't want to discuss the details of the clean-up operation. Suffice to say it involved a bucket full of cold water, and an ocean full of cold humiliation.

I've read stories about people who have embarrassing episodes involving the toilet. Hayley had some trashy comedy book that I scanned through a couple of years ago, which had a guy accidentally crapping into a pedal bin thanks to a bout of food poisoning. It seemed pretty awful at the time.

I would like to find the guy who wrote it and reassure him that his mortification at ruining a date thanks to some dodgy chicken, is nothing compared to holding out a ball of ripped-up newspaper from the 1960s at arm's length, and parading it past your sister, a team of beefy workmen and a BBC cameraman, on the way to the wheelie bin.

I slam the lid down and look back at everyone, trying not to burst out crying.

'I once got the shits on a job,' Spider says in a thoughtful voice.

'Oh yeah!' Baz laughs and points at him. 'You was up the scaffold, wasn't you? I could see skid marks from the ground! What was it we called you for the rest of the month?'

'Brown Spider,' Spider says, possibly highlighting why brickies don't have alternate careers as stand-up comedians.

'That's right! Brown Spider!' This sends Baz off into a gale of laughter. Then he sees the glum look on Spider's face and instantly sticks an arm round his friend's shoulder to make him feel better.

'I followed through in the truck once,' Fred says. 'Three-hour journey up to Lincolnshire for a new stove, as I recall. Dad wasn't best pleased, I can tell you.'

'I peed over Trevor McDonald once,' Pete pipes up. We all turn to look at him aghast. 'Yep. Got pissed at a wrap party and fell over at the urinal. He never knew what hit him. Some of it went in his eye.'

I try for a moment to work out the logistics of such a feat, but it eludes me.

I know what they're trying to do, but it's not helping. I'm fully aware that other people have highly embarrassing episodes in their lives, but I'm the one who's just had to walk past a group of people carrying my own shit in a scrunched-up roll of paper, so unless one of them wants to squat here in front of all of us, I'm just going to carry on feeling epically sorry for myself.

'I'm going home,' I tell them in a flat tone of voice. Nobody puts up an argument. And who can blame them?

'I got caught kissing Claire Wright at university!' Hayley squeaks. Now it's everyone's turn to look at her.

I'm aghast, but everyone else is suddenly smiling. Hayley looks at us nervously, realising that sharing this kind of information isn't quite the same thing as letting people in on your embarrassing episodes of public incontinence. 'We were only experimenting a bit in the common room after everyone else had left. Gav the Chav came back to get his coat and saw us over by the Space Invaders machine.' Hayley sees my expression, stops talking and looks down at her feet.

'I'm definitely going home,' I repeat and stalk off towards the motorbike, hoping to Christ that nobody else is going to let me in on one of their past humiliations just to try and make me feel better. Then, a thought strikes me, and I'm striding back towards Pete in a split second.

'Hand it over,' I tell him.

'What?'

'Hand it over, Pete!' I snap.

He sighs and pops the digital tape out of the camera, handing it to me reluctantly. 'Those things are expensive, you know,' he moans.

'I'll buy you another one,' I reply, trying to resist the urge to hit him over the head with it.

This time there are no interruptions to my walk of shame, and I manage to get on the bike and ride away without doing further injury to both my body and my sense of self-worth.

I think today has taught me a very valuable lesson. Don't get ideas above your station, because the chances are you'll just end up burning the station down, with hordes of screaming commuters inside.

From now on I think I'll stop trying to integrate myself into the Daley Farmhouse workforce, and just be content to be the client paying for them to do a better job than I can.

On my way home I stop to get some petrol – and a variety pack of Monster Munch. It'll save time tomorrow.

HAYLEY
July
£59,327.92 spent

I mean, come on, how hard can it possibly be to use a nail gun?

'*Miss Daley? Can you hear me, Miss Daley?*'

I can feel someone pinching my earlobe. It hurts.

My eyes flutter open as I hear my brother's tremulous voice. 'Is she going to be alright?'

'Have I got this done up alright?' I ask Spider, showing him my efforts to get into the dark blue overalls.

'I dunno, Hayles. I never wore one of those things before.'

My brow creases. 'You've never worn overalls to work?'

'Nope.'

'But the bloke in B&Q told me that if I was going to do some DIY, I should wear them.'

Spider smiles thinly and rubs his bald head. 'Yeah, I bet he did.'

I catch the tone. 'So, you're saying I got ripped off?'

* * *

Spider holds up his hands. 'I ain't saying that, Hayles, but I never saw no one wearing one of those things on site before. Not when you can just wear your hi-vis over your T-shirt and jeans.'

Well, I don't care what Spider thinks. I reckon I look *smart* in my overalls. I particularly like the shiny cuffs and bright white piping going down both sides. I feel like a Power Ranger who's lost a lot of weight recently.

If I'm going to have a go at some DIY, I want to look the part, don't I?

And that's been the problem. All I've been doing is *looking*. Looking at other people doing all of the hard work. I've stood around and done bugger all, except fill out countless spreadsheets, and make phone calls to people who want to take all of my money away from me.

For the first few weeks the idea of doing any manual labour turned my stomach, but as time has gone by and I've spent more time on the site, I've become more and more aware that I have an itch that I really want to scratch.

It's quite fascinating to see Daley Farmhouse change for the better in front of my eyes, and when it's complete I want to be able to say that I contributed to that change. There's nothing wrong with that, is there?

Danny's having no problems. Okay, it took him a good fortnight to return to the renovation after that incident in the loft, but since then he's got on with the job alongside the rest of Fred's team quite well. If anything, I think they all actually like him *more* since he took a shit in the loft. It's almost as if that one act of disgusting behaviour has integrated him into their ranks more than any actual contribution to the build.

I will never understand men as long as I live.

This has left me as the only person involved in the build that hasn't actually done anything yet, other than push paper about and stand around feeling awkward in wellies. Even Gerard O'Keefe mucked in a couple of days ago on one of his occasional visits. One minute he's standing there delivering an update into Pete's camera, the next he's trowelling mortar next to Fred, and slapping bricks onto the back wall of the new extension.

Speaking of which, the extension is really coming along nicely now. By the time it's done the whole rear of the ground floor will be a lot more spacious, and I can't wait to see what it looks like.

Mitchell's design is fabulous, I have to say. By extending several metres back from the old rear wall of the house, we'll open out the kitchen and the lounge into one huge, light-filled space. This also gives us room to put in a downstairs cloakroom, which should increase the house's value even more.

Fred and the boys have already knocked down the wall between the kitchen and the lounge, and have put a strong RSJ in its place to hold the first floor up. It really is quite incredible what you can do to a property once you have the plans in place, and the expertise to see them brought to life.

Which is why I'm standing here in a brand-new set of overalls. I want to be a part – however small – of seeing those plans turned into reality, just so I can stand back when the house is finished and know that a tiny part of it includes Hayley Daley's blood, sweat and tears.

'*Oh God! She's bleeding!*' Danny moans. 'Can you stop it?'

'Please stand back, Mr Daley.'

The paramedic's jacket has the same shiny cuff as my overalls.

'Everything's gonna be fine, lad,' I hear Fred say. 'Let's just move back and let him patch your sister up.'

'Right, what can I do?' I ask Fred Babidge expectantly.

He gives me the narrowed eyes. 'What would you like to do?'

I wave a hand. 'Oh, I don't know. Anything really. As long as someone shows me the ropes, I'll be fine, I'm sure.'

Fred's doubtful expression fills me with feminine rage.

'What's the matter, Fred? Don't you think I can do anything?' My tone is haughty. My face is sharp. 'Is it because I'm a *woman*?'

Fred sighs and puts down the hammer. 'Hayley, my youngest, Trina, would be here working on this job if she hadn't got pregnant. My wife has forgotten more about furniture-making than I'll ever know, and my old mum – may she rest in peace – could put up a set of shelves blindfolded in a hurricane. This has nothing to do with you being a woman.'

'Then what is it, Fred? What is it?'

'You've never done a day's DIY in your life, have you?'

My hands go to my hips in indignation. 'And what makes you say that?'

'Well, firstly, you're wearing a set of overalls that most labourers wouldn't go within a thousand feet of. Then there's the fact that last week you asked me what a spirit level was, and when I asked you the other day to order us some more two-by-four, you told me that buying a new truck would be far too expensive.'

I don't have an answer to that. My anger is instantly quashed, as I realise that Fred is not being a sexist pig – he's just got a set of eyes and a functioning brain.

'But I want to do something, Fred!' I say in a whiny, nasal tone that I intend to regret for the rest of my life. Every feminist on the planet would be tutting louder than the cement mixer if they were here.

Fred folds his arms. 'Okay, I get you. This always happens on a job. I once had a seventy-five-year-old grandmother of six up on a ladder doing a little light plastering before her hip gave out.'

'Well, there you go then! If you got her working, you can give me something to do as well!'

Fred's eyebrow arches. 'The old dear was in hospital for a week. You should have seen the paperwork I had to fill out.'

I stamp my foot. Somewhere in the world a cold shiver has just run down Germaine Greer's back. 'Oh, come on Fred! I'm not going to hurt myself!'

'Now I'm just going to give you a small injection for the pain, Miss Daley.'

I nod and squeeze my eyes closed.

'Then we'll get you into the ambulance, and to the hospital as quickly as we can.'

Fred looks over at where Spider and Weeble, the smallest member of our building team, are putting floorboards down in the massive new lounge. Spider is holding the boards in place while Weeble nails them into the joists with a very loud and very powerful nail gun. 'Boys? You got anything Hayley here can do?'

The look of veiled terror is priceless. If I look closely, I can actually watch the blood run from Weeble's face. I can't do the same with Spider as all those tattoos are in the way.

Fred sucks in air over his teeth. 'I tell you what, there's some wood needs cutting for the studwork. Do you think you can handle a saw?' he says to me.

I nod enthusiastically. That sounds like just the kind of job I can do: simple, easy and straightforward.

Fred takes me out of the extension and onto the patio area, which has been cleared somewhat thanks to Baz's efforts with an old industrial strimmer.

Fred walks over to what looks like two thick black plastic hurdles. 'Now these are sawhorses, Hayley. You stick your wood across them, and saw through them.' He picks up a long length of thin wood and places it over both of the plastic hurdles. 'So I want you to measure out lengths of three metres, and cut twelve separate bits. You got that?'

I nod slowly.

'Good stuff.' He takes out a tape measure and a thick black marker and hands both to me. 'Remember, three-metre lengths, alright?' Fred then retrieves a long saw from beside the sawhorse and hands that to me as well. 'You good?'

I nod again, faster this time. I want to show willing.

'Smashing! Off you go then!' Fred gives me a pat on the shoulder and returns back to where he came from, into the bowels of the house and out of sight.

For a few moments I just stand staring at the hurdle things. I was rather hoping for some more complete instructions, but it appears that Fred is one of those minimalist types, who prefers to give people the bare facts and let them work things out for themselves.

Fair enough, I suppose. This will be my chance to endlessly impress him with my independence, and ability to pick things up quickly. Germaine will be so proud!

I go over to the pile of wood and immediately get two splinters. Carrying a length very carefully over to the two hurdle things, I place it on top of them and use the tape measure to section out three metres, which I mark with the pen. So far, so good. Then I grab the saw, take a deep breath and drag the teeth across the wood. Fairly quickly, I build up a nice rhythm, and the sharp saw neatly cuts through the wood in no time at all. Before I know it the two pieces of long wood are falling apart. I have successfully cut my first piece of wood!

I look up to see Fred standing where the double doors to the extension will eventually be. He smiles and gives me a thumbs up, which I return with enthusiasm. 'Keep going then,' he tells me, before disappearing off into the house again.

And keep going I do, for an hour. By the time I have finished, there are six splinters of wood in my fingers, and a big pile of three-metre timber lengths. The job is done and I couldn't be happier about it. Not least because those splinters are really hurting. I should have worn gloves.

'So, how do you fancy screwing those bits of wood together into a framework for me?' Fred offers as we stand eating sandwiches in the sunshine.

'Er . . .' I reply, looking down at my hands. I'm going to need a good couple of hours with the tweezers and Savlon as it is.

'Go on, sis!' Danny encourages. 'It'll save me having to do it!'

'Yep,' Fred adds. 'Then you can get on with treating the floorboards, my old cupcake,' he says to Danny.

Ah, I see what's going on here. Fred has cunningly made sure there are enough easy jobs lying around the place to keep both Daleys busy and out of his hair. The studwork had obviously been earmarked as a Danny job, but with my, er, *helpful assistance*, he can do something else that the average five-year-old could probably have a decent go at.

We are both being *smoothly* handled.

'Uh, okay,' I agree, with visions in my head of walking around the completed house, patting the stud walls affectionately, as someone offers me a million quid for the place.

And so, a short time later, I'm back on the patio surrounded by wood, with Fred once more giving me a detailed set of instructions.

'Right, you put three down this way round,' he says, placing the bits of wood down on the flagstones. 'Then two this way round.' Another two lengths are put at either end of the other three. 'Then you use the stud brackets to screw 'em all together using the inch-long screws, and the drill with the screwdriver attachment over there. Just make sure the middle one is exactly one and a half metres in the centre and you'll be golden. Do six of them, and then I'll come back and we'll do the supporting struts in between, alright?'

Not really.

'Yes, I'll be fine, Fred,' I assure him. 'Off you go.'

I could, and should, get him to go through all of that again in finer detail, but I figure I'm on a roll now, and probably don't need any more assistance.

Fred claps his hands together. 'Lovely jubbly. If you need any help, just ask.'

And with that, he leaves so I can continue with my new career in advanced carpentry.

Sadly, it turns out I wasn't on any kind of roll.

The only thing rolling around here are my eyes, in frustration every time I have to use that bloody drill.

You see, the wood is hard, and the screws are quite blunt. The cordless drill is also large, heavy and quite unwieldy. Persuading the screws to go through the holes in the bracket and into the wood straight is a virtual impossibility. I struggle for fifteen minutes with the first frame, and end up with something more warped than the Starship Enterprise. The only wall you'd want to build with this thing would be one in a house of horrors at the funfair. I pull out the screws and do it again, but try as hard as I might, I just can't get everything to marry up straight, even if I stand on the wood while I'm screwing.

There must be any easier way to do this . . .

'There must be a better way to get to the ambulance,' I moan through the fog of pain.

'This is the best way, Miss Daley,' the paramedic replies, strapping me onto the wheeled stretcher.

'Just mind the new floorboards!' I wail, as my head swims with the pain medication he's just administered.

* * *

I make my way back into the house to find that everybody has buggered off.

The kitchen extension and lounge are empty.

Looking out of the broad front windows I can see why. Danny has been out and apparently bought doughnuts. The entire workforce is crowded round him and tucking into a large box of Krispy Kremes.

Why did nobody tell *me* there were bloody doughnuts?

I am most, most put out. I have been forgotten about. Because I have been out in the back garden struggling with the studwork for hours, it has become a definite case of out of sight, out of bloody mind.

Men!

There's no way I'm going out there to ask for help now – and I'm not going to ask for a doughnut either. They can just feel incredibly guilty later when they realise that they forgot all about me. Yeah. That'll do it.

I turn to stamp back out to the garden, when out of the corner of one eye, I spy a tool that may well make my job outside much, much easier.

The nail gun is even heavier than the drill, but it looks like quite a simple contraption. It also looks ancient. There's grease and other substances I can't identify covering the thing, and a strong smell of oil emanating from it. There's every chance I'll need to disinfect myself once I've finished using it, but I'm sure as hell going to give it a go on the studwork, as it might save me a lot of bother.

I walk back out to the patio and over to my bits of wood.

'Right then, you bastards,' I whisper to the nearest two pieces. 'Let's see you put up such a big fight when I use this.' I shake the nail gun triumphantly over the wood, as if they weren't completely inanimate and totally unable to appreciate the import of my words.

With renewed resolve, I put the two bits of wood at right angles to one another, bracing one with my left foot. I place the bracket between them, put the end of the nail gun where the bracket hole is, and grit my teeth.

I press the trigger and . . .

WHAMP!

A six-inch nail shoots through the hole, into the wood, out of the other side and right into my foot.

There's no pain.

Not at first.

Just shock.

'Mib,' I exclaim in a weird squeak. 'Mib mib,' I repeat, my bottom lip quivering.

I can see the nail's grey steel entering the side of my dirty white trainers. Judging from the size of the nail, a good two inches of its length are now inside my body.

Are now *inside* my body.

The world starts to go fuzzy at the edges.

'Mib,' I say for a fourth time. Quite what this means I have no idea. Maybe in my state of shock I'm channelling some long-dead language of my ancestors, and 'mib' is what they used to say when they accidentally drove a foreign object into the side of their foot.

I pull my foot away from the wood, and feel the nail sliding out as I do so. As soon as the nail is free of my shoe, I instantly see the edges of the trainer turn from mucky white to bright red, and the world goes even fuzzier. I stumble, and plant my injured left foot hard on the ground to stabilise myself.

Ah, there's the pain.

A bright, lancing spear of agony shoots up my leg, through my body and out of the top of my head. I let out an involuntary scream.

Sadly, that's not the only involuntary action the shock of the pain hitting me causes. My finger also flexes on the trigger of the nail gun.

WHAMP! WHAMP! WHAMP! goes the infernal machine, sending nails ricocheting off the patio. Two cracks appear in the flagstone beneath my feet, and somewhere I hear the sound of breaking glass as one of the flying nails finds a target.

With another scream – one of terror – I throw the nail gun across the patio. When it hits the ground, another four nails come spitting out of it in quick succession. Luckily – oh so very *luckily* – the gun is pointing away from me as it does so. Not so luckily, it's now skidding along the concrete paving stones and will very soon hit a bank of earth. When it does, it will rebound, and there's no telling where the nails might end up if it fires any more off.

'What the hell's going on?!' I hear Danny exclaim from the extension doorway.

I spin around and in full-on commando style I screech, 'Get down now!' As I do, I crouch, ignoring the fresh burst of pain from my left foot.

'What do you mean, get d—'

WHAMP! WHAMP!

The corner of the brick to the left of Danny's head explodes as another ricocheting nail flies from the gun, hits one of the lengths of wood I've been wrestling with for the whole day and shoots past my brother's head.

'Jesus Christ!' he screams, and assumes a crouching position.

I look over at where the nail gun has come to rest. It's not spitting out six-inch death bullets any more, but it is making an ominous clicking noise, indicating that if it finds another nail in the magazine, we could still be in serious trouble.

'Fuck me!' Fred Babidge roars, striding past both crouching Daleys. He grabs the nail gun, immediately flicking a switch on the side that makes the thing silent. 'What the hell were you *doing*, Hayley?' he spits at me.

I instantly go shamefaced. Fred has never once raised his voice to either of us, but here he is, doing it now while holding an implement that nearly killed both my brother and me.

It's all my fault!

'I was . . . I was trying to get the studwork done,' I say in a meek voice.

His eyes bulge a bit. 'With a bleedin' nail gun? Christ, girl. What do you want to do next? Prune a few rose bushes with a chainsaw?'

My face falls. 'The screws wouldn't go in properly,' I complain.

He looks at me for a moment, words forming on his lips. Then he appears to remember that I am in fact a client paying him a great deal of money, so he breathes deeply, and obviously thinks better of voicing his opinions about my DIY skills. 'Well, at least neither of you got hurt.'

'Ah,' I say, holding my finger up. 'That's where you're wrong.'

I lift up my foot to show him the damage. A few drops of blood hit the patio and I immediately go fuzzy again. 'I think I'm going to faint . . .'

And indeed, I do.

Thankfully, Danny is there to catch me. Otherwise I'd be adding a heavy concussion to severe foot trauma.

The world goes black – and not a moment too soon.

'It's no good, the stretcher's too heavy with her on it,' I hear one of the paramedics say as I swim in and out of consciousness.

I grab him by the shiny yellow coat. 'Are you saying I'm fat?' I drawl at him, trying not to drool from the pain medication he's just pumped into me.

'What?'

'Are you saying, Mr Paramedic, that I am *fat*?'

'No, Miss Daley! It's just that we could carry the empty stretcher across the lounge, but there are too many floorboards missing for us to wheel it back with you on it.'

'Because I'm *fat*. Correct?'

Danny appears at my side. 'Just ignore her. She gets like this when she's not feeling well.'

'Not feeling well?' I snap. 'I've just stabbed myself with a six-inch nail!'

'Only a tiny bit of it, sis. I had a look.'

'Oh, bugger off, Danny. You once cried for a week when a bee stung you on the bum.'

Danny's face flames red as the paramedic tries to suppress a smile.

'We can carry it for you,' Fred offers, the rest of boys standing around him looking muscular.

Bless them. They want to help me in my hour of need, even though my hour of need was scheduled entirely by my own stupidity.

The paramedic shakes his head. 'We can't do that. Health and safety. If anything happens to her, it'll be on our heads.'

I grab his jacket again. 'What could possibly happen to me that's worse than getting a six-inch nail through my foot?'

'Inch and a half . . . Two at most.'

'Shut up, Danny!'

The paramedic gives me an apologetic look. 'Sorry, we just can't let them take you.'

Fred grunts in disgust. 'Well, how about round the side of the house then?'

I look at him wide-eyed. 'What? Across the battlefields of the Somme, you mean? That'll be even worse!'

To explain: both sides of the garden have been mud bogs for the past few weeks. When you have heavy machinery trundling across them every day, the soft earth and grass doesn't stand a chance, especially with the usual amount of summer and autumn rain you get in the UK. While I was pleased to see the back of the gigantic bramble bushes and overgrown trees, the uneven hills and troughs of mud have not been much of an improvement. I'm amazed none of us has come down with trench foot yet.

In fact, the job I should have been doing today – instead of being the DIY disaster I quite clearly am – was to find a decent landscape gardener to come and fix all that mess once the house is finished.

Getting me across that mud bog on a big ambulance stretcher will be a nightmare.

'We can lay down some planks to get you over the worst bits,' Fred suggests to the two ambulance men. 'It won't be a problem.'

Another fresh wave of pain emanates from my foot. It seems the medication isn't as strong as it could be. 'Oh, whatever!' I say, trying not to faint again. 'Just get me somewhere clean and smelling of Dettol!' I lie back down on the stretcher properly and cross my fingers.

What follows could easily be filmed by Pete the cameraman and released on YouTube to the delight and edification of anyone who enjoys watching others in extreme distress.

The two paramedics start to wheel me across the mud, with my brother, Fred and the rest of them all watching on with nervous expressions on their faces.

At first things don't go too badly. We edge around the side of the house until we are in view of the ambulance. It's only when the muddy ground starts to get really uneven that we encounter difficulties.

'Watch the wheel on the edge of that plank!' Danny warns – sadly too late.

'Ow! Bloody hell!' I cry as my foot bangs painfully against the stretcher's side.

'It's okay, I've got it!' Paramedic One assures me as he wrenches the stretcher back onto the precarious track that Fred and the boys have constructed across the muddy battlefield. He gives me a reassuring smile as he does so.

Then he instantly disappears from view as he steps into the mud and his leg goes out from under him.

'Oh bugger!' Paramedic Two shouts. 'I don't think I can hold the—'

And he's gone too. It's like they've both been sucked under by a bog monster, leaving me high and dry on a stretcher in the middle of no-man's land. I crane my neck round to the small crowd gathered off to one side. 'Aren't any of you going to bloody help me?'

'No, no!' A muddy hand appears, waving frantically. 'We've got everything under control!'

Paramedic Two is back upright again. He is also now covered from head to toe in mud. Those shiny cuffs are well and truly in need of a good hosing down.

'Are you alright, Alistair?' he asks the other guy.

'Not really. I think I've sprained my ankle,' Alistair replies in a reedy voice, still out of sight.

'Do you think you can help me with the patient?' Paramedic Two asks.

'I don't think so . . .'

'Oh.'

Silence descends. I look up at Paramedic Two, getting a really good view of his nasal cavity.

'Do you think you could get me to the ambulance?' I ask, trying to stay calm. 'I am in rather a lot of pain, you know.'

He looks down at me. 'But what about Alistair?'

'I DON'T CARE ABOUT ALISTAIR! My foot is about to fall off!' It's not, but it certainly feels like it might if I have to lie here on this stretcher for much longer. 'Let them help you!' I order.

'But health and safety . . .'

I don't grab his jacket, because I don't want to get any mud on me. 'I'm marooned in a bog with one foot bleeding all over the place, with one paramedic down and the other resembling a fresh turd. I think health and bloody safety have gone right out of the window! Danny! Fred! Get over here and get me to the ambulance!'

Thankfully, the paramedic makes no more objections when the boys slip and slide over to me, picking the stretcher up between them and carrying me over to the ambulance. They then go back and pick up Alistair, who has gone very grey. That sprain might well end up being a break.

In no time at all, I am loaded into the ambulance and awaiting departure.

'I'll ride down behind you,' Danny says.

'Thanks.' The anger is gone from my voice again, now it's all about the pain.

Paramedic Two fires up the ambulance as Alistair limps in and sits next to me. He looks down at my foot again, checking the temporary dressing.

'So, how exactly did this happen?' he asks in a tight, pained voice.

'Well, it was like this,' I reply, matching the tone of his perfectly. 'My grandma left me a house, and I thought it would be a good idea to fix it up. So now I have a giant hole in my foot.'

'I see.'

'No, you don't. You really, really *don't*,' I disagree, closing my eyes and trying to ignore the throbbing coming from my lower left extremity.

I expected Daley Farmhouse to throw up a lot of difficulties, but I was rather counting on being able to tackle them without bleeding everywhere.

In the end, I get two stitches in my foot for my troubles, a tetanus injection and a big box of lovely painkillers. Danny offers me a ride home, but I wisely decide to take a taxi instead.

That evening I am feeling decidedly miserable, and very sorry for myself. My foot aches like mad, and the painkillers are making me woozy and fuzzy-headed, which is horrible. I'm about to limp up to have a bath (with a plastic bag round my foot so the dressing doesn't get wet) when my phone rings.

'Hello?'

'Hello, Hayley? It's Gerard. I heard about what happened. Are you alright?'

Well, this is unexpected.

'Not really. My foot hurts,' I reply, voice treacherously quivering somewhat.

'Ouch. Tell me all about it.'

So I spend the next twenty minutes explaining what happened to Gerard, who listens quietly until I am finished, and then sympathises with me in that soft tone of voice he has no doubt practised a thousand times in interviews with people as incompetent as I am at house renovation.

By the end of the chat I am actually feeling a lot better.

I put the phone down and allow myself a little smile. What a nice thing for him to have done.

Hang on.

Oh no.

Oh no, no, no.

This is an utter *disaster*.

The last thing I want right now is a charming, rich, famous man being nice to me. That way madness lies. I swore off men for life after Simon ruined me.

How could I be any different after what happened? I got swept off my feet by the best-looking man in the nightclub, found myself married to him a mere three months later because he was the most exciting person I'd ever met, spent five years thinking I was living with the man of my dreams, and then had everything torn away from me when that bitch turned up on the doorstep in her stupid plastic high heels.

I do *not* need the kind of temptation that Gerard O'Keefe represents.

It may all be charm and smiles and concern right now, but in five years? All that charm is being directed at two other women, and the concern is only for his own well-being when I find out he's been cheating on me!

Now, come on Hayley. Gerard isn't the same man, my internal voice of reason says.

Yes, he bloody well is. They're *all* the same!

I'm not going to fall for it again! I'm not!

What I am going to do is scream and reach for the painkillers, as I've just forgotten about today's injury, and stamped my foot on the ground in determined anger.

How hard can it be to use a nail gun? Extremely easy, if what you're trying to do is get yourself a month's supply of ibuprofen tablets and work yourself up into a rage about how useless men are. If you're putting up shelves though, I'd stick to a tube of No More Nails and save yourself the bother.

DANNY

July
£76,546.39 spent

The house is coming along nicely. Nearly three months in and we're motoring along *marvellously*.

All the boring stuff is pretty much done. The foundations are secure. The roof is fixed. The walls are strong. The woodworm has been killed. The floorboards have been replaced. The extension is built. The list goes on and on.

Sadly, virtually none of these enormous improvements are visible from the street, which is a tad disheartening, to be honest. When you spend over seventy thousand quid, you expect there to be something to show for it. But thus far, Daley Farmhouse looks like it's been barely touched.

I'm led to believe this is fairly typical of major house renovations like this. If you're looking for immediate gratification, pick something else to do as a hobby is my advice.

Still, we're at the point when we are ready to start on all the fun stuff, and thus far we've had very few big problems come our way. Hayley is still limping about the place a bit, but the doctor has assured her she'll be fine in a couple of weeks. Fred and the lads will just have to find a different impression to do than Long John Silver.

Nope, everything is ticking along nicely.

Now, if I could just get rid of that bloody cow, everything would be truly fantastic.

Three weeks ago I was helping Spider strip the last of the old plaster from a corner of the dining room.

'I'm going for a piss,' I inform him.

He gives me a look. 'I think Fred's in the Portaloo.'

'Oh. Then I guess I'll have to brave the jungle outside.'

We haven't started on the expansive back garden yet, apart from clearing the immediate area around the house. The rest of it is still the overgrown wilderness it was when Hayley and I first came here.

'I'd wait for the Portaloo,' Spider replies.

'Why's that?'

He grimaces. 'There's way too many spiders out the back there.'

I'm stunned. 'Spider – your name is *Spider*.'

'So?'

'Well, how can you not like spiders, if your name is Spider?'

'That's what my mum always says.'

'So what's your real name?'

'Charlton.'

'Come again?'

'M'name's Charlton. My dad's a Man U fan.'

'I think I prefer Spider.'

'Me too.'

This is easily the most profound conversation I've ever had with the tattooed, bald brickie, but my bladder is making noises that I can no longer ignore. 'Hold that thought, I'll be back in a minute.'

It doesn't take long to reach an area of the back garden that is out of sight and within moments I am breathing a blessed sigh of relief as I water one of the gnarled old apple trees that dot the garden.

'Moo.'

What the fuck?

'Moo.'

I spin around, penis still in hand, to see a cow staring at me from less than four feet away.

No, not a cow. *The* cow. The same cow Hayley and I first encountered all those weeks ago. It has the same black patch around one eye and the same searching expression coming from those big, brown cow eyes.

And here I am, presenting my genitals to it. Probably not appropriate, all things considered.

I spin back around and finish urinating. By the time I am done and the old chap is popped back in, I fully expect the cow to have moved away.

Nothing of the sort. If anything, it's a foot closer.

'Watch yourself,' I tell it. 'I've just peed there.'

'Moo,' the cow replies, and doesn't budge an inch.

I regard the cow with a look of extreme suspicion. 'Where the hell did you come from?' The cow has not been seen again in the garden since that first encounter. Possibly all the heavy machinery put her off, but now the big noisy work is done, she's returned. Quite how is still beyond me. I've walked around the whole gigantic field that passes for a garden at Daley Farmhouse, and can see no evidence of where something as big as a cow could gain entry to it. It's quite unfathomable.

'I feel as if I should call you Houdini The Cow,' I say to the cow, continuing my train of thought out loud. 'But you don't look like a Houdini.' Inspiration strikes. 'I shall call you Pat The Cow. How does that sound?'

'Moo.' I swear there's a derisory tone to that response.

'Please yourself. I never said I was a creative genius.'

Pat The Cow takes another step towards me, so her head is within touching distance. 'There, there,' I say, and pat Pat The Cow's head gently.

Pat The Cow seems to be quite happy with this state of affairs. 'Moo.'

'You're quite sweet really, aren't you?' I tell Pat The Cow.

'Moo,' Pat The Cow agrees. 'Moo mooooooo.'

'Why thank you, Pat The Cow,' I tell her. 'I'm glad you think I'm sweet too.'

From over by the house I hear Spider calling me. Pat The Cow looks around, chewing the cud slowly as she tries to spot this new interloper. She then turns back to me, gives a look with her big swimmy cow eyes that seems to say 'mention nothing of this' and turns to walk away into the long grass.

'Danny! Where the hell are ya?' Spider calls.

'Over here!' I call back and start to make my way back towards him. I turn and throw one last glance in Pat The Cow's direction to say goodbye . . . But she has disappeared! The big bovine is nowhere to be seen.

Spooky.

I return to Spider. He notes the look of confusion on my face. 'What's up?'

I open my mouth to tell him all about my encounter with Pat The Cow, but then I remember the expression on her face and keep my trap shut. Pat The Cow is obviously part ninja, and I don't want to end up skewered on the end of an expertly thrown ninja cow dagger.

My next encounter with Pat The Cow happened a mere couple of days later. I was sitting on one of the old patio chairs out the back, enjoying a nice chicken Cup-a-Soup and some sun, when Hayley limped over to me, carrying a small trowel.

'Having fun with the pointing?' I ask her.

'Not really. I should never have asked Fred what pointing was. He's had me filling in gaps between bricks for the past two hours.'

'At least you're still showing willing.' I grin. 'You are being careful not to stab yourself though, aren't you?'

She gives me a withering look. 'Very funny. Baz handed me the trowel covered in bubble wrap when I started.'

I laugh. 'Well, look at it this way, at least they see you as one of the boys now!'

'I don't want to be one of the boys. The last time I tried that, I ruined my chances of competing in any upcoming marathons.'

'How is the foot?'

She shrugs. 'Could be better. Could be worse. At least I can put some of my weight on it now. Still hurts like buggery, though.' She looks around. 'Where's the Big Black Bucket of Water? I need to give this trowel a clean.'

You may think that something as prosaic as a bucket of water would not need capitalisation, but trust me: it deserves that amount of importance. On a building site such as this, the Big Black Bucket of Water is easily one of the most valuable things to have at hand. Don't believe me? Try spending three months of your life surrounded by mud, dust, plaster, wood chips, construction adhesive, mortar and more mud. The Big Black Bucket of Water is an absolute must.

'I haven't seen it,' I tell Hayley. 'Could be in the kitchen, though.'

'Thanks. I'll have a look.'

Hayley limps slowly off across the patio and in through the brand-new double doors that lead into the kitchen area. I have to refer to it as a 'kitchen area', as we still haven't put the actual kitchen in yet. The concrete took longer to set than anticipated, and the plumbers still haven't been round to extend the pipes back.

There's nothing much in the broad expanse of empty space right now, other than a pasting table, on which sits a kettle from 1985, more Pot Noodles than you can shake a fork at, enough tea and coffee to drown a hall full of insomniacs, and a bag of sugar that would last an entire African village until the end of time.

Nothing dangerous, weird or scary.

Which is why it comes as something of a surprise when I hear a blood-curdling scream come from my sister.

Wondering what she's managed to impale herself upon now, I get up off my chair and go inside.

The sight that greets me is a true tableau of bovine terror. Hayley is backed up against one wall, the trowel held out in front of her, while Pat The Cow is slowly edging towards her, still chewing the cud, and with the same implacable look on her face.

Hayley spots me. 'Get it away from me, Danny! Aaargh!'

'Calm down! Pat The Cow isn't dangerous!'

Terror turns to disgust. 'You've given it a bloody *name*?!'

I stride forward, wanting to get myself in between the two of them before Pat The Cow treads on Hayley's foot, and gets a smack between the eyes with a trowel for her troubles. 'Just calm down, sis. She just likes to be patted, don't you Pat The Cow?' I give Pat The Cow the now customary pat, which she seems to appreciate.

'Moo.'

Hayley isn't so impressed. 'Move it away from me, Danny. I keep thinking it's going to charge me at any moment!'

'It's a cow, Hayley. Not a bull. The only way Pat The Cow will charge is if you stuck a cattle prod up her arse. I thought you were the one who didn't think cows were dangerous? Pat The Cow is not dangerous. Smelly, but not a risk to life and limb.'

Pat The Cow supplies me with a reproachful look. At least I think it's reproachful. It could just as easily be wind.

'Just give her a pat. I'm sure she'll move away then,' I suggest to my sister, who, with nose wrinkled and trowel still held up defensively in her other hand, reaches out and issues Pat The Cow with a timid couple of light taps to the forehead.

This seems to be enough as far as Pat The Cow is concerned, as she backs away from Hayley, nearly knocking over the pasting table snack bar.

'One question,' Hayley says.

'Yep?'

'How the hell did it get in here?'

Now this, in any other circumstances, would be a very sensible and unanswerable question. But we are dealing with a very special cow here. One able to vanish without a trace, like Batman.

'I'll just lead her back outside . . .' I venture, not willing to answer Hayley's question for fear of sounding like a lunatic.

Luckily, Pat The Cow is not feeling in an intransigent mood today, so when I gently put my arm over her neck and start to pull her round to face the doorway, she doesn't put up a struggle.

'What the living fuck?'

This comes from Fred Babidge, who has just appeared at the patio doors, no doubt wondering what all the fuss is about.

'It's alright, Fred,' I assure him, 'I'm getting her out.'

'You'd better! That concrete's only just set. Those hooves could do some real damage!'

I think Fred's being a bit melodramatic, but I figure it's best not to argue with him. To that end, I start to pull Pat The Cow's head towards the door. She moves, but when she reaches the threshold, she stops dead, giving Fred a look.

'Er . . . I think you'd better pat her,' I tell Fred.

'What?'

'You have to pat her. It's what she wants.'

He looks at me aghast. 'It's what she wants? It's a flamin' cow, chief!'

'Just do as he says,' Hayley tells Fred. 'Otherwise we might be here forever.'

Fred huffs, and shakes his head in disgust – but also reaches out a hand and smacks Pat The Cow once on the top of the head. It's not so much a pat, as it is a slap for being naughty, but Pat The Cow doesn't mind. She's made of strong stuff.

Fred has to dodge out of the way as Pat The Cow makes her exit, easily avoiding doing any damage to the patio doors. Pat The Cow may not be svelte, but she's not big enough to trouble such a wide exit either. The several hundred quid we spent on the big glass doors to provide great views of the garden and easy access to the patio are starting to pay for themselves already.

Pat The Cow does not hesitate once she's outside. She trots off back towards the jungle garden without a look back at any of us.

'Maybe we should follow it,' Hayley says. 'Find out where it's getting in.'

'Don't bother,' I reply, knowing full well the extent of Pat The Cow's supernatural abilities.

'In all my years of doing this job,' Fred says, 'I've never known anything like that.'

'Pat The Cow is quite special,' I reply, regretting it as soon as it's out of my mouth.

Fred looks in disbelief at Hayley. 'He's *named* it?'

Hayley grimaces. 'It appears so.'

Fred Babidge has several laughs.

There's the 'someone's just told a dirty joke of which I wholeheartedly approve' laugh. There's the 'don't try and pull a fast one on me, son, I've heard it all before' laugh. And everyone's favourite, the 'Danny Daley has just said or done something ridiculous, and boy do I find it hilarious' laugh. I'd like to say the first two are far more common than the third, but I'd be lying through my teeth.

Fred walks off back to where the rest of the crew are busily pointing the side of the house, leaving me to ponder where Pat The Cow might have gone . . . and my sister pondering where my sanity might have gone.

Which brings us to our third and final meeting with Pat The Cow thus far, and blimey if it isn't the weirdest one yet.

Picture, if you will, a cold, windy, summer's morning. A typical July day of 18 degrees and cloud.

The weather, having recently been very mild, has changed for the worse, bringing in a gusty wind that tempts you to put the central heating on in the middle of what could be laughably termed the English summer.

Given the fact that most of the doors and windows haven't been fixed yet, Daley Farmhouse is falling prey to the wind, and is rather like a wind tunnel when we all arrive early that morning to start work again.

I am, unusually, the first to arrive. The reason for this is simple. My next-door neighbour is an arsehole. While most people are sleeping soundly at 5 a.m. on a Saturday morning, she is just getting in from a night out. And boy does she like to let everybody know about it. There's nothing like hearing Taylor Swift at high volume seeping hideously through your adjoining wall to really ruin the (very premature) start to your day. Having lain there trying to get back to sleep while Taylor tells us about how all of her ex-boyfriends are pricks, I eventually give up, when Taylor is replaced by Beyoncé, who, if anything, sounds even more grating than the elfin-faced pipsqueak at that time in the morning.

Therefore, Fred and the boys are all amazed to see me standing next to my bike and munching on a stale cereal bar when they drive up at the crack of dawn.

'You're keen today, captain,' Fred observes.

I smile. 'What can I say? I just can't wait to get started on that plaster in the master bedroom.' There's no need to tell Fred the truth at this point. It would only disappoint him. Besides, I very much doubt he has any idea who Taylor Swift is, and it's too early in the morning to try and explain.

I swap a little morning banter with the crew as we make our way towards the house. As he opens the brand-new oak front door, Baz asks me for the hundredth time whether I'd like him to bring me in a big wooden box for later, when I need a mid-morning crap. I decline his kind offer and recommend that he stick his head up his arse.

Each of the six-man crew heads off to whatever job he's currently working on.

'Take these upstairs,' Baz says to me, handing over a couple of chisels and hammers from a large pile in the lounge. 'You get started and I'll be up once I check the wind's done no damage out back.'

'Okay,' I agree and take the tools from him, making my way up the stairs and along the landing with a large and expansive yawn. I start to sing Taylor Swift's 'Blank Space' under my breath. The bloody tune has earwormed its way into my brain thanks to the early morning wake-up call. 'Nice to meet you, where you been,' I sing badly under my breath, 'I can show you incredible things . . .'

I walk into the master bedroom, and boy do I get to see an incredible thing, alright.

The tools fall out of my hands in amazement.

My gob is well and truly smacked.

For a second I stand stock-still, simply unable to believe what my eyes are quite clearly telling me. Then my brain starts to function again and I stir back into life.

'Er.'

This is quite ridiculous.

'Um . . . Morning, Pat The Cow?' I say, uncertainly.

'Moo.'

Yes, that's right. A half-ton cow is standing in the *upstairs* master bedroom of a Victorian farmhouse.

Let's think about the logistics of that for a moment, shall we?

No, then again, let's not. We could be here all day.

It's a testament to how involved I am in this house renovation that my next thought is how impressed I am that the new floorboards are quite easily taking Pat The Cow's weight. Fred will be pleased.

Alternatively . . . No, he bloody well *won't*, because there is a cow in the *upstairs* master bedroom.

'I don't think you should be up here, Pat The Cow,' I tell her, voicing what must be the most obvious statement ever uttered by a human being.

'Moo,' Pat The Cow retorts, defending her position magnificently. She then wanders forward, and sticks her head through the tarpaulin covering the large glassless sash window for a look outside.

Well, I suppose that's a start. Her head has left the bedroom now. We just have to get the rest of her out.

'Was that Taylor Swift you was singing then, Dan?' I hear Baz say as he reaches the landing. 'Only I downloaded the album the other day and it ain't actually that ba— *Fuck a donkey!*'

'Pat The Cow, be polite and say good morning to Baz,' I say to my bovine friend. Pat The Cow chooses to ignore me. There must be something very interesting going on outside.

'Why is there a fucking cow's head poking out of that window?' I hear Fred exclaim loudly from the front garden. Ah, it appears the interesting thing is our master builder falling into apoplexy at the vision of Pat The Cow's head appearing majestically through a blue tarpaulin, several metres above where it can be found in more customary circumstances.

'This ain't good,' Baz says.

'This ain't possible,' I tell him in the same bemused voice.

Baz blinks hard a couple of times, as if willing the sight of the upstairs Friesian away. He looks vaguely disappointed when Pat The Cow does not disappear in a cloud of brown smoke.

I hear Fred stamping up the stairs, followed by some of the others. He comes in to the room, and does something we rarely see on site, he takes his flat cap off. Fred Babidge normally only ever takes his hat off when something very serious is going down. Whenever it is removed, Hayley and I start to panic, because it invariably means something very expensive.

I start to wonder how expensive it will be to have Pat The Vertical Cow removed from the first floor of this house, but am interrupted by Fred the Incredulous Builder. 'Did you do this, captain?' he asks me. 'Some sort of prank, is it?'

'Are you *mental*? What do you think I did? Got myself a nice bale of hay and came down here in the depths of night?'

'You was here before the rest of us this morning, Dan,' Trey the Barbadian Sweatbeast points out, rather unhelpfully.

'I had nothing to do with this!' I snap at all of them. 'Do you think I want any damage done to those bloody floorboards when I'm the one who paid for them?'

'S'a good point boss,' Baz remarks.

Fred squints at me disapprovingly for a moment, before his face relaxes. 'Alright, fair enough. But it doesn't really matter how it got up here, how the hell are we going to get it out?'

I have to disagree with Fred somewhat. How Pat The Cow got up here is a *very* important question, as far as I'm concerned. One for the ages, in fact.

'Will it go through the window?' Baz enquires. 'Some of us can stand underneath it and catch it in a blanket. We had to do that with my mum's dog once when it got stuck up a tree.'

Fred puts his head in his hands. 'Baz, that cow weighs half a ton. It'd kill all of us.'

Baz looks crestfallen. I feel a bit sorry for him.

'We'll have to kill it,' Trey intones ominously. 'Chop the damn thing up and carry it down in bits.'

Pat The Cow has heard this threat to her life and responds by removing her head from under the tarpaulin and giving Trey a look that suggests any attempt to chop her into little bits will be met with many hooves and head butts.

'It'll cause a right bloody mess,' Spider argues. 'Blood's hell to shift, and the place will stink. I like Baz's idea better.'

'Moo,' Pat The Cow agrees, still not taking her eyes off Trey.

'We're not chopping it up or pushing it out of the window,' Fred says. 'If it got up here, we must be able to get it out the same way.' This sounds like the most sensible suggestion yet.

He walks over to Pat The Cow and grabs it by the ear. 'Come on you, let's get you out of this room,' he tells the bovine interloper, and attempts to pull her in the direction of the door. Pat The Cow is having none of it.

'Move, you big bitch!' Fred barks, and slaps Pat The Cow on the head.

Pat The Cow gives Fred the same look she just gave Trey, looks away from him in disdain, lifts her tail and deposits an enormous pile of dung behind her, in what I can only assume is a dirty protest at her treatment.

'Oh shit!' Baz cries, extremely accurately.

The stench of rich cow dung instantly fills the bedroom, forcing us all out onto the landing.

'What the 'ell do we do now?' Weeble asks in a high-pitched voice. Thus far he has remained silent, but it appears the pressure is getting too much for him.

Fred rolls his tongue around his teeth thoughtfully for a few moments before speaking. 'Baz, go get the nail gun. Trey, go get some saws.'

'No!' I shout. 'You can't kill Pat The Cow!'

'Have you got any better ideas?' Fred snaps.

'Just . . . Just give me a minute,' I tell him, re-entering the room and trying not to breathe too deeply as I do.

'He gave it a fucking name?' Trey whispers under his breath to Weeble, who shrugs his shoulders and shakes his head in disbelief.

Yes, I did give 'it' a name, thank you so very much, Trey. Pat The Cow is a special cow, and deserves better treatment than to be sawn up by a bunch of brickies.

'Think of something quick, Dan,' Fred tells me, 'or we're having hamburgers for lunch.'

I swallow hard and make my way back to where Pat The Cow is still standing defiantly in the centre of the room.

'Um . . . Now look here, Pat The Cow. You need to leave, otherwise my friends here are going to do something very nasty to you, do you understand me?'

'Moo.'

'We need to get you back downstairs.'

'Moo.'

'Um . . . Please?'

'Moo, moo.'

Pat The Cow starts to walk towards the door. Once again I have successfully appealed to her better nature – and to her sense of self-preservation.

'Blimey,' Baz says, 'he's got her moving.'

'He's a bloody cow whisperer,' Spider adds.

The crew make way for me as I lead Pat The Cow out onto the landing. We all wince slightly as the floorboards take her weight. These ones haven't been re-laid yet and there's every chance we're all going to get relocated to the ground floor in a few split seconds unless we can get the animal off them quickly.

Now just comes the problem of the stairs.

Quite how the cow made her way up to the first floor in the first place is a mystery, but how we eventually manage to get her down to the ground floor again is most certainly not.

It involves a lot of pushing, pulling, swearing and loud exclamations of pain every time one of us gets squashed up against the wall. It also requires no less than four separate lengths of sturdy rope . . .

. . . And *four hours.*

Four sweaty, noisy, distressing hours of my life that I never want to repeat again as long as I live. I will happily shit repeatedly into a wooden box every day for the rest of my life, if it means I never have to coax a full-grown cow down a flight of broad Victorian stairs again.

'Will she go through the front door?' Fred gasps. He is red-faced, and covered in a film of perspiration. The flat cap was discarded hours ago, along with his jacket. I've never seen him work so hard.

'Let's bloody 'ope so!' Spider says. 'Getting Pat The Cow through the kitchen without breaking any of the new cabinets will be a nightmare.'

This is a good point. The kitchen has finally started to go in, and the last thing we need is Pat The Cow destroying any of the new units.

Fred reaches out a hand and attempts to open the front door. The handle doesn't budge. 'Who locked the bloody door?' he cries in exasperation.

'I did. It's good security, innit!' Baz replies defensively.

'Well, have you got the key then?'

Baz pats his pockets. 'Er . . . must have put it down somewhere. Anyone else seen it?' he asks the rest of us.

We all shake our heads. 'I thought you had it, Baz,' Spider says. 'Not any more. Danny?'

'I haven't got it,' I say wearily.

Great. We've got Pat The Cow downstairs, but now we can't get her back outside.

Salvation comes when we all hear a key turn in the lock from the other side. The front door swings open to reveal Hayley and a man who must be a local farmer, judging from his dungarees, gingham shirt and muddy welly boots.

'I'm sure your cow isn't here, Mr Blenkins,' Hayley is saying to him, looking at his angry face and not at us, 'but I'll ask my building team. Maybe they might have seen it—'

Hayley turns her head and takes in the grand tableau in front of her. A group of full-grown and exhausted men, standing red-faced around a cow who looks exactly how you'd imagine a cow to look after being manhandled for the past four hours.

'Oh good fucking grief,' Hayley moans.

'Thas moi bluddy cow!' Mr Blenkins exclaims, in the most clichéd accent I've ever heard in my life. 'What 'ave you perverts been doin' to her?'

Perverts? What's he mean, perverts?

Oh, yeah. I see.

I wave my hands. 'No no! It's nothing like that!' I cry. 'We just had Pat The Cow up in the bedroom, and we were trying to get her out before any more damage was done—'

'What?!' Blenkins shouts in disgust. He then gives me the farmer's stink eye. 'Why're you callin' 'er Pat The Cow? Her name's Angelina!'

'Danny! What the hell is going on? What have you done?' Hayley yells at me, as if this entire thing is my doing.

I point at Angelina The Cow. 'Don't blame me. This is all her fault!'

Angelina – no, fuck it, I still prefer my name – Pat The Cow looks up at me with an expression that seems to suggest that at some point I'll be hearing from her lawyer.

'Moo,' she says, in a tone that brooks no argument. Pat The Cow then barges past all of us, including her irate owner, and squeezes out of the front doorway, trotting rapidly off up the garden path in Friesian disgust, no doubt.

'She's a roight one, that one,' Blenkins tells me as he closes the gate on his own pasture land, some five hundred yards down the road from the entrance to Daley Farmhouse. I've spent the last ten minutes explaining what exactly was going on, and he seems to have accepted my account with only a raised eyebrow here and there. Convinced that I'm not the head of a sex ring of cow perverts, he's allowed me to help him walk Pat The Cow back to where her rightful place in the world is. 'Always buggerin' off somewhere, she is.'

'Like a ninja,' I add.

'Loike a what?'

'Never mind.' I look out to where Pat The Cow has joined some of her bovine sisters. 'Still, at least she's back where she belongs now.'

'Yep. For the toime bein' anyway,' Blenkins remarks gravely.

'What do you mean?'

'Oim 'aving to sell up, mate. Farm's too expensive to run these days. Oim retiring with the wife to the Lake District. We've gorra a nice cottage near Windermere.' He spits onto the ground. 'Oi reckon thas why old Angelina keeps makin' a break for it. She knows somethin's coming, loike.'

'Something's coming?'

'Yep. They'll arl be slaughtered,' Blenkins says matter-of-factly. 'Only thing that ever 'appens when a farm closes.'

I'm *aghast*. I'm *dismayed*.

I'm still not sure about that accent.

A thought occurs. A strange and bizarre thought that is bound to get me into trouble with my sister. 'Er . . . How much does a cow cost these days?' I ask Blenkins hesitantly.

He turns in surprise, claps me on the back and laughs. 'Well now, young man. Thas an interestin' question you're askin' there.'

HAYLEY

August

£92,203.34 spent (plus £250 for Pat The Cow)

'Get out of the way, you stupid bloody cow!'

'Moo.'

I put down the large laminated piece of bathroom vanity unit I've just lugged over from the van and stare daggers at Danny's new pet. Pat The Cow has decided that today she wants to stand directly in the middle of the garden path, which is extremely helpful, as we've had a delivery from the bathroom company. What we haven't got with that delivery is any help carrying all the bits and pieces into the house, so Team Babidge are having to do it all themselves. Around the bloody cow.

'Danny! Can you please get this idiotic animal out of the way!' I scream at my brother as he emerges from the house. 'It's stopping us from doing any work!'

'Oh, don't be so melodramatic, Hayley,' he replies. 'Pat The Cow just likes you and wants to say hello.'

I look heavenwards in frustration. 'Will you please stop calling it Pat The Cow? It stopped being funny about five seconds after you first said it. Just call it Pat!'

Danny contrives to look offended on the cow's part. 'But her name is Pat The Cow.'

'Well, you had better make sure that Pat The Cow is back down at the end of the garden before the camera crew turns up in an hour! The last thing I need is the sodding creature trotting across the shot as Gerard is examining the pointing!'

Danny comes over and puts a hand on my shoulder. 'Alright, alright, calm down. I'll take Pat The Cow away. No need to have an aneurism.'

I grit my teeth and resist the urge to insult both him and his ruddy cow even further. As I watch him lead the big smelly thing away, I have to count to ten to calm myself down a bit.

I am rather stressed out this morning. Okay, more than that, I'm a complete basket case.

Why?

Because *Great Locations* are turning up for more filming on the property now it's advanced along to the point where there's actually something to film that isn't old, rotten or broken. But, unlike the previous three times they've been here, today's filming will be done for *a live episode of the programme.*

Yes, you heard me right. At precisely 11.30 this morning, the BBC will be throwing over for an entire thirty-minute live episode of *Great Locations* all about Daley Farmhouse.

The BBC like to do this every once in a while. They imaginatively call it *Live Week*, when some of its more popular daytime TV shows are broadcast as they happen. *Great Locations* is one of the jewels in this event, and Gerard O'Keefe is very excited that Daley Farmhouse is the project that they have chosen to cover.

I put up several lucid and perfectly acceptable arguments as to why it's a bad idea, of course. All of which were either shot down by my brother and Fred, or neatly explained away by Gerard.

'Think of the publicity,' Gerard said.

'Think of the promotion for my business,' Fred said.

'Think of how it'll improve my chances of getting into Mischa's knickers,' Danny said.

So, I capitulated, because I am an idiot.

Oh, alright. That's not entirely the truth.

This project is actually starting to come together now and I'm very proud of the way I've— Sorry, *we've* managed it. From a derelict shell we have turned Daley Farmhouse into something on the cusp of being great, in only a few months. I see nothing wrong in wanting to show that progress off to everyone. Especially my bloody mother and father, who are *still* on their stupid round-the-world cruise. You would have thought that they would want to keep some of Grandma's money back for a rainy day, but no, it appears that they've decided never to have a rainy day again by staying on a large boat near the equator for the rest of their lives. We get emails once every so often regaling us with tales of how wonderful the Caribbean is, or how fantastic the Maldives are. You can imagine how *wonderful* that makes me feel when I read them, standing in the British August rain, slowly feeling my feet rotting from inside the green wellies that have now become a far too regular part of my wardrobe.

But the cruise ship they are on appears to get the BBC in some sort of world service deal, and that means Mum and Dad will be able to watch the programme. They've managed to miss the previous episodes we were featured on, so I made sure to call them and order them to watch this one.

Think of how proud they will be!

Think of how jealous they will be that we're on national TV and they're not.

I recognise this is not a healthy thought process, but they called me *Hayley Daley*, for fuck's sake, so please cut me a little slack.

None of this is getting the vanity unit up to the main bathroom any quicker, so I put my thoughts aside and continue with the important business of destroying my spine by lugging this heavy thing up the stairs.

'Here's the side bit,' I tell Weeble as I plonk the laminated wood down in the doorway.

'Cheers,' he replies, as he moves the roll-top bath a few inches to the left. Weeble is our resident bathroom fitter. Everyone, including Fred, defers to him in all matters bathy.

'It's looking good, Weeble,' I say to the chubby workman. 'It'll look great in the show.'

Weeble makes a face. 'I would have liked to have got it all finished for it, but with the floor tiles coming late, that pipe needing replacing, and the problem with the sink, it's got away from me a bit.'

I give him a sympathetic smile. 'Don't worry about it. Gerard knows we're still only halfway through this thing. He's not expecting anything to be finished.'

Which is just as well, as the house still looks like exactly what it is – a building site. Only these days it's a building site where things are being put *in*, rather than taken away.

Everything structural is done. The large rear extension is finished and looking super. All the windows and doors are in, the external brickwork looks like it was put up yesterday, and even the basement has been fully rendered and rewired so it's now a useful extra storage space, rather than a place to hide the bodies of your victims.

We've reached that wonderful point where Daley Farmhouse now looks like a blank canvas, ready to be filled with all of Mitchell Hollingsbrooke's exciting design features.

Even the back garden has been attacked. Only by Spider and Baz with two industrial-sized lawnmowers, so it's not exactly what you'd call *landscaped*, but at least the grass isn't two feet tall any more, and you can fully appreciate just how big the plot of land is. Unfortunately, you can also appreciate Pat The Cow a lot more easily as well, whether you want to or not. Danny has strung up a large tarpaulin and dumped a load of hay in the back corner of the garden for the silly thing. But it is an inquisitive animal and takes every opportunity it can to come over and see what we're all doing.

All in all though, I'm pretty pleased with our progress, and can't see any problem with showing the place off to the BBC. Now all I have to do is stop worrying about embarrassing the hell out of myself with a camera in my face, and I'll be fine.

I look at my watch. It's nearly 9 a.m. They'll be here soon. I try to ignore the feeling of my heart skipping out of my chest as I walk back down the stairs, marvelling at how smooth and lovely the bannister wood feels under the palm of my hand.

This place is really starting to get to me.

I've never been one for appreciating craftsmanship, but when you see that craftsmanship happening in front of your eyes, it does rather lend an added perspective. If nothing else, you understand just how much hard work goes into it.

The BBC truck rolls into view at 9.30 a.m., just as I come back out of the house, having delivered yet another box of tiles to Weeble.

'Good morning, Hayley!' Gerard O'Keefe says with far too much enthusiasm for this time of the morning. 'Looking forward to it, then?'

I smile a bit awkwardly. 'I think so.'

He laughs. 'Don't worry. It's going to be easy. I'll lead you through the whole thing.' He puts an arm round my shoulder. I'm disgusted to realise that this feels very nice. 'I've done hundreds of these things with people far, far less capable than you, so I'm sure you'll be fine.'

He's very reassuring, but equally, he doesn't know what's going on inside my head. If he did, he may have to rethink just how capable I am when compared to all the other luckless individuals he's featured on his TV show.

Today, we don't just have Pete in attendance with his one camera. On this very special occasion, there are no less than *three* cameramen – all of whom must have been trained in the same school of camera-manning that Pete was. They all wear dishevelled black BBC polo shirts and jeans that have seen better days. All of them smoke roll-ups, and all of them look like the last thing they want to do is hold a video camera.

Also in the BBC entourage is Monica, the show's producer. A woman of few words, she favours a practical all-black ensemble and the kind of tight ponytail that would be guaranteed to give me a splitting headache in five seconds if it were on my head.

Gerard rounds all of us up so he can run through what's going to happen during the half-hour the show is on for. The seven of us listen closely, all sharing the same look of mild apprehension on our faces. We're far from magnificent, but I hope that we can all at least manage *competent* for the BBC audience.

'So, I'll start the show with an intro,' Gerard says, 'then I'll come for a chat with Hayley and Danny. Next up we'll all walk over to Fred and the gang for a talk with them, and after that I'll go over the house, pointing out some of the more interesting features of the property, like we discussed the other day. Hayley, Danny and Fred, I'd like you with me for that.'

We nod dumbly.

'Then it's just a matter of a quick wrap up. That should easily cover the half an hour.'

That surprises me. You'd think a couple of conversations and a tour of the place would be over in ten minutes. I say as much to Gerard.

'Ah, you'd be surprised,' he tells me. 'Trying to squeeze too much in is where you start to run into problems. Trust me, we'll fill the running time. I'll have Monica talking into my earpiece, letting me know the time, so I can pad things out, or cut things down as seems appropriate.'

You can tell he's done this time and time again. I begin to feel a little more relaxed.

Relaxation turns back to severe doubt when Mitchell Hollings-brooke arrives on the scene some ten minutes later in his rusty old 2CV.

'I thought you were up in the city today, Mitchell?' I say to him as he hurries down the garden path towards me and Gerard, dodging one of the camera crew as he does so. Mitchell is flamboyantly dressed, and flamboyant to Mitchell Hollingsbrooke is positively clown-like to everyone else on the planet. The pink polka-dot cravat is lovely. The orange cords are even worse than the usual purple ones. The red smoking jacket is a sight to behold, as is the blue hat.

Mitchell reaches us and flaps his hands around. 'They cancelled at the last minute,' he says, face like thunder. 'I should have known. London couples with too much money and too little sense. I wonder why I ever get involved with them!'

'The huge percentage you can charge?' Gerard says with a cheeky grin.

Mitchell looks daggers. 'That's enough from you, O'Keefe.'

'So why are you here?' I ask him.

He turns to me. 'Well, I thought you might like me along for your little show this morning. Hence why I have made an effort with my outfit.'

An effort to look like a children's entertainer, apparently. 'Er, I don't know, Mitchell,' I reply. 'It's up to Gerard and his producer, I guess.'

Gerard can't help but look a little anguished as he takes in Mitchell's outfit, but within a moment, the doubtful look has been replaced with one of what I feel is rather faked enthusiasm. 'Of course! The show wouldn't be complete without you, my friend. Perhaps you can join us on our walk around the house, and let us know what your plans for it are?'

Mitchell looks beside himself.

I *wish* he *were* beside himself, then he could see how awful he looks and possibly do something about it.

'Excellent!' he crows. 'Make sure to ask me what I plan to do with the bathroom. I have a little surprise for Hayley and Danny that I just know they're going to love!'

Really? That sounds a bit disconcerting. I'm all for our architect throwing in new ideas, but I'd rather he didn't bring them up on live TV.

'Well, that sounds wonderful,' Gerard tells him, his voice betraying the uncertainty he's resolutely keeping away from his face. 'I'm sure your contribution will be great!'

Mitchell gives voice to a rather strange squeak of pleasure, hugs Gerard, hugs me and then takes off back towards his 2CV at a rate of knots. I give Gerard a look.

'It'll be fine,' he tells me. 'I can keep him under control.'

'You can keep a man who wears orange cords without irony under control?'

Gerard doesn't have an answer for that. Today promises to be unpredictable, if nothing else.

What *is* massively predictable is that my brother loses his mind when Mischa turns up to assist her boss.

'Gaah,' he says, as he spots her pull up in her Mini. 'I didn't know she was coming today.'

'Neither did I.' This could be disastrous. Dan has to be on camera today as much as me, and he'll have enough problems doing that without being stared at by the object of his affections. 'Will you be able to do this?' I say to him as I watch the small BBC crew and Gerard make their final preparations for the live show. It kicks off in ten minutes, and the last thing I need is Dan having a libido-induced breakdown, thanks to the presence of five feet and ten inches of lusty Eastern European female sexuality.

He looks away from where Mischa is sashaying over to her boss. It shouldn't be possible to look sexy in a parka and walking boots, but she manages it anyway. 'I'll be fine,' Danny tells me, face resolute.

I'll have to take his word for it, I suppose. 'Good. I need you with me on this.'

'You nervous?'

'Aren't *you*?'

'Oh, well of course I am, but then I'm *me*. You're a lot stronger when it comes to this kind of stuff than I am.'

'Thanks, Danny,' I say, quite touched.

He smiles. 'No worries, sis.'

A few minutes later Gerard approaches us, rubbing his hands together. 'Okay then. We're just about ready to do this. Let's get you all in a suitable position to open the show with.' He shuffles us back a bit, so we're both standing by the new front door of the house. 'This'll do fine. I'll do my intro up the path near the front, then I'll walk backwards to you and we'll get going with the interview. That all sound good?'

Danny nods erratically.

I go, 'Meep.'

Gerard puts a hand on my shoulder. 'Honestly, Hayley, you'll do great.'

My turn to nod erratically.

Gerard moves away from us back up the garden path, and I grasp hold of my brother's hand tightly.

'Good luck, sis,' he says to me, his own hand tightening a bit.

'Yeah, you too,' I reply, wishing I was anywhere else in the world right now than here. I close my eyes, take a deep breath and try to compose myself.

The credit sequence of *Great Locations* is just what you'd expect. Images of grand houses, sweeping countryside and long sandy beaches, all caught under the kind of bright blue British summer skies that only exist in people's memories. The theme tune that plays with the credits is the bland kind of muzak that plays when you're in an elevator, or on hold with the gas board. It's inoffensive, light and easy to hum along to.

When the credits end, and the live show begins, the camera finds Gerard O'Keefe looking resplendent in his usual collection of army surplus gear, standing by the front gate to Daley Farmhouse with a welcoming grin on his face. His thatch of brown curly hair has been arranged artfully by a make-up girl, and he's even had a bit of foundation applied to take the glare off his forehead in the morning sun.

'Good morning everyone,' he says brightly down the camera lens, with practised ease. 'I'm Gerard O'Keefe. Welcome to a very special live episode of *Great Locations*, coming to you from the gorgeous Hampshire countryside. You may have seen our previous features on the renovations of the Daley Farmhouse. We're here today to catch up on its progress, and speak to everyone behind the reclamation of this wonderful Victorian property from its previously derelict state.'

Gerard then does something that should be impossible. He starts to walk backwards down the garden path as if it's the most natural and normal thing in the world. It's like he's just beamed down from a strange and alien civilisation where they all walk backwards, to teach us how to do it before the galactic invasion force arrives to subjugate the planet.

Not only does he effortlessly walk backwards, he also carries on talking about the farmhouse renovation without missing a beat.

By the time he reaches Danny and me, he's neatly summed up the project so far and is already into his introduction of us both.

'Hayley and Danny were left the house in their grandmother's will, and they really are honouring her with such a wonderful renovation of the property. But let's allow them to speak for themselves, shall we?' Gerard parks himself next to me, and the camera looms large. 'How do you feel the renovation is coming along Hayley?'

I stare down the camera lens. A million bored housewives and unemployed people stare back at me. 'Er—'

Oh god, no. Please, please, *no*.

Don't let my brain freeze up before I've even got one constructive syllable out of my stupid mouth.

Come on Hayley, say something!

'It's, it's going quite well!' I spit out triumphantly. A little too triumphantly, as the words are accompanied by a fair amount of unwanted spittle. I now look like a raving madwoman to the housewives and the jobless, but this is still preferable to looking like a terrified, frozen statue. 'I'd say it's all going according to plan.' I consider this statement for a moment, and feel a twinge in my left foot. 'More or less,' I add.

'Excellent!' Gerard beams, happy that I've not let the nerves get the better of me. 'And you, Danny? How do you feel right now?'

By the look on his face as he stares over at Mischa, I'm going to say *horny*.

'Danny?' Gerard repeats, his voice a tiny bit strained.

'Hmmm?' my brother eventually responds.

'How are you feeling about the project's progress?' Gerard repeats.

Danny composes himself and deliberately stares at the TV presenter, ignoring any female architectural assistants who may be in the vicinity. 'I'm happy, I think. It looks more like a house than a bombsite now,' he tells Gerard.

'Yes, indeed it does!' Gerard exclaims. 'Our viewers can see for themselves just how much work has been done since we were here last. You're all doing a fantastic job.' He holds up a hand. 'But before we get into the renovation itself, let's find out a bit more about the both of you. How did you come to inherit this place, and what made you decide to fix it up?'

And so we're into the chat that Gerard has been coaching us on for the past couple of weeks. He did such a good job that we manage to rattle through the background to the project pretty quickly, and before you know it we've finished, and the loyal viewing audience are now up to date – whether they necessarily want to be or not. You'll be amazed to discover that I neglect to mention the nail gun through the foot, and Danny doesn't talk about shitting into a wooden box. I'm all for getting the details right, but let's not go too bloody far.

'Well, that's a fascinating story, Hayley and Danny, thanks for telling us all about it.' Gerard looks back down the camera again. 'You heard Hayley mention the architect on this project, Mitchell Hollingsbrooke. We'll be catching up with him shortly, but first, let's make our way over to where the building team are waiting to speak to us.'

And with that, Gerard is off over to where Fred and crew are standing around a cement mixer looking like they're about to be brought up in front of a firing squad. Danny and I trail along behind Gerard like the good little puppies we are, being careful not to trip over on the uneven muddy ground as the camera follows all three of us.

'Hello there!' Gerard says to Fred, offering his hand out like he's never met the man before.

Fred takes it gingerly and gives it a gentle shake.

'Ladies and gentleman, please say hello to Fred Babidge and his team of brilliant builders and tradesman. They're the ones who are bringing this lovely old house back to life, aren't you, Fred?'

''Es,' Fred says, in a barely audible voice.

It's amazing what being on live TV will do to a person. In Fred Babidge's case, it's turned him from a bluff, loud cockney chancer into a seven-year-old girl starring in her first nativity play.

'And what did you think of the project when Hayley and Dan first approached you, Fred?'

'I liked it.'

'Sorry? What was that?'

'I thought it was a good 'un.'

'Did you?' Gerard looks a bit worried, and Pete the cameraman is adjusting something on the camera's microphone. This isn't going well.

Gerard then tries to turn his attention to one of the other builders. Out of the four of them, only Spider looks like he is still able to function. But it's frankly touch and go. His eyes aren't quite as bulgy as the others, but he has gone a rather disturbing shade of red.

'And what about you, Spider? What's this farmhouse like to work on?'

'Great!' Spider bellows. 'It's a nice house!' We've gone from one extreme to the other. Poor old Pete winces in pain and immediately fiddles with the microphone again.

Gerard soldiers on. 'I bet you're all pleased with how much you've managed to improve the property in the five months you've been working here, aren't you?'

'Yes! It looks much better than it did!'

'Much better,' Fred chimes in – barely.

'It was in quite the dilapidated condition when you first got here, wasn't it?' Gerard asks them both.

'It wasn't great, no,' Fred says.

Spider goes even redder. 'Yeah! The boss is right! It was a right shit tip!' Spider immediately realises he's just sworn on live daytime TV and puts a hand over his mouth. 'Oh fuck! Sorry!' he virtually screams at Gerard.

And there we have it. Ten minutes into the show and we have our first swear words. I can now look forward to watching us all on *Points of View* in a month's time.

Gerard physically backs away from Spider, as if the builder is about to explode. He turns to the camera and composes his face into an expression of trite apology. 'We're sorry for Spider's fruity language, everyone. Builders will be builders!'

Nice attempt at saving it there, Mr O'Keefe, but I don't think it's going to stop the letters of complaint rolling in somehow.

'Why don't we have a look in the house at some of the work that's been done?' Gerard suggests to his vast, unseen audience. He starts to walk back towards the front door, prompting Danny and I to follow with a barely visible flick of one wrist. He's keen to get away from the team as quickly as possible, and I can't say I blame him that much. Asking them any more questions may either result in Fred Babidge weeing in his knickers, or Spider's use of the word 'cunt' for the first time on daytime TV.

We're on much safer ground once we've moved away from them and have entered the house. Gerard spends the next few minutes of the broadcast showing the audience all the improvements that have already been made to the house, and boy does he sell them *brilliantly*.

The way he waxes lyrical about the new woodwork, brickwork, plastering and the new extension, makes it sound like we've restored the Sistine Chapel in the middle of the Hampshire countryside.

Danny and I duly trot along behind him as he goes from one room to the next, two of the three cameramen following to provide coverage and close-ups of both us and the renovation work.

Within a few minutes Gerard has made a whistle-stop tour of the downstairs, pointing out each and every thing that he deems worthy of the nation's attention. He's particularly delighted with all the original features we've been able to retain. Nothing gets Gerard

O'Keefe more excited than a newly painted ceiling rose, or a freshly sanded doorframe.

Even the basement is visited on the live TV tour of Daley Farmhouse, where Gerard takes great lengths to show off the new plastering work and concrete. I can't say that if I were sitting at home watching this programme I'd be all that enamoured with such broad expanses of greyness, but Gerard seems convinced that it's all very fascinating, so who am I to argue?

Eventually, we do make it upstairs, after Gerard has made a comment about the lovely new bannister on the way up.

'So this is the master bedroom,' he says, arms open wide as he goes in. 'And what's been done in this room, Hayley?'

Oh blimey, it's my turn in the sun again. I'd better be thorough with my answer.

'Er . . . All the floorboards have been replaced after the old ones were destroyed by woodworm. The windows have all been done as well. We managed to salvage a lot of the frame up here, which is nice. The ceiling's been plastered, all the skirting boards have been replaced, the whole room's been rewired, and the fireplace has been restored as well.' I look around the room, which, while nice and clean now, is a tad on the bland side. 'Obviously it still needs decorating,' I add, just in case anyone at home thinks we're going for the grey plaster look up here too.

Gerard points to his left. 'And what about the en suite?' he asks.

Bugger! I completely forgot about the new en suite. That's fine though, it's only the biggest job we've done in here.

I am an idiot.

I splutter for a moment as Gerard points towards the new doorway that leads to the bathroom we've put in.

'We've had to take some space from the main room,' Danny interjects, saving me my blushes. 'But the bedroom is still very big anyway.'

'It certainly is,' Gerard agrees, obviously happy that Danny is contributing something useful at this stage.

'The plumbing's not all done yet, so most of the actual en suite stuff like the shower and loo haven't gone in, but once it's finished, it'll be cracking,' Danny continues.

'Absolutely!' Gerard says, his enthusiasm infectious.

I somehow doubt most of the audience back home will be quite as enthusiastic. After all, they're being treated to a tour of a house that isn't finished. If I had a penny for every time one of us has said 'when it's finished' today, I'd probably have enough to pay my licence fee for the month.

'Has the chimney been cleared?' Gerard asks, walking over to the fireplace, with Pete the cameraman in tow. His colleague is loitering by the doorway, filming Danny and me. I hope he's getting my good side – if I have one, that is.

'I don't know,' Danny responds to Gerard's question. 'Hayley?'

Oh thanks, bruv. Put me on the spot, why don't you? 'Um. As far as I know, it hasn't been.' I give Gerard a pained look. 'Does it need to be?'

Gerard shrugs. 'It depends on if you want to use it.' He bends down in front of the fireplace and sticks his hand up the chimney breast inside. 'Let's have a feel, shall we? I should be able to tell if it's blocked up or not.'

What follows is a few excruciating seconds of dead air as Gerard temporarily forgets his role as beaming TV presenter, in favour of enthused chimney prospector. I am acutely aware that camera number two is still filming me, and is likely transmitting my rather gormless expression to the world at large as I watch Gerard having a rummage.

'Aha!' he says triumphantly. 'I've got my arm up over the damper, and there's definitely something blocking the way here on the smoke shelf.'

Is there really Gerard? Well, thanks for that.

'Got it!' he exclaims happily and pulls his arm back. With it comes what appears to be a large, old, yellow floral curtain, bundled up. Inside the bundle something is making a metallic clanking sound.

'Well! This is curious!' Gerard says, placing the bundle on the floor in front of him so Pete can get a good close up. 'Any ideas what's in here?' he asks us.

'None,' I say, hesitantly.

'Okay, shall we take a look then?' Gerard suggests, his eyes gleaming with interest.

'Um . . . I suppose so?' I reply, not sure whether this is actually a good idea or not. Still, I'm guessing Gerard has decided this makes great TV, so I don't really think I have much of a choice in the matter.

Gerard looks at the camera. 'Okay then, everyone. This is totally unscripted and unrehearsed, I assure you. We don't know what's in here any more than you do!' He then pulls the curtain bundle apart, revealing . . .

Handcuffs. Four pairs. Rusty and broken.

Also, a brown leather riding crop, in surprisingly good shape, it has to be said.

There's a couple of face masks in there too, but both are so faded and rotten from age, it's hard to tell what they once depicted. I think they must have been like those Italian theatre masks I once saw on a trip to Venice.

'Well, well, well,' Gerard says breathlessly. He also now sounds pretty damn apprehensive. Not surprising, considering he's just uncovered what looks like a stash of bondage gear on live TV before midday.

'What's that thing?' Danny asks, pointing at the last object in the bottom of the bundle. It's still wrapped up in a fold of the rotten curtain, but looks pretty bulky.

'Let's have a look shall we?' Gerard intones, unsure of himself. I get the impression he's wishing he never embarked on this journey of chimney-based discovery, but has now committed himself, and must unveil the last item for the world to see.

It takes him a few moments of pulling and yanking to get the thing out, given that it's wrapped up very well in the curtain folds, but with one last strong tug, it comes free. This leaves Gerard O'Keefe, celebrated BBC TV presenter and all-round expert on all things property based, holding up a large metal butt plug for his audience to feast their eyes on.

Yep. A butt plug.

A tarnished, golden, metal butt plug. And not a small one, either. From the looks of things, Pat The Cow might just be able to manage it, but the thought of a human being inserting that thing anywhere brings tears to the eyes. It's a good eight inches wide at the bulbous bit in the middle.

'That's a butt plug,' Danny helpfully points out in astonishment, just in case everyone at home has led a sheltered life.

Gerard, finally realising what he's actually holding, yelps in terror and drops it like it's a hand grenade with the pin pulled. He instantly covers it up again with the tatty old curtain, along with all the other newly unearthed sex toys.

With a look of fleeting panic on his face, Gerard stands back up and looks at me. There's a question forming on his lips. If it's the one I think it is, my appreciation of Mr O'Keefe is about to take a downhill slide.

'So, Hayley,' he says. 'Do you have any idea where those things may have come from? Are they yours?'

Yes, indeed. That's the bloody question, alright.

I put my hands on my hips. 'No, Gerard,' I reply emphatically. 'I do *not* know where those things have come from, and they most certainly *are not mine*!'

But it doesn't matter how emphatic I sound, does it? Because now Gerard's put the idea in the heads of all those people watching at home that I am a sex pervert who likes to stash her butt plugs up the chimney. It doesn't matter how hard I protest, they're not going to believe a word I say. I am now Hayley Daley, queen of awkward insertions.

Danny jumps in to try and deflect the situation. He only manages to make it worse. 'Perhaps they belonged to Grandma?' he suggests.

I give him an enraged look. Now everyone out there will be picturing our poor deceased grandmother about to do something very unpleasant with a butt plug. This is supposed to be a TV show about property renovation, for crying out loud. It should not evoke images of pensioners indulging in pornographic activity!

I choose not to answer Danny's question, and look back at Gerard, who now looks every bit as terrified as Fred and his crew did a few minutes ago. I have to get us out of here.

'Shall we go and have a look at the bathroom?' I propose to him in a strong tone.

It has the desired effect. 'That's an excellent idea, Hayley!' he replies, shooting a meaningful look at Pete the cameraman, who starts to move rapidly backwards out of the bedroom. Gerard immediately follows, walking away from the bundle of sex aids in the same manner you'd move away from a lit firework.

'Where the hell did that shit come from?' Danny whispers to me as we follow Gerard out, keeping his voice down so as not to be picked up by the second cameraman.

'I have no idea,' I whisper-snap back at him. 'But I'm pretty bloody sure they didn't belong to our sodding grandmother, you idiot!'

'I panicked!'

'Yes, apparently so!'

Now we are in a situation where the audience is likely to remember nothing else about this live tour of our farmhouse other than the sex toys. It doesn't matter how impressive a job you've made of the skirting boards and pointing, nothing is going to override the image of a middle-aged TV presenter holding aloft a golden butt plug. We could have discovered the last resting place of the Holy Grail in the bloody loft and it wouldn't have made a damn bit of difference.

Nope, we're just going to have to accept that the viewing public will only remember one thing about today's show.

But then, I've forgotten about Mitchell Hollingsbrooke, haven't I? Can a slightly unstable architect dressed like a clown detract from an enormous bottom plug? Let's see, shall we?

Gerard enters the main bathroom to find Mitchell stood by the brand-new roll-top bath with an expectant look on his face. Before the show started he had requested that he be interviewed in the new bathroom, for reasons I am afraid we are about to discover.

Gerard stands next to him and looks back into the camera. 'Now, everyone, I'd like you to meet Mitchell Hollingsbrooke, the architect who has designed the renovation for the Daleys. Good morning, Mitchell.'

'Hello, Gerard,' Mitchell replies, and then stares down the camera lens like he's trying to set it on fire. 'Good morning, people at home.'

It's funny how different people react to a camera, isn't it? Fred Babidge turns into a small girl, Spider becomes a town crier – and Mitchell Hollingsbrooke unveils his very best impression of a serial killer.

'Have you enjoyed working on the house, Mitchell?' Gerard asks, attempting to draw the architect's gaze away from the lens.

Mitchell is having none of it, though. He continues to stare intently straight down the barrel. 'Yes, thank you, Gerard. It has been a fascinating and fulfilling job.' His voice has become robotic and monotone. I'm reminded of The Terminator, only with more brightly coloured clothing. 'I look forward to seeing my concepts and designs realised in this bucolic setting,' he adds in the same dead voice.

If there are any children watching at home who haven't as yet developed a fear of clowns, this will tip them over the edge.

'Well, that's lovely,' Gerard responds despondently. He knows this whole thing has gone south faster than a nuclear-powered duck.

'I have a surprise for you,' Mitchell says sharply.

'Really?' Gerard sounds genuinely scared for his life now.

'Yes. A lovely surprise for the Daleys.'

Oh god, he's about to murder us right here on national TV.

Instead of whipping out a bread knife and going at us hammer and tongs, Mitchell bends over a cardboard box just to one side, opens it, and searches around in the polystyrene balls inside.

'Isn't this exciting, everyone?' Gerard says to the audience, who by now are probably on the edge of their seats, I would imagine. After all, they expected a rather dreary live broadcast from a house halfway through a renovation, and what they've had so far is swearing, sex aids and a maniac in a bowler hat.

'What is it you're looking for?' I ask Mitchell, attempting to parrot the light, breezy tone Gerard is adopting.

'Taps!' he bellows without turning round.

'Taps?' I ask.

'Yes, taps!' Mitchell replies.

'That's wonderful!' Gerard exclaims. 'It'll be fantastic to see some of the final elements of the bathroom's design before they actually go in. Gives us a good chance to get up close and personal with them, doesn't it?'

'I think you're going to be pleasantly surprised!' Mitchell says. 'I found these in a catalogue from Italy. Very exclusive design. They will work wonderfully with the aesthetic I'm trying to create in here!'

And with that, Mitchell pulls two taps from the box, holding them up for the camera to get a good look at.

They are . . . very *interesting*.

For starters, they're mixer taps. One for the bath, one for the sink. Big ones too. In a lovely chromed finish, the long, thick shaft of the tap curves gently upwards and over, before culminating at the business end in a graceful flared metal bulb.

Yes, I am pretty much describing a penis here, aren't I?

Mitchell is holding two large chrome – and no doubt hideously expensive – cock taps. Whoever ends up buying Daley Farmhouse will have the joy of bathing themselves in water ejaculated from taps that would look perfectly at home sat on a shelf next to the golden butt plug we've already inflicted on the great British public this morning.

Or is it just me?

I haven't had sex in longer that I care to think about, so maybe the taps aren't all that phallic after all. Maybe it's just my suppressed libido trying its hardest to get noticed again.

I look at Danny's and Gerard's expressions.

Nope, the taps definitely look like dicks. There can be no other explanation for the strangled look on Gerard's face, and the smirking schoolboy look on Danny's.

'What do you think?' Mitchell asks, still sounding rather like The Terminator. The effect is now ruined somewhat by his hilariously shaped bathroom fittings. He waves both in our general direction. I feel like I'm being sexually assaulted.

'They're very large,' Gerard says.

'Indeed!' Mitchell replies. 'I wanted to make a statement with them.'

'Oh, they're definitely making a statement,' I say, giving Gerard a sideways look.

'A very interesting design,' he ploughs on, with a degree of bravery I have to admire.

'Bulbous,' Danny points out, trying hard not to snigger.

Mitchell's face clouds. 'Do you think so? I think the shape is more graceful than that.' He puts one of the taps back in the box and concentrates on the other. 'I was fascinated with the curve and tone of the shaft. The smoothness of its arch recalls the form of a rolling wave at its zenith, or the back of a leaping dolphin.' To demonstrate how much he appreciates the curve of the tap, Mitchell gently takes hold of it and runs his hand from the bottom of the tap to the top.

'I see what you mean!' Danny says, shoulders starting to shake with mirth. 'Could you just repeat that motion a few times so I really understand?'

Mitchell duly obliges.

And now, for the delight and edification of the BBC audience, we have a man in a clown costume wanking off a tap at five to twelve on a Wednesday morning. It doesn't help that Mitchell has returned to looking down the camera with that intense stare.

'Thank you so much, Mitchell!' Gerard cries, grabbing the architect's arm and pulling the tap out of shot. 'Why don't we all make our way back outside and take one last look at the farmhouse as a whole before the show finishes?'

This particular show might not be the only thing finishing here today, I reflect as we troop back down the stairs. Poor old Gerard's ratings hit *Great Locations* might well be finishing here for good if enough complaints roll in over the next few days. I'm not sure Mitchell has done his architectural practice many favours either.

In fact, what with Spider's swearing, and Fred's lost little girl impression, there's every chance that Danny and I are the only ones who have come out of this thing relatively unscathed.

Time to wrap things up.

Gerard strides back up the garden path, still talking to his audience, this time about how they can find out more on how to renovate their own properties. He doesn't give them any advice on where to buy the best butt plugs or cock taps though, which I feel is something of an oversight on his part, as I'm sure at least a few of them will be interested.

The others peel away out of shot, leaving just Gerard, Danny and myself at the gate to the front garden.

'So, how long do you think the rest of the project will take to complete?' Gerard asks us.

I rock a hand back and forth. 'We'll have it done by the end of November with any luck.'

Gerard's eyebrows shoot up. 'November, eh?'

'You don't think that's likely?' I enquire doubtfully.

Gerard laughs abruptly. 'I've seen enough of these projects to know that timescales can go out of the window before you know it. Problems and issues can arise from where you least suspect them. You can never be prepared for all eventualities. You might find yourselves having to make changes and alterations when you didn't expect to.' His tone has taken on a somewhat patronising quality I'm not enjoying one little bit. Gerard O'Keefe the friendly TV presenter has become Gerard O'Keefe the pretentious construction expert in three seconds flat.

I bat my eyelashes at him in a winsome fashion. 'Do you think so, Mr O'Keefe? Do you think we might have to make changes?'

'Yes. Probably.'

I now affect a shocked expression. 'It's the taps, isn't it? The taps need changing.' I look around. 'Let's get Mitchell back over here. Perhaps the audience can help us decide whether we should use them or not!'

Gerard's face crumbles in panic. The last thing he needs is more tap wanking. I know it. He knows it. His rapt audience knows it.

'No no no! I'm sure they will be fine. They looked lovely!' Gerard says.

'And bulbous. Don't forget bulbous,' Danny remarks, stirring the pot again.

Gerard chooses not to take the bait and addresses the audience again through Pete's lens. 'That's about all we've got time for on the programme today, everybody. I do hope you've enjoyed our look around Daley Farmhouse, and are looking forward to seeing the finished article in a few months.'

Gerard then starts to talk about all the interesting features the audience can find on the BBC's interactive services. What he doesn't realise is that while he has been talking, Pat The Cow has wandered over from where she was happily chewing on a clump of old grass in the far corner of the front garden. As Gerard is telling his audience about what time the show will be on next week, the cow has come up behind him, looking for her customary pat. Gerard now sees the cow, but as he's in full flow, he ignores her, which is a mistake of epic proportions. Danny's cow doesn't like to be ignored, so as Gerard is saying a final awkward goodbye to the public, Pat butts him heavily in the side, sending the poor bugger teetering off balance. The last thing the million or so viewers see of their favourite TV presenter is him stumbling out of shot with a squawk of surprise.

'That's it. My career is over,' Gerard moans from where we sit watching the TV crew pack up the equipment.

I pat him on the shoulder. 'Don't worry. I bet it won't be that bad.'

He gives me a look. 'Butt plugs? Cock taps? Cow assault? The F-word?'

'Fair point, but it was a live show. Things always go wrong on live TV, don't they?'

'Yes, and people invariably lose their jobs because of it.'

I can't help but feel at least partially responsible for Gerard's glum mood. This is, after all, my house of horrors, and my team of renovators. 'Sorry, Gerard.'

He smiles at me. 'It's not your fault. How were you to know?'

We both lapse into silence. There doesn't seem to be much more I can say to console him at this stage.

'Hayley?'

'Yes?'

'There might be something you can do that might make me feel a little better.' Gerard's tone has changed. The glumness is gone. Now he sounds nervous.

'What's that?' I reply, suspicion dawning.

'I . . . I'd like to take you out to dinner. Would you come with me?'

Okay, so that's *not* the question I thought he was going to ask me. I was expecting him to want another live TV broadcast out of us to make up for this one, not a date. I'm struck dumb for a moment, unable to respond.

He sees this. 'I'm sorry! It was a stupid suggestion.'

'No! Actually, it's a very nice thought.'

'It is?'

'Yes.'

It really is, as well. I'm very flattered that a celebrity would want to take me out to dinner. If life had dealt me a better hand recently, I might have accepted.

I take Gerard's calloused hand. 'It's a very nice offer, but I don't think I'm ready for anything like that. It hasn't been that long since my divorce, and—'

'Oh god, I'm sorry!'

'No. No. It's not you. It's me.' Captain Cliché, eh? 'It's just that Simon, my ex-husband, he was very bad to me . . .'

Gerard puts his other hand over mine. 'Don't worry, Hayley. I completely understand.'

'We're ready to go, Gerard,' Monica the producer calls over from the BBC truck. She looks even more worried about her immediate future than he does.

The presenter stands up. 'Well, that's that then,' he says matter-of-factly. 'I'm sure we'll be back again soon. Take care of yourself, Hayley.'

'And you, Gerard. And thank you again for the offer.'

'My pleasure,' he replies with an uncertain grin, and walks over to his waiting colleagues.

As the BBC van drives away I feel a sudden and very much unwanted anger rise from the depths of my body. It's been nearly two years since I threw that bastard out of my life, but here he is again, ruining my life without even having to be in it. I've just turned down a date with a famous – and handsome – TV presenter because of the emotional baggage Simon Claremont has left me carrying around like a ton of bricks.

When the hell am I ever going to get over this? When the hell am I going to be able to trust a man again?

I stand up and walk back towards Daley Farmhouse, trying to put such black thoughts at the back of my mind.

To help me do this, I think again of the golden butt plug and rusty handcuffs.

Someone put those bloody things up in that chimney. But who? And *when*?

I'm not a fan of mysteries, and I resolve quietly to myself that I will get to the bottom of this one before the renovation is complete.

DANNY

September

£112,291.45 spent

In the end, our very special episode of *Great Locations* ended up being the third most downloaded programme on the BBC iPlayer for the month of August. Gerard O'Keefe was praised by his bosses for 'handling a difficult situation' – along with a metal butt plug – and the programme was once again renewed for another series. This all goes to show that if you surprise the audience with something they weren't expecting, the chances are you're onto a winner.

Not long after the broadcast I discover that I am resolutely *not* onto a winner when I get steamrollered into doing something concrete about the bloody garden.

I would like to just concrete the whole thing *over*, as I'm sick of looking at a vast combination of mud, badly cut grass and gnarled old trees, but this won't do. If nothing else it'll play havoc with Pat The Cow's hooves. Therefore, I am tasked with finding an appropriate landscape gardener to have a proper go at it.

We've obviously picked the ideal time to find a gardener – the arse end of the summer. I'm sure most of them are planning to disappear down a burrow soon to hibernate until March. Still, somebody started Find a Trade for a reason, so I spend an hour or so browsing the selection of gardeners in the local area who might actually be agreeable to coming out and doing some work as autumn hits us square in the face.

I find a likely looking company called Willingham Landscape Creations, who certainly sound like they know what they're doing, just from the name. I give them a call and have a brief chat with the head of the company, a middle-class-sounding but very friendly woman called Sally.

'It sounds like an interesting project,' she tells me, after I've filled her in on all the gory details. 'It'd have to be a simple design to start off with, I think. Once winter has passed we could look to putting more in, as and when it is needed.'

I grimace. The idea of working on this house next year is not one that fills me with pleasure. There's still so much to do, and everything will slow down once bad weather hits.

Sally (who I assume is the Willingham of the company's name) agrees to come over later today to have a look at the place. This pleases Hayley no end. Whether that's because she didn't think I could find a gardener in the local area, or whether it's because she didn't think I could find a gardener because I am an *idiot*, I will never know. Still, the appointment is booked. I have done a good job, and probably deserve a nice pat on the head.

It occurs to me though, as I look out at the mess that is our garden, that when Sally turns up I am going to have some explaining to do. I confess that we have not treated this garden with anything like the kind of love and attention the house has been getting. It's been a complete afterthought, and boy is that screamingly obvious when you look at it. I have never met Sally Willingham, but by the sounds of her on the phone I can imagine her as tall, robust and likely to look down on me with a mild loathing when she sees the mess we've made of such a potentially lovely stretch of greenery.

'Well, there's not much we can do about it now,' Hayley says to me, when I voice this concern. 'Go and have a poke about, and see if you can neaten it up a little. At least cut the hedges back a bit at the sides. That'll improve things.'

I open my mouth to protest, but frankly, I have nothing else to do today. The electricians are in the house now, doing the rest of the wiring – a job that has to be left to the professionals, lest you want to die at the end of 40,000 volts and burn your house down at the same time. Even Fred's crew have knocked off for the day, leaving their boss and my sister loafing about, keeping an eye on the electricians and advising them when necessary.

I could go into work and catch up on all the jobs I should have had done ages ago, but I can't frankly be arsed. I have to admit that my eighteen hours a week at the Emberland House Museum have shrunk to more like fourteen, given the amount of time I'm bunking off to come here and work on the house. But what can I say? I am far more invested in making this place look good, than I am in trying to maintain a badly neglected city museum on the brink of closure. If we sell this house at a premium, I'll earn about ten years' wages in one fell swoop.

So, given my inability to run wiring through a loft space, and given my supreme indifference to my part-time day job, I really have nothing better to do than a spot of light gardening, in order to tidy the place up a bit before the landscape gardener comes over. This is rather like washing your dishes before putting them in the dishwasher, but I try very hard to ignore this fact as I pull out a few battered and rusty gardening tools from the back of Fred's Transit van.

'Good luck using them, colonel,' he tells me, as I walk past him down the left-hand side of the house. 'The last time I did any proper outside work, Callaghan was prime minister.'

'They'll do. I only want to neaten up the hedges a bit.'

Actually, that's about all I can do, anyway. The gnarled trees look like they could withstand a nuclear blast, and the expanse of grass is just too huge to have a serious go at without industrial lawn-mowers. Besides, I wouldn't want to deprive Pat The Cow of her favourite foodstuff, now would I?

Speaking of whom, I find my bovine pet standing at the rear of the garden, looking into the small patch of forest that stands at the garden's edge. I haven't investigated this area in the entire time we've been here, which is something of a surprise as when I was a boy I liked nothing more than having a good explore in a bit of woodland.

I pat Pat The Cow in customary fashion. She looks up at me with a content expression on her face, chewing the cud lazily, as she is wont to do. She then returns her gaze to the forest again.

'What is it, girl? Have you spotted something?'

I sound like I'm talking to Skippy the Bush Kangaroo.

The image of Pat The Cow leading emergency services to the site of the abandoned well that little Timmy has fallen into suddenly springs into my head. I can picture the police and fire crew following her through the fields, mesmerised by her swinging udders.

This leads to a five-minute laughing fit that Pat The Cow wants no part of. She ambles away from me as I begin to get myself under control.

Pat The Cow may have lost interest in the patch of forest, but now my curiosity has been well and truly aroused. Figuring that I'm under no time limit, and whistling the *Skippy the Bush Kangaroo* theme tune, I wander over to the hedge that divides the forest from the garden and have a closer look.

There's not a whole lot to it, to be honest. Bordered on three sides by our garden, and two fields belonging to Pat The Cow's ex-owner, the woodland is a clump of beech and oak trees, interspersed with brambles, small bushes and leaf litter. Looking just over the hedge, I can see a large clump of some sort of tall plant, flourishing nicely in the late September sun. In fact, the closer I look the more of the broad, leafy plant I can see spread out in front of me. There's something familiar about it, but I can't quite put my finger on what it is. Some of the plant has invaded the boundary hedge of our garden and is growing through it, making the hedge even untidier than it needs to be.

Right then – there's my first gardening job of the day. I'll have to trim the hedge back to make it neater, and I suppose I'd better climb over into the woodland to yank a load of it out so it can't grow back through the hedge again at a later date.

Feeling good that I have actually managed to identify a job to do, I get to work with the set of old garden shears I found underneath a bag of nails in Fred's van.

The shears are blunter than an Australian sheep farmer. It takes three or four rapid chops to get through even a couple of hedgerow branches. The leafy green plant is easier to cut through, thankfully.

Two sweaty hours later, the whole back hedge is looking much, much neater. I check my watch and groan out loud. It's lunchtime. At this rate, I'll never get the other side of the garden cut before Sally Willingham turns up to judge me. Still, I've pigging well started now, haven't I? I can't just do this one edge and not the others, no matter how big and daunting the job appears. It would be rather like cutting the top of somebody's hair and leaving the back and sides long.

I take a deep breath, an even bigger swig of water, and set to work on the rest of the job.

Luckily, the hedges on the left- and right-hand sides of the garden are easier to deal with. They're less brambly for starters. It only takes me an hour on each side to wrestle them under some kind of control with the old shears. It helps when Fred provides me with a whetstone halfway through, and tightens the bolt in the centre of the shears for me. The two things help them cut a lot better, and by two o'clock the hedges have been trimmed all the way to the house.

I now have a slight problem, though. What the hell to do with all the greenery I've just chopped down. I can't just leave it there. It looks awful. Pat The Cow may be a bovine masticating machine, but not even she can eat her way through that lot before Sally Willingham arrives.

'Burn it,' Fred suggests. 'There's a can of petrol in the van. Just make sure you do it well away from the house.'

'But what will the landscape gardener say?'

Fred's eyebrows knit with disdain. 'What are you bellyaching about now?'

'Well, she might not like it if I burn all that stuff.'

He rolls his eyes. 'Don't be such a goon, chief. That's the way they do things out here in the country. Look.' Fred points at the horizon to a column of smoke in the distance. 'You ain't gonna be the only one having a bonfire today.'

Well, that settles it. If it's good enough for the locals, it's good enough for me.

It doesn't take me long to gather all the mess up and collect it in a nice big pile in the right-hand corner of the garden. I make sure to site the bonfire away from any of the overhanging trees in the woodland. We don't want this thing getting out of control, after all.

To that end, I'm quite sparing with the petrol. Too sparing to begin with, as the fire is hardly going before the combination of light wind and green branches put it out in a haze of smoke. The smoke makes me hack and cough a bit, so I have to take a step back to have a bit of a rethink, while the pile gently puffs white clouds into the air.

Second time around I pour more petrol on. Trying to be at least a little sensible about the whole thing, I light a piece of cardboard and throw it on the pile, rather than try to light the petrol up close. I enjoy having eyebrows, and don't think the soot-blackened-face look would suit me.

This time the fire roars into life in a far more satisfactory manner. The amount of petrol I've poured on overcomes how green and fresh the branches are, and in no time the fire is a good three feet high and crackling away nicely.

I feel an immense feeling of manly pride.

This is par for the course any time a man lights a fire. Whether it is a bonfire, a barbecue or a campfire, we take great delight in the act of setting fire to stuff. It must be something written in our DNA from the time we were all cavemen.

I suppress the urge to find a woman to hit over the head with a wooden club and step back a little from my fire, so I'm not breathing in quite so much smoke.

To tell the truth, I'm beginning to feel a bit giddy from smoke inhalation right now. My head is swimming, and my face feels a bit numb.

I step back even more from the blaze and the vast clouds of smoke emanating from it. Most of the smoke appears to be coming from that big leafy plant I extracted from the hedge.

As the fire burns I stand there and daydream a little. At first I think about how nice the house is going to look once we've finished the renovation. This leads me to picture the enormous £4,000 TV I'm going to buy with the money I make from the sale. Then, as is usual when I'm in a daydreaming mood these days, I think about Mischa in her underwear. Finally, I go back to thinking about Pat The Cow as a member of the emergency services. I can imagine her in her own TV series, saving small boys and elderly ladies from a variety of horrible dangers. A theme tune springs into my head and I start to make up some lyrics to go along with it.

'It's Pat The Cow, she's Pat The Cow,' I sing to myself. 'If you're in trouble, she'll come right now. She'll save your life, she'll save your wife. She'll be right there, if you're in strife.'

An enormous bray of laughter erupts from my mouth. I can't quite believe how *astronomically* funny my new tune is. And *how* creative am I being? To think of not only a theme tune, but the *lyrics* to the theme tune, all in the space of a few seconds? Amazing!

I continue to sing, marvelling at my inventiveness.

'If you're up a tree, or you've hurt your knee, Pat The Cow is a sight to see. Her udders are round, her eyes are brown, let's make her the queen, let's give her a crown.'

The image of Pat The Cow dressed in full ermine cloak and golden crown, sat on her throne in the House of Lords, instantly fills my imagination, and I start laughing again.

Twenty-five minutes later, I'm still laughing. There's every chance that if I don't get this giggling fit under control, I'm going to pass out from oxygen deprivation.

What the hell is wrong with me? Why is the image of my pet cow in a crown so bloody funny? I look over to where Pat The Cow is staring at me in bewilderment, and I mentally place a crown on her head. This sends me off into another fit of laughter that lasts a good quarter of an hour.

Through tear-streaked eyes I look up to see Fred and Hayley walking down the garden towards me. With them is a tall blonde-haired woman of about forty-five, who must be the eponymous Sally Willingham. She's wearing green wellington boots and a cable-knit sweater. Her hair is held back in an Alice band and she has the kind of suntan that only comes from extensive time spent outside.

I wonder if she'd like to hear my song about Pat The Cow?

I try to get the giggles under control as the others get closer, without much success.

'Danny? Are you alright?' my sister asks. 'You've been down here for ages. The gardener is here to talk to you.'

'Yes! Yes, I'm fine!' I reply, tittering slightly.

Don't think about a cow in a crown. Don't think about a cow in a crown.

'Pleased to meet you, Danny,' Sally Willingham says, offering me a hand. I go to shake it, but miss completely, as a wave of nausea blows through me.

'Oh dear,' I say. 'I appear to be feeling a little light-headed.' I attempt to grasp her hand again, this time with more success. I pump it up and down once before letting go. 'So! What do you think of our garden then?' I say in an inexplicably loud voice.

Sally Willingham is taken aback. 'Um, it's very large. But there's plenty we can do with it.' She points at the bonfire. 'Mr Babidge told me you were down here clearing some cuttings away.'

I gaze at the fire.

I continue to gaze at the fire.

I continue to continue to gaze at the fire.

In fact, the fire is all that exists in the universe. Its flickering flames, its burning inner light, its curling, wonderful swirls of smoke that I could get lost in for hours . . .

'Danny!' Hayley snaps. 'Sally is talking to you!'

'Hmmmmmmmmmmmmmmmmmmm?' I reply, sounding like a malfunctioning electrical transformer.

Hayley looks exasperated. 'I said, Sally is talking to you.'

What is a Sally? Is it an alien creature? Or maybe it's a small turtle from beyond Atlantis?

Maybe Sally is a cow, just like Pat The Cow. They could rule us together as our benevolent cow overlords. The world would bow to their bovine might. We would tremble! Tremble, I say!

I collapse into another fit of giggles. The three of them stare at me as if I have gone completely off my rocker, which to a certain extent, I have.

Maybe that's it . . .

Maybe I've gone stark staring insane in this garden. After all, people do go insane, don't they? Maybe this is how it happens. Maybe one minute you're a perfectly normal human being cutting down some hedges, the next you're visualising cows as world leaders with tears of laughter streaming down your face.

That must be it.

Oh God! I've gone mad!

I instantly sober up as I realise that for me, the universe has now become a dark and cold place. Has the sun gone in above my head? Yes, it has! The world has darkened! The creature comes for me!

What slouches towards Bethlehem? I do! I am cursed by the demon! Star Wormwood! The end of days!

I give my sister an imploring look. 'I . . . I think there might be something wrong with me,' I tell her in a raspy voice.

Sally Willingham has been studying me closely for a few moments, with a speculative look on her face. She takes a couple of steps past me, and sniffs the air closer to the bonfire.

'Ah, I think I see what's happening here,' she tells us all.

'Is it Satan?' I ask, terrified. 'He's come to claim me, hasn't he?'

'I very much doubt it, Mr Daley.' She points at the burning plant material. 'That's your problem.'

'What is?' Hayley asks.

'I believe your brother's bonfire consists largely of marijuana,' Sally states, trying not to laugh.

Fred has no problems expressing his amusement. 'Ha! I don't believe it! The captain's gone and got himself stoned!'

I am not laughing – far from it. I've reached a stage of such sublime paranoia and dread from the vast amounts of marijuana smoke I've inhaled that I'm pretty much terrified of everything. Out of the corner of one eye I see Pat The Cow ambling towards us. Except that it is no longer Pat The Cow. It is Pattus Cowisicus, Roman deity of death and destruction. She has come to claim me! Claim me for her own!

And with that, I'm off and running.

'Danny!' Hayley shouts, but I hear none of it. Pattus Cowisicus is right behind me! I must flee for my mortal soul!

Sadly, standing between me and the ability to flee from the Friesian Death Goddess, is one of the twisted old apple trees, whose trunk I choose to run into at full speed.

Did I say apple tree? No. What I meant is Arborus Applosicus, Roman deity of torture and severe bowel cramps brought on by sorbitol intolerance.

'Mehunga!' I screech. I have no idea who or what a Mehunga might be. Perhaps I am praying to a sworn enemy of my two foes, in the hopes that he or she may appear out of thin air to save me from a fate worse than death.

This does not happen, of course. Rather, I stumble backwards away from the apple tree and lose my balance, collapsing onto the uneven grass. To me, this does not feel like rough, uneven ground covered in stones and clumps of dying grass. To me, it is a soft and comfortable mattress made of woven cloud, upon which I can rest my weary head for the rest of eternity.

Not even Pattus Cowisicus and Arborus Applosicus can trouble me here. In this place, all is well. All is good. All is peace.

'Had we better call an ambulance?' I hear the disembodied voice of my sister say.

'Yes, I'd say so,' Sally Willingham replies. 'From the looks of his reaction, that was some very strong stuff he burned. Probably a strain of outdoor skunk.'

There's a pause.

'My brother is a police officer,' Sally Willingham continues. 'You learn things.'

Instantly, my peace is shattered. The police! The man! 5-0! The Rozzers! The Peelers! The Old *fucking* Bill!

I'm a man stoned out of his brains on skunk. They will arrest me, chuck me in the nearest cell and throw away the key!

My becalmed state is immediately replaced by the paranoia and fear again. This time it's not cow gods I am afraid of, it's having my poor innocent bottom ravaged by a never-ending queue of hardened criminals.

I must get away!

I'm back on my feet before anyone can stop me, and within seconds I'm careening down the side of the house with my sister, builder and potential landscape gardener in hot pursuit. They catch up to me as I'm sat astride my motorbike, trying to kick-start it into life.

'Danny! What are you doing?' Hayley demands, pulling at my arm.

I slap her away. 'No! No! Leave me alone! My poor bottom! They will destroy my poor bottom!' I wail, still feverishly working at the kick-starter with one trembling leg.

Fred Babidge assesses the situation and decides to take a decisive course of action. 'Right, my old china, that's quite enough of that. I once had to calm my cousin Clive down when someone slipped him a mickey in his drink. Let's see if the same method works on you.'

Fred stands beside me, measures me up, and gives me a hard bop on the side of the head with his fist. This has the desired effect. I fall limply off the motorbike and crumble to the asphalt. This does not feel like a comfortable mattress in any way, in fact it feels like precisely what it is – a hard black road surface, designed to carry heavy vehicles. In the sane part of my brain that has been locked away by all that inadvertent marijuana abuse, a coherent thought forms: I must be coming out of it. The weed must be losing its potency.

I no longer think monster cows are after me. I do, however, start to feel the massive bump on my head incurred from hitting that apple tree at full pelt.

'Can someone help me back inside please?' I ask the three of them. 'I think I might need an aspirin.'

Four aspirin and two pints of water later, the ambulance arrives. Hayley is dismayed to see that one of the paramedics is Alistair, the poor bugger she abused some time ago when she shot herself with a nail gun. He doesn't look happy about being called back to this house either. Last time he was here, he nearly broke an ankle. I'm sure he wants to see the back of the place this time as quickly as possible, before it can do him any more injury.

To that end, he and his female partner deal with me swiftly. They take my blood pressure and run a few other checks to see that my vital signs are all okay. Alistair also treats the bump on my head with some antiseptic, which stings like hell.

'You know, we have to tell the police about this,' he says to me.

'Yeah. I figured as much.'

To tell the truth I'm not all that concerned about the police coming down here, now that the drug high has worn off. If nothing else, I want them to get rid of the rest of the marijuana at the bottom of our garden.

'How the hell did it get there? Who put it there?' I ask the tired-looking policeman who turns up to the house about half an hour later. The paramedics have gone by this time. As he left I'm sure I saw Alistair sketch the sign of the cross, which I felt was a little over the top.

The copper shrugs. 'Could have been anyone really. These more remote areas are popular for growing outdoor marijuana plants. It's probably kids.'

'I thought you had to grow that stuff in a greenhouse or something?' Hayley pipes up. This is a good question. If I knew marijuana could grow outdoors in the UK I might have realised what I was burning before it sent me loopy.

'Nah. Some strains can grow outdoors here,' the copper replies. 'It just needs a bit of sun and warm weather.'

Well, there you go. You learn something new every day – even if you didn't want to. I've never smoked cannabis in my life, so all of this has been a real eye-opener for me.

Then Hayley gives voice to a question that makes my blood run cold. 'What if whoever planted them comes back?'

I hadn't thought of that! What if it isn't kids? What if it's hardened Eastern European criminals, covered in tattoos and just itching for the chance to remove the testicles of anyone who burns their cash crop?

The copper sees my look of terror. 'I wouldn't worry,' he says, in a soothing tone that he probably learned in police school. 'It's not a lot of grass. Certainly not enough to be owned by anyone you have to be concerned about. I'll send a crew down in the next few days to gather the rest of it up and dispose of it properly.' He gives me a meaningful look. 'Just be a bit more careful when you're clearing vegetation in future,' he tells me, as if I'm likely to stumble across hordes of psychedelic plants whenever I break out the garden shears.

'Thanks, officer, I promise I will,' I reply meekly for some reason. It must be the stab vest. It makes me nervous – and very, very compliant.

The policeman leaves, having done his job to the best of his abilities. This leaves me with some apologising to do.

'I'm so sorry about all this, Sally,' I tell the landscape gardener as she sips her cup of tea. Hayley and Fred have gone off to fill the electricians in on what's been going on. I'm sure they'll embellish the story magnificently, because nobody likes a good tall tale more than a bunch of tradesmen.

'It wasn't your fault,' Sally says. 'How were you supposed to know?'

I grin in sheepish fashion. 'Do you still think you could do anything with the garden?' I ask her.

'Oh yes!' she says enthusiastically. 'It's a simple plot, and I like a blank canvas to work with. Give me a week or so to come up with a design and I'll get back to you.'

'Thanks very much,' I say. 'Though, could you keep it nice and simple, please? Our budget's already getting pretty stretched.'

Sally laughs. 'No problem. I'll cancel the water feature and the ha-ha then.'

'The what now?'

Her face pinches. 'Never mind. After inhaling half a ton of marijuana smoke, I don't think you're in the best mental state for me to try and explain what a ha-ha is.'

I look it up on Google after Sally leaves, and immediately have to agree with her. It sounds like a jolly strange thing even when you're straight as a die. Trying to have the finer points of a compli-cated landscaping structure explained to you while you're still com-ing down from a massive psychedelic high is a hiding to nothing.

Miraculously, I manage to end the day with a landscape designer secured, and a lengthy term in a psychiatric ward avoided. We'll call that breaking even – and move on as swiftly as possible.

For the whole of the next week, I keep one eye on the bottom of our garden. The tired copper may have assured us that no crim-inal gangs will be turning up on the scene to reclaim their prized hoard of illicit drugs, but then I watched enough episodes of *The Bill* when I was younger to know that coppers don't always tell the truth. Especially when it comes to extramarital affairs with the nearest detective sergeant.

It's only when I start to pay attention to that end of the property's land that I realise how easy it would have been for my imaginary criminal gang to come and go without being seen by any of us. The end of the garden is so far away, and slopes downhill to the woodland, so unless you're craning your neck, or standing on the first floor, it's extremely difficult to get a clear look at what's going on down there. About the only person in our work crew who may have seen anything is Pat The Cow, and, as we've firmly established, she is not the type to be assisting in the apprehension of the criminal underclasses.

Good to his word, the copper sends out a clean-up team to eradicate the rest of the marijuana from the woodland and the back of the garden. It ends up being quite an impressive haul. They need three bin liners to take all of it away.

Surely this destruction of the crop will bring the evil Tattooed Weed Gang down on our heads? They will surely seek their revenge on us!

You see? I don't need to be high as a kite to be paranoid.

Of course, I do not see any members of a criminal gang (tattooed or otherwise) for the whole week, no matter how many times I look up from whatever job it is I am doing. Not even when I volunteer to paint the window frames in the back bedroom. This gives me perfect line of sight to where the marijuana was, but other than a few birds and Pat The Cow, there are no signs of life whatsoever.

And so, I forget about my constant vigil. My attention span is minimal at the best of times, and even the threat of death by a criminal maniac can only keep me interested for about a week, before my mind wanders off to somewhere else.

That somewhere else for me is Mischa in her underwear. Again. What can I say? I am a man of little imagination when I'm not on drugs.

As I finish off the last of the undercoat on the windowsill, I start to have a particularly pleasant daydream about the unreachable object of my affections – one that would be instantly banned from cinemas, if it were ever exposed to celluloid. As I'm reaching a fairly graphic part that causes my hand to get a little unsteady as it guides the paintbrush along the woodgrain, I spy something out of the corner of my eye: a brief flash of red coming from the woodland.

I am instantly transfixed. There's somebody down there!

There's a person in the woodland. That flash of red was a hooded top, I'm *sure* of it.

And what do hardened criminals like to wear? Hooded tops, that's what! We've all seen *Crimewatch*. We all know how they like to skulk around in the shadows with their hoods up, waiting to smack the next unsuspecting person around the head and take their wallet.

My heart starts to race. What do I do? Do I confront this evil-doer alone? Do I recruit some of my burly building colleagues to help me apprehend the monster? Do I call the police?

Or do I calm down a fucking bit, take a few deep breaths and go have a better look, before I jump to any more ridiculous conclusions?

I put the paintbrush down, walk downstairs and go out into the garden through the kitchen, eyes locked on the woodland and whatever miscreant may be hiding down there.

'Where are you goin'?' Baz asks me from inside the front room, as he notices me creep past the patio doors.

'Um . . . Pat The Cow. She needs feeding,' I tell him.

Baz looks confused. 'I only fed her an hour ago with that stuff Blenkins sold us.'

Pat The Cow has become the de facto mascot for Daley Farmhouse now, and everyone has embraced her as a large, smelly pet. Everyone except Fred, who refuses to have anything to do with her. Poor cow.

'Well, I heard her mooing,' I tell Baz. 'You must not have fed her enough.'

Baz looks crestfallen, and I feel awful. But what else am I supposed to tell him? That I'm jumping at red-hooded shadows? They all had a jolly good laugh at my expense (again) when the full details of the marijuana bonfire came to light. I hardly want to give Baz any more ammunition for a good giggle by telling him I'm off to investigate who put the bloody stuff there in the first place.

With some trepidation, I make my way down to the bottom of the garden. Pat The Cow is actually nowhere to be seen. I can't rely on her for back up, it appears.

As I reach the hedge, I duck down and crab my way along it, listening for more evidence of human activity. I get it when I hear some sulphurous swearing coming from just the other side of the hedge.

'Fuck! Fuck! Bollocks!' the voice says. 'Where's it all bloody gone? Fuck!'

Rather than the gruff, harsh tones of a gigantic man who has stabbed more people than he cares to remember, this is the voice of a very angry, but also very teenage, *girl*. Unless I haven't been watching the right episodes of *Crimewatch*, this doesn't strike me as the type of person who would be part of a gang of international marijuana smugglers that want to use my genitals as earrings.

I'm not taking any chances though, and remain hidden, listening intently to the one-sided conversation going on beyond the greenery.

'India? Is that you?' I hear the girl say, apparently into a phone, unless she's gone mad with the grief of losing her drugs. 'Where's Cindy? Is she there?' A pause. 'Who do you think it fucking is, you idiot? It's Mel! I've got to talk to Cindy. All the bloody plants have gone!' Another pause. 'I don't know, do I? I just got down here, and someone's nicked them!'

Aha!

So it's not a gang of Eastern European thugs then. Just some teenage girls.

'I'm gonna get out of here,' Mel continues, 'before he sees me.'

He?

Does she mean me? Has my lonely vigil been noticed?

It's probably about time I confronted this girl, before she has a chance to slip away.

Emboldened by the fact that I'm fairly sure I could hold my own in a fight against someone who sounds about sixteen years old, I stand up, gird my loins and leap over the freshly cut hedge like Batman on a particularly bad day.

'Stop right there!' I cry manfully, which makes Mel scream, somewhat unsurprisingly like a teenage girl.

'Who the fuck are you?' she hollers.

'Me? I'm the man who's been waiting for you, young lady!'

Mel the teenage drug-dealer's eyes widen. 'Paedophile!' she screeches.

'What?'

The girl bends down and picks up a large, thick branch, which she then proceeds to hit me with.

This is not going the way I thought it would. This girl is meant to be terrified, knowing that her criminal ways have been discovered by an upstanding member of society. She is not supposed to mistake me for a child molester and start hitting me about the torso with a short length of beech tree.

'Ow! Ow! Stop it!' I wail. 'I'm not a bloody paedophile!'

'Yes, you are! I know your type!' Mel argues. 'Britney got jumped out on the other day when she was walking home from Budgens. He waved his willy at her and asked her to touch it. And Britney is a right fat lard ball, so he must have been a weirdo! Just like you!'

She swings the stick at me again, but this time I manage to dodge it, my arms flailing wildly as I lose my balance and fall back into the hedge. This gives Mel the hooded terror the opportunity to advance on me, stick held aloft. 'I'm not touching your willy!' she screams.

'Everything alright here, is it?' Baz says conversationally, from where he's peering over the hedge at proceedings.

'Baz! Help me, Baz!' I implore.

'This bastard wants to fiddle with me!' Mel rages at him.

Baz calmly pokes a finger in one ear and has a bit of a rummage. 'I doubt it, luv,' he tells the girl. 'You're not his type.'

'Thank you, Baz!'

'If you was from Europe and liked to design houses you might stand a chance.' Baz chuckles. 'Not like he does though, eh, Danny?'

'Here! That's not fair!' I argue, temporarily forgetting that I have an enraged and tiny teenage girl standing over me, ready to bash my brains in with a big stick.

'Sorry, Danny. Couldn't resist,' Baz tells me, and climbs over the hedge himself. 'Gi's that, luv. Can't have you smashing the boss's head in.'

I'm touched by Baz's use of the word 'boss' in relation to my good self. It's a slightly misconstrued description, but I'll take it nonetheless.

'He's a paedo!' she snaps.

'No, he ain't,' Baz disagrees, snatching the stick away. 'But you're a druggie, right?'

Mel's face goes white. 'What do you mean?'

'You're the one who planted all them Mary Jane plants that Danny found the other day. The coppers cleared it all out though, there ain't nothing left.'

'Coppers?!' Mel says in a terrified tone.

'Yeah!' I interject. 'The police are onto you!' I tell her, trying to get back to my feet as I do.

Mel backs away. 'Oh God! Please don't take me to them! Please don't let them know it was me!' She shakes her head back and forth. 'It was Cindy's idea. She got the seeds from her brother! She said we should plant them here cos of my dad!'

'Your dad?' I ask, confused.

Mel's eyes go wide. 'Please don't tell my dad! He'll *kill me!*' Tears start to well up at the corners of her eyes.

'Here, steady on,' I say. 'Don't cry.'

Baz rolls his eyes. 'Let's get back over this hedge and up to the house.' He points at Mel. 'If you try to run away, I'll grab you before you get far, alright?'

I know Baz is a right soft touch, but he is still six foot three and built like a brick shithouse, so I can understand the look of fear that crosses the girl's face.

It doesn't go anywhere while we frogmarch her up to the house, and it gets even more pronounced when Fred's entire crew crowd around her.

'You're in a lot of trouble, petal,' Fred tells Mel and points at me. 'Your drugs made poor old Daniel here think a demon cow was after him.'

Oh, *thanks*, Fred.

Mel gives me a long look. 'Really? Cos all I get off that stuff is a buzz. Cindy says she sees tracers, but I don't believe her. You really saw a demon cow?'

'Maybe,' I reply in a very small voice. Now I have the distinct pleasure of knowing that I have less resistance to strong marijuana than a bunch of teenage girls.

'Who's your dad?' I ask her, changing the subject. Her face blanches.

'Look, flower,' Fred says, 'it's either we tell your dad, or we tell the coppers. Choice is yours.'

'Shouldn't we just tell the police anyway?' Hayley says.

Fred shrugs. 'What good would it do? She's fifteen years old.'

'Sixteen,' Mel says with a huff.

'*Sixteen* years old. They won't charge her with anything. I reckon her dad will be a better bet, punishment wise. If she tells us who he is.'

'I ain't saying nothing,' Mel says, crossing her arms.

It's at this point that Pat The Cow appears in the doorway, looking at Mel intently.

The girl turns around and says something that gives me a bloody good idea of exactly who her father is, whether she wants us to know or not. 'Angelina?' the girl says incredulously. 'What are you doing here?'

I put two and two together.

'Blenkins!' I shout. 'Your dad is Blenkins! He owns the farm next door.'

Mel cringes. She knows I've got her pegged! She starts to cry. 'He's going to kill me! He's going to bloody kill me!'

'Moo,' Pat The Cow intones, as one who has finally seen justice served this day.

En masse, we deliver Mel back to her father.

As she predicted, he is not best pleased. 'Growing drugs on moi land!' he snaps at her. 'You're in a lot of trouble here, missie! You just wait until I tell your mother!'

The farmer turns back to us. 'Are you gonna tell the police on her?' he asks.

'Nah,' I reply, to his visible relief. 'If Mel here promises not to do it again, we'll say no more about it.'

In truth, getting the police back would be more hassle than it's worth, and I have no real desire to ruin the life of a small girl just because she made one stupid mistake.

'Thanks very much,' Blenkins says. 'How's Angelina workin' out for ya?'

'Pat The Cow is a legend,' I tell him. Everyone behind me nods in agreement.

Then they stop, realising how stupid they look. Pat The Cow's influence runs deep.

We exchange a few more words with the farmer while Mel squirms and looks at her feet. I have a feeling that her mother is the disciplinarian of the family, and will be meting out the kind of justice that the police probably couldn't get close to if they tried.

We part company with Blenkins and Blenkins Junior, satisfied that this matter can now be put behind us.

As I wander back to the house with the others, I am forced to reflect that without Pat The Cow's timely intervention, we may have never discovered who Mel's father was.

Maybe my idea for a cow-based TV series isn't so ridiculous after all. All together now:

It's Pat The Cow, she's Pat The Cow,
If you're in trouble, she'll come right now.
She catches thieves, she catches thugs,
She'll tell your dad if you grow drugs.

HAYLEY
October
£129,734.28 spent

Wh, hen we began this crazy renovation I did a lot of reading about the pitfalls and problems that you can – and probably will – encounter during the project. I am a girl who likes to plan ahead, and I most certainly do not like surprises. You can imagine how disconcerting I found it when pretty much the first thing I read about house renovations was to 'expect surprises'. Nevertheless, I spent a great deal of time familiarising myself with the kind of bombshells we might encounter, just to be as ready as possible for any eventuality.

And so far that prior planning has paid off. There have been some shocks and surprises along the way, but each and every time, they were the kind I half expected to happen at some point. Take the subsidence, for instance. That ended up costing us thousands more than we thought, but while it was painful in the pocket, it wasn't a complete and total surprise. Therefore, my stress levels remained in the yellow zone. More floorboards needed replacing due to the woodworm as well. Again, this was expensive and time-consuming, but was a fairly typical problem with a property of this age and again, my stress levels didn't tick into the red zone once.

Yes, indeed, I thought that whatever Daley Farmhouse wanted to throw at us, I was ready and prepared to deal with it. Woodworm, rising damp, broken sewage pipes, bad wiring, bad weather, bad insulation – Hayley Daley was ready to cope with all of these things, and many more!

However, in all those online articles I read, in all the books I bought, in all the TV shows I watched, not once, not bloody *once*, did anyone mention that during a house renovation you might come across *unexploded ordnance*.

Yes, that's right. A fucking *bomb*.

An unexploded shell from the Second World War, to be more precise.

I mean, come on people. That's entirely unfair!

If we were fixing up a house on the Normandy beaches I could accept it, but not in the middle of the bloody Hampshire countryside!

And everything was going so well.

'Looking lovely, isn't it?' Fred remarks as I gaze at the nearly complete bathroom with misty eyes. I am a woman who enjoys a good bath, and this is most certainly a *good bath*. In fact, it's a *great* bath. A *fabulous* bath. The kind of tub you would only be marginally annoyed to drown in, given that there probably isn't a nicer place in the world to shuffle off this mortal coil than a brand-new, bespoke, luxury bathroom suite.

'It's stunning.'

'I'll give Mitchell some credit. He may dress like my uncle after he'd lost his marbles, but the boy knows how to design a house,' Fred says, nodding his head. 'And source the fittings. I have no idea how he managed to find this lot at such a good rate.'

'Mmmmm,' I reply, only half listening. I'm imagining myself in here on my own of an evening, with a glass of wine and an iPod dock.

The bathroom is absolutely in keeping with the modern farmhouse aesthetic we've gone for. The roll-top bath is exquisite. The large, broad sink unit is magnificent. Even the toilet looks like a work of art, what with the cistern on the wall way above it, connected by a polished chrome pipe. The tiles that line the walls and floor are a heady combination of black and white that shouldn't work, but just *do* – effortlessly so.

I turn my head to where Weeble is standing behind me with an expectant look on his face. 'Well done, Weeble,' I tell him. 'You've done an amazing job in here.'

Weeble smiles the smile of a man well pleased with both his work, and the compliments it has received. 'Thanks, Hayley. It's one of the best ones I've done.'

Fred clamps a hand over Weeble's shoulder. 'No arguments there, my boy,' he says, with father-like approval.

'Of course, there's no water yet,' Weeble continues. 'We're still having issues down at the main pipe from the road, so it'll be a while.'

'It'll be a while yet' is now the catchphrase of this renovation.

I can't help but feel a bit disappointed. When presented with such a lovely place in which to bathe your cares away, it would be nice to actually have the water with which to do so.

I grit my teeth. There I go again – picturing a life for myself in this house, when it will be someone else who gets to enjoy it, when all is said and done.

I try very hard not to heave a sigh, fail miserably, and turn myself away from Mitchell Hollingsbrooke's work before I get any more morose.

'How's the front garden coming?' Fred asks me as we amble back downstairs.

I give him a look. 'Just go outside and find out, Fred. It's fairly obvious what Sally and her team are doing out there.'

'No it ain't, love. Me and gardening do not get on at all. I haven't a clue what they're up to out there. All I see is a bunch of people in dungarees bent over and fiddling. I haven't got the first bloody clue what they're actually doing.'

I think for a moment, trying to recall what my brother had told me yesterday. 'Danny says they're plotting out a classic English country garden in the front, designed to draw the eye—' I pause. 'Designed to draw the eye somewhere. I can't quite remember where. I want to say to the horizon, but that doesn't sound right. Maybe the front door?'

'Well, that's where I'd want my eye drawn, cos that's where I'd be bloody heading,' replies Fred sagely. 'What about the back bit?'

I wave a hand. 'No idea. They've got enough trouble wrestling the mess out the front into something attractive, let alone sorting out Pat The Cow's field.'

The rear garden has become the property of Pat The Cow over recent weeks. She will not be happy once Sally Willingham gets out there and starts cutting all that lovely grass down.

'Whatever they're planning, they need to get it done quickly,' I continue. 'The weather will be caving in pretty soon. This Indian summer won't last much longer.'

'As long as they keep out of our way,' Fred warns. 'We're still nowhere near done yet. The electricians need to come back; the plumbers still have to get through. Then there's the kitchen.'

For all his bluster and bravado, Fred Babidge can be a right worrywart sometimes. I put a hand on his arm. 'Don't worry, Fred. Danny will make sure they're kept out of your way. Why don't we go have a look outside at what they're up to?'

Fred shrugs his shoulders. 'Alright. Can't hurt, I suppose.'

It's not exactly said with enthusiasm, but if I can just get Fred to appreciate how important it is for the garden to look as good as the house, it'll go a long way to making sure the two teams get on with each other.

We traipse over to where Sally and Danny are standing by a hole in the left-hand corner of the front garden. Around them are a team of three gardeners, currently all busying themselves with clearing the garden of detritus in preparation for what I assume will be the planting of bright, waving flowers.

'Oh no, nothing that grand yet,' Sally tells me when I voice this assumption. 'Autumn's no time for planting anything like that. We're strictly here to re-turf, re-grass, build a border pattern, and put in some simple violas and pansies for the minute. The showpiece stuff will have to wait until spring.' She catches the look on my face. 'Don't fret. The garden will still look lovely, you mark my words. It'll just be a subtle design. Which, as it happens, works better with a grand old farmhouse like this. You've all done such good work making the place look as magnificent as it does, I wouldn't want the garden to compete with it.'

Fred glows with pride at these words. So much for me needing to get him and Sally on the same page. She's done it for me with a simple but effective compliment that will ensure harmony at Daley Farmhouse for some time to come, with any luck.

'What's the hole for?' I ask her.

'There was a rather nasty old yew stuck in there. Half rotten and good for nothing. It had to come out. Left a big hole to fill, though.' Sally indicates a rather chubby young man in a work shirt digging in the hole with a spade. 'Jez is just making sure there's no root matter left before we fill it in. How's it going, Jez?' she asks him.

'Not too bad, boss,' he replies, thrusting the spade head back into the ground as he speaks. 'Think we've got all of it. I'll poke around for another few minutes or so, just to make sure we—'

CLUNK!

The sound is low, metallic and hollow.

'What was that?' Danny asks, moving forward.

'I don't know,' Jez replies. He lets the spade fall out of his hand, and bends down to scrape the mud away from something under his feet with both hands. In a few seconds he has revealed the round end of a metal object about eight inches wide.

'What is that? A tin can?' Danny asks.

'Too big for that,' Jez responds, brushing off even more dirt. 'Looks like it's got funny fins down the sides. And what's that writing mean?' He manages to reveal a good foot and half of metal before Fred issues a sharp intake of breath and steps forward with both hands out.

'Stop!' he orders.

Jez looks up. 'What's the matter? The quicker I get it uncovered, the quicker we can get it out.'

'Trust me, lad. You don't want to mess with that bloody thing any more!' Fred insists.

'Why?'

'Because it's a bomb, son,' Fred tells him matter-of-factly. 'German probably,' he adds.

If you ever have the urge to watch a chubby man in his twenties leap ten feet into the air in a split second, simply tell him he's standing in a hole with a seventy-year-old unexploded bomb.

'Everybody back!' Danny wails, somewhat unnecessarily, as we've already all started to back-pedal like maniacs.

'Into the house!' Fred orders.

Much to my dismay, Sally's team of dirty, mud-encrusted gardeners all pile through the front door to Daley Farmhouse, and onto the crisp, clean, polished floorboards inside.

It is testament to my obsession with this place that even in the face of potential explodification, I am still more concerned about the bloody house than my own well-being.

Mind you, if the bomb goes off, a few dirty footprints will be the least of my worries. I can't imagine that bomb-damaged properties sell for much on the open market, no matter how nice the roll-top bath is.

'Er, I guess we should call the police?' Danny suggests as we all crowd in one corner of the living room.

'Good idea,' Sally agrees.

'Do you think it'll go off?' Jez asks no one in particular.

'Let's hope not,' Sally replies. 'I've left my favourite hoe out there.'

It seems I'm not the only woman in the world who has slight problems getting her priorities right when faced with the prospect of a bomb going off.

Danny takes out his mobile and hits the usual three digits. What follows is a unique conversation I am only privy to one side of.

'Hello? I need the police!' Danny says in a strangled voice. 'There's a bomb in my front garden!'

He listens for a moment. 'No, I'm being bloody serious! We've just found a bomb!'

He listens again. 'How should I know? It's big, metal and missile shaped!'

Listens. 'No, it's not fucking *ticking*! This isn't a Bugs Bunny cartoon, mate!'

Fred whips the phone out of Danny's shaking hand. 'Let me speak to them,' he says. 'Can we please have the police here as quickly as possible?' he tells the operator in a much calmer tone than my brother. Then he explains the situation, gives the guy on the other end the address and hangs up. 'They'll be here within the next few minutes,' Fred tells us, handing the phone back to Danny.

Baz then appears from upstairs. 'What's going on?' he asks us.

Danny gives him a look of abject terror. 'There's a bomb in the garden, Baz!'

Baz looks out of the living-room window, cocks his ear to the faint sound of sirens, and nods his head. 'Right then.' He walks back out into the hallway and shouts upstairs, 'Tea break, lads!'

Not just us women with the misplaced priorities, then.

Twenty minutes later a small police car turns up at the front gate, being driven by an even smaller police officer.

'Blimey,' Danny says when he sees the pocket copper climb out of the car. 'He's a little one.'

'He looks like my grandson,' Fred remarks, peering through the front-room window.

'Copper too, is he?' I ask.

Fred gives me a look. 'No. Eight years old.'

The policeman steps over the broken garden gate – we really have to get that sorted out soon – and makes his way rather nonchalantly down the garden path.

'We did say we thought there was a bomb in our garden, didn't we?' I murmur as I watch the policeman show absolutely no signs of concern about the massive explosive device sat in the hole off to his right-hand side.

'I thought I made it pretty bloody clear,' Fred says, and walks out of the room. He opens the front door and points at the bomb hole. 'You might want to walk a bit quicker there, officer.'

'Why's that then?' the copper replies, with a cheery smile on his face.

'There's a bomb in that hole over there,' Fred tells him.

The copper continues to show no outward signs of distress. He waves a hand. 'Oh, we get these calls all the time. It always turns out to be a tin can, or an old bit of pipe.'

'Ah, does it?' Fred replies, eyes narrowing. 'Do the tin cans or old bits of pipe often come with fins down the sides and the words *Warnung Explosiv* stamped on them?'

The copper's face goes a little grey around the edges. 'Fins?' he says in a reedy tone.

'Yep. Big ones.'

'Er, I think I'll come inside then.'

'That's your best bet, squire.'

The copper is in the house faster than you can say doodlebug. He's on his radio even faster than that. 'Victor One from Papa 72, are you there, Victor One?' he says breathlessly.

'Receiving, Papa 72,' a bored voice on the other end says.

'Um. There's a bomb here, Victor One.'

'Are you mucking about, Kev? Only the inspector warned you lot about mucking around on the radio last week in that email.'

'No, Tracy, I am not mucking about! There's a ruddy Second World War bomb here! I need more units and the sodding bomb squad as quickly as they can get here!'

'Received, Papa 72. I'll get them out to you as soon as possible,' the call taker responds, this time with a satisfying sense of urgency to her voice.

'Received, Victor One.' The copper pauses and looks round at all of us. 'I think I'll evacuate these people into the back garden, as far away from the device as possible.'

'Wise move, Papa 72. Wise move.'

Kev the copper gets off the radio and tries to issue us all a reassuring smile. It fails miserably.

'Okay, everyone. Why don't we step out into the back garden?'

'Alright,' I agree.'

'And everyone be nice to Pat The Cow,' Danny adds. 'Too many people on her patch makes her, um, *frisky*.'

With the warnings given, we all traipse out into the garden to await the arrival of people who, with any luck, will know what the hell to do with a seventy-year-old explosive device.

Sadly, the people in question are sequestered on the nearest army base, which is a good hour away in the car, so we're forced to stand around like a bunch of lemons awaiting the bomb squad's arrival. In that time another ten police officers turn up to see what all the fuss is about. By midday the immediate area is swarming with coppers. About the only constructive thing they do is erect an exclusion zone around the bomb with bright yellow tape that stretches from back up the road to where we're all stood at the far end of the garden.

I look at my watch every thirty seconds or so. All this hanging around is costing us valuable time that could be spent on the house renovation – not to mention all the money it's costing Danny and I, as our team of builders and gardeners stand around doing nothing at our expense.

Eventually I see a large green army truck roll up at the front of the house. Four men get out dressed in military garb. I'm very pleased to say they all look calm about the whole thing. This can only be a good sign.

One of them skirts the edges of the garden, keeping as far away from the bomb as possible, and makes his way through the mud towards us. 'Morning, folks,' he says. 'I'm Corporal Smith. Looks like you have an old Luftwaffe shell in your garden, eh?'

'Apparently so,' I reply. 'Can you get rid of it?'

'Oh, I'm sure we can. Done quite a few of these over the years. A lot of the German shells were duds when they were dropped, you know. That's what comes of enlisting prisoners of war and the poor old Jews to build your bombs for you. They're bound to do a bad job, quite deliberately!'

This man seems quite jocular about the concept of innocent people being enslaved by the Nazis, but I think I'll let it pass, as it's now one in the afternoon, and those skirting boards aren't going to fit themselves.

'How long will it take?' I ask Corporal Smith.

He sticks his chin in the air in deep thought. It's a very odd gesture to make. I guess it looks perfectly fine if you're in the military. 'Depends on the shell, my dear. If it's an SC50*BI* it'll be quite quick. If it's a *JB* though, then that could take a while.'

This makes absolutely no sense to me, obviously. But I'll take his word for it. As long as he knows what he's talking about, then everything is fine. As fine as it can be with an unexploded bomb less that a hundred metres away, anyway.

Of course, Sod's Law being what it is, the bomb is indeed a bloody JB. And boy does it take the bomb squad an age to sort the ruddy thing out. I'm not privy to the actual analysis and defusement of the device, as I'm still stuck with the rest of my clan at the rear of the garden. About the only thing we've got to look at is Pat The Cow chewing cud and looking decidedly grumpy about having her private patch of grass invaded by quite so many people.

It's gone *five p.m.* when Corporal Smith jogs back over to us to let us know that the bomb has been removed from the garden. 'All done!' he says cheerfully. 'Looks like the fuse was missing completely. It couldn't have gone off. You were all perfectly safe.'

This is very good news indeed. We may have lost a day, but at least the situation is resolved.

'However—' Smith continues.

I don't like the sound of that *however* one little bit. Nothing good can come of it.

'However, the JBs were often dropped in clusters,' Smith tells us.

'Which means?' I reply, dread creeping into my voice.

'Which means there's every chance that there could be more of them in the area, also unexploded. The prisoners would often sabotage these things in entire batches. Could be quite a few of them lying around under the soil. We have protocols in place for such an eventuality, of course.'

'What kind of *protocols*?' I ask, my heart racing in panic.

Corporal Smith catches my mood and gives me a sympathetic look. 'We have to do a sweep of the area. All standard stuff, don't you worry. It just might take a little bit of time.'

I can almost hear the money draining from my bank account as I ask my next question. 'How *much* time?'

'Depends on what HQ says about the likely spread. But we've had to do this a couple of times, and both searches took a good week to complete. You can't be too careful.'

A week!

A bloody *week*!

Smith looks even more apologetic. 'And we'll have to get into the house with the metal detectors too, I'm afraid. There could be a device underneath it. You wouldn't want one going off, now would you?'

Oh god! The floorboards! The poor bloody floorboards!

I start to go a bit weak at the knees.

'What if you find a bomb under the house?' Danny asks.

'Oh, we'll whip it out, don't you fret!'

Whip it out?

Whip it out!

It's not like pulling out a splinter, you camouflaged idiot! If there's a bomb under the house, things will need to be *ripped up* to get at it! Torn apart! All our hard work will be destroyed!

Okay, I know I'm going a bit overboard here, but I've just been told that my lovely new renovated farmhouse could be hiding several unexploded Nazi bombs, so I'm understandably a little *fraught*.

'What should we do now?' Fred asks Corporal Smith.

'Oh, we'll have the police escort you all off the property,' he tells him.

'What about Pat The Cow?' Danny asks.

'She'll be fine down the bottom of the garden,' I reply. 'That cow is more than smart enough to stay away from an unexploded bomb.'

'We'll get to work on the sweep tomorrow,' Smith says.

I'm speechless. This is a *disaster*.

Not only are we going to lose days of work while this man and his mates poke around our house for bombs, but if they find one, there's every chance that they'll have to destroy some of our renovation work to extract the thing. That's provided they don't set the sodding thing off! How much damage will be done to my lovely new house then?

I gasp out loud. What the hell have I become?

If a bomb does go off, Corporal Smith and chums will be blown into tiny smithereens, and all I care about is what happens to my massive financial investment. How crushingly *awful* is that?

Daley Farmhouse is turning me into something I don't like very much – an obsessive sociopath.

I need to get away from this place as quickly as possible before it turns me completely to the Dark Side.

'Okay, we'll get out of your hair,' I tell Corporal Smith. I then look around at everyone else. 'We could all do with a few days off, couldn't we?' I spout in a tremulous, sing-song voice.

'Er, we've only just got here?' Sally Willingham points out. I choose to ignore her, as this is no time for level-headedness.

'Yes! A nice week off will do us all the world of good!' I repeat, my voice as brittle as eggshells.

'Are you alright, sis?' Danny asks.

'Fine! I'm fine!' I reply. How can I explain that a vast irrational fear has suddenly come over me that this house has corrupted my mortal soul in ways I daren't speak of? Best to just get the fuck out of here as quickly as possible, preferably in the direction of the nearest bar.

'Right, you heard the lady,' Fred says to Kev the mini-copper, who has been stood at the back of our small crowd, trying to stop Pat The Cow from nibbling on his baton. 'Lead us away, sport!'

Kev pushes Pat's head away from his waist. 'Thank God for that. I think this cow is about to commit a common assault on me.'

It is with some relief that I drive away from the farmhouse that evening, leaving the police and bomb squad to their risky search. While I would prefer not to have to delay work on the house any longer than necessary, it has become quite apparent to me that I need some time away from the place. It's all I've thought about for months, and having one thing fill your thoughts twenty-four hours a day for so long is not healthy in the slightest.

I will use this bizarre and strange series of events to get away from the renovation completely, and give my brain a bit of a rest.

I might read some books, catch up on some Netflix, and go for a few nice walks in the countryside. It'll be lovely. A whole week without thinking about Daley Farmhouse once!

At 7.30 a.m. the next day I'm standing at the police tape strung across the road leading to the house with an anxious look on my face. What the hell are they *doing* down there?

My much-needed break from Daley Farmhouse lasted about an hour and a half, until I remembered that the gas man was supposed to be coming out on Wednesday to run a safety check. This threw me into a panic that ensured I got about three hours' sleep. By six in the morning I was wide awake and picturing the bomb squad ripping up the entire basement because they'd found a five-hundred-pound bomb down there, with Hitler's corpse draped over it.

You can imagine how delighted poor old Corporal Smith was when he saw my anxious face coming towards him as he stood by his army truck having a nice cup of tea poured directly from one of Her Majesty's thermos flasks.

I fired twenty questions at him about what they were planning to do in their search today, none of which he gave me any particularly useful answers to.

I ended up standing forlornly at the police tape for a good two hours before deciding that I was being very silly, and should go home and try to forget about it.

I'm very pleased to say I successfully managed to do this!

Until 6.25 a.m. the next day, when I turned up at the house before Smith had even got the top off the thermos flask.

On the third morning the tea-drinking bomb disposal expert is conspicuous by his absence. Word has also obviously got around about me to his colleagues, as the exclusion zone around my good self is just slightly larger than the one around the house. Therefore, all I can do is stand and watch various men in green fatigues traipsing to and from the farmhouse in the kind of hobnailed military boots that can destroy the average brand-new floorboard in no time at all.

'Hayley?' a voice says from behind me. I turn to find Gerard O'Keefe walking down the road towards me, an old grey Jaguar parked behind him. I didn't even hear him pull up; such is my obsession with damaged floorboards.

'Gerard! What are you doing here?'

'Mitchell called to say that work had halted thanks to a bomb scare?'

'Yeah. That's right. If it's going to happen anywhere, it's going to happen at Daley Farmhouse!' I'm trying to make light of it, but inside I think I could just about cry right now.

'So, no work at all for a week then?'

'Nope.'

Gerard winces. 'Costing you a fair bit, is it?'

My wince is much bigger. 'Oh yes.'

He gives me a sympathetic look. 'Fancy a hug?'

I nod. 'Yes, Gerard. That would be very nice.' I point over to the army lads. 'They're all ignoring me.'

'Come here, then.'

The hug is warm, comfortable and smells faintly of paint thinner. All in all, quite the pleasant experience, I have to say.

'So what do you plan on doing?' he asks me once the hug is over.

'I don't know. I probably should go off and have some kind of life, but I can't draw myself away from the place. Any second now I keep expecting them to find a massive bomb that means they'll have to rip the flooring up. It's potentially heart-breaking.'

Gerard puts his hands in his pockets. 'Well, I'm not up to much today. I'll hang around here with you, if you like.'

'Wow. Thank you. It is a bit lonely stood here on my own.'

'I've got a couple of camp chairs in the boot. I'll go get them.' Gerard turns to go back to his massive old Jag.

As he pulls the chairs out I have a little think. Gerard lives a good sixty miles away. He could have just called. But here he is, at the house, having come all the way down here on the off chance one of us might be around.

On the off chance you *might be around, you silly sod.*

My heart races. He's still interested. Even though I turned him down for that date. So what do I do now? My reticence to get involved with another man still stands, but he's come all the way down here from London and has brought a chair for me to sit on.

'Here you go,' Gerard says, plonking down a camp chair in front of me and unfolding it. He parks the second chair close to it and sits himself down, looking up at me expectantly. I sit down as well, making sure I've still got a decent line of sight to the army truck and the road up to the farmhouse. If anything destructive is likely to happen, I want to know about it.

'So, tell me a bit more about yourself,' Gerard says.

'Huh?' I reply, forcing my gaze away from the house.

Gerard laughs. 'Tell me a bit more about *you*. We're probably stuck here for a while, so we may as well have something to chat about!'

'Fair enough,' I say, returning the smile.

The next couple of hours are spent in idle chit-chat with Gerard, and not once do I feel bored, restless or anxious. This is a completely new experience for me, as the last man who I had such a long conversation with that wasn't my brother was my ex-husband Simon. Conversations with him were usually stressful, unpleasant and demeaning – towards the end of the relationship anyway. Having a decent chat with a narcissist and a misogynist all rolled into one human being is nigh on impossible.

Gerard, on the other hand, is funny, insightful and thoroughly fascinating to talk to.

And did I mention the blue eyes?

They're quite magnificent as well.

'Can I say something that you might find a little . . . *personal?*' he says to me, after finishing an anecdote about his elderly mother's penchant for aerobics that has me guffawing like a madwoman for a good couple of minutes.

'Yeah, okay.' I reply a little uncertainly, still chuckling at the image of a rambunctious seventy-three-year-old woman in Lycra at a spinning class.

'I think you have no idea who you actually are.'

'I'm sorry, what?'

I wasn't expecting that. I thought he was going to tell me I had a nice nose – or that I sound like a hyena when I laugh.

'You think you're two steps away from a meltdown, and that you're not a strong person,' Gerard continues, his deep blue eyes fixed on my face intently. 'I think that ex of yours did you a lot of damage, and if I ever met him, I think I'd pull his kidneys out.'

I blink a couple of times. No one has ever offered to do brutal and amateur surgery on Simon before. The thought has a definite appeal. 'Thank you, Gerard,' I tell him. 'I'm not sure I'm quite as tough as you think I am, but thanks for saying so anyway.'

Gerard holds a finger up. 'And beautiful, Miss Daley! You are also quite, quite lovely to look at.'

There go my knees. Traitorous bloody things that they are. It's a good job I'm sitting down.

I'm also apparently leaning forward in my seat to get closer to Gerard.

This is very strange. I'm not doing it consciously. It's just happening without my say so. It's almost as if my body has had quite enough of my timid brain and is taking matters into its own hands.

Gerard's eyes go a little wide, but then he leans towards me too.

From the outside this all looks astronomically awkward I'm sure. I don't recommend attempting a first kiss in a foldaway camp chair. There's an unwholesome amount of straining and lurching involved that doesn't lend itself to passionate romance in the slightest. Nevertheless, our lips are now almost touching.

'Er, hello?' Corporal Smith says from beyond the police tape.

I jump a mile.

Gerard and I both instantly lean back away from the kiss and look up at Smith, who has the good grace to look extremely awkward. 'Um. Sorry to interrupt. Thought I'd better let you know that we've finished with the sweep.'

'Already?' I say in disbelief. 'I thought you said it could take a *week?*'

'I did, but the land has been easier to scan than I thought it would.' He smiles. 'Job's done!'

Excellent!

For a moment I forget that this man has ruined my first kiss with a man in years. He's just given me some very good news, after all. 'You mean we can get back in the house *today?*' I ask him excitedly.

'Yep. We can be packed up in an hour.'

'Thank you, Corporal Smith!' I turn back to Gerard, who is looking faintly disappointed. 'Isn't that great, Gerard?'

'Yes. That's wonderful,' he says, sounding more than a little forced.

'Er, there's something else,' Corporal Smith says. 'We didn't find any more shells, but we did find *something.*'

'What?' I ask, wondering what the hell he's on about.

'I think— I think you should come and look for yourself,' Smith suggests. 'We put it in the living room for you.'

I look down at a large black trunk, encrusted with mud.

'Where did you find it?' I ask Smith.

'Down the right-hand side of the house, close to the fence. Private Carmichael picked it up on his detector. We all held our breath for a quite a while before we got it unearthed. Thought it could have been another bomb. Turned out to just be this trunk, though.'

'People have a habit of hiding things away in this house,' Gerard remarks from beside me. 'First all that stuff from up the chimney, and now this.'

He has a point. I still have no idea who secreted all the kinky stuff up that chimney. Maybe the same person is responsible for burying this trunk?

'Is there anything in it?' I ask the corporal.

Smith smiles. 'Oh yes!'

He flips the trunk lid open to reveal a very old projector and four cans of film.

'Good god!' Gerard exclaims. 'It's an old 8 millimetre! A Bell & Howell if I'm not mistaken!'

'You know about these things?' I ask him, gobsmacked.

He rolls his eyes. 'I work for the BBC, Hayley. We're pretty much required to be steeped in useless knowledge about this type of stuff. Never ask me to tell you about eight-track recording. You'll want to kill yourself within five minutes of me opening my mouth.'

He pulls the projector out of the trunk. It looks exactly the way you'd expect an old film projector to look. Two big wheels on top, big camera lens at the front, lots of complicated-looking switches and spindles on the side.

Gerard examines the thing for a few seconds. 'It's in very good nick,' he says at last. 'That trunk must have been pretty much air-tight. Even the power cord still looks fine. I'd have to rewire it with a modern plug, but other than that, it'd be good to go.'

'Do you think it'll work?' Corporal Smith asks, apparently caught up in the excitement of the find.

Gerard shrugs. 'I have no idea. There's no electricity here yet, so I don't think we could get it working anyway.'

'You could fire the generator up,' I respond. Even I'm curious to see whether this antique still works or not. 'There's an extension cord over there. You could plug it in and have a go.'

Gerard's eyes light up, as do Corporal Smith's.

Within a few minutes Fred's generator is up and running, Gerard has found a modern plug and rewired the power cord, and the projector has been propped up on one of the stepladders that lie around the house.

'It's got power!' Gerard says with excitement, examining the side of the projector. 'We could actually get this thing working!'

I look through the four round metal cans of film inside the trunk. Two aren't labelled, and the film looks to have crumbled to dust, but two are in better condition, with the film still intact. They both have scuffed and faded black lettering on the outside of the can. One says 'A Special Evening' and means nothing to me, but when I read what's written on the other, my excitement levels sky rocket. 'Oh my God,' I say breathlessly.

'What is it?' Gerard asks.

I hold up the film can to show him the title on the side of it.

'"Genevieve in the Summer Garden",' Gerard reads. 'What does it mean?'

'Genevieve was my grandma's name,' I tell him. 'This is a film of my grandmother!'

His eyes go wide. 'Fantastic!' He holds out a hand. 'Let's get it in the projector and see if it runs.'

I hand the film can over with one shaking hand. This is *incredible*. There's every chance that I am about to see my grandmother fifty years ago, when she wasn't that much older than I am now.

And the house! I'll get to see the house before it fell apart!

I stand nervously chewing on one fingernail while Gerard goes through the complicated business of spooling the film into the projector. After ten minutes of swearing and grunting he announces that it's ready to go. 'It might not look very bright,' he warns, 'but this room is quite dark and the plaster on the walls is white, so we should see something. If the projector works.'

'What about sound?' Corporal Smith asks.

'Oh yes, these old beauties had sound on them as well. But it might be very bad quality.' He hovers a finger over the on switch and looks at me. 'Hold your breath,' he says, and flicks it.

The projector starts to make a loud, rapid ticking noise as the film starts to feed from one spool, through the projector and onto the other. A bright light erupts from the lens and casts a vaguely square image on the plaster wall in front of it. The picture is a bit blurred, but otherwise Gerard has done a fine job getting the old projector to work.

'Yes!' he crows triumphantly.

'Good bloody show!' Corporal Smith shouts.

I can't say anything, as I am transfixed.

In the blurry projector's image is a summer garden, bathed in warm sunlight.

I was *right*, it *is* the garden here at Daley Farmhouse. The back garden to be precise.

Where now stands a cracked and disused patio, covered in weeds and old bits of rusted garden furniture, there once was a wooden gazebo, covered in trailing vines and flowers. The very same rusty garden furniture is in this shot, only looking in much better shape. Not brand new by any means, but still perfectly useable.

This is a description I could use for the whole house, actually – what I can see of it at least, in this shaky, blurred image. There's a shabby chic quality to it that I rather like. You can tell it was an old Victorian home, even back then, but it was still in good enough shape to be inhabited. It'd take another fifty years of neglect for it to get to the dilapidated state Danny and I found it in.

In one of the patio chairs sits a woman in a light summer dress. It's my grandmother. A very young version of my grandmother, anyway, with a neat early 1960s bob haircut. She looks *beautiful.*

'Now I see where you get your looks,' Gerard murmurs from my side.

My grandmother smiles, waves at the camera and stands up. 'How long are you going to do that?' I hear her say. The sound quality is atrocious, but even through its thick layer of static I can hear how strong and vibrant Grandma's voice was when she was a young woman. I've been so used to hearing her at an old age and beyond, that it comes as a pleasant surprise to listen to her light, young and lyrical tone.

The person on the other side of the camera does not respond, but moves the camera towards her. She laughs, crosses her eyes and pokes out her tongue, and ducks out of shot. The camera wobbles for a moment, before the screen goes black.

'That's it,' Gerard says.

'Play it again,' I tell him.

He duly obliges and I once again get to spend a few short seconds with the woman who left me this house in her will – and all the problems and complications that have gone with it. I just wish she were still here for me to thank her.

'There might be more of her on the other reel,' Corporal Smith points out.

'Of course!' Gerard agrees, and starts to replace the first old roll of film with the second.

I wait with bated breath to see if Smith is right.

'Okay, this one is a bit longer,' Gerard says. 'Let's see what we've got, shall we?' he adds, and flicks the on switch.

What we have is a bedroom. The master bedroom. I can tell by the position of the fireplace off to the left-hand side, and the height of the skirting boards behind the large four-poster bed.

It's a little hard to stay concentrated on the room's décor though, given that there is a fat, sweating man of about sixty lying naked on the bed with his arms and legs strapped to the four posts.

'Bloody Nora!' Corporal Smith exclaims.

'Oh my,' Gerard adds.

I am speechless.

'I've been a bad boy!' the fat man says to the camera, his large, distended belly wobbling grotesquely as he does so.

'Yes, you have,' a voice says from behind the camera.

My breath catches in my throat. That's Grandma's voice again!

Sure enough, from the right of the shot my sainted grandmother appears – but this time she's not wearing a light summer dress. This time she's wearing a black basque, and a set of stockings and suspenders that must have taken her an hour to get into.

There are many things in life that can traumatise you. Burying a beloved family pet, for instance. A six-inch nail disappearing into your own foot.

But nothing can quite compete with the vision of your grandmother's pert 1960s bottom, clad in a lacy pair of knickers and sashaying its way over to where an obese old fart is awaiting his punishment.

Said punishment seems to consist of being lightly whipped on the stomach with a riding crop.

'Oh yes! I've been such a naughty boy!' the fat man wails.

'Yes, you have!' Grandma replies in a husky voice, slapping the riding crop across his gut one more time.

All three of us are transfixed, unable to move.

I'm horrified. Gerard is shocked. I'm hoping and praying Corporal Smith isn't *turned on.*

'Yes! Yes! Punish me!' Fatso continues.

Grandma Genevieve stops slapping the obese pervert and leans over him. 'You know what I think you should do, Clive?' she asks her captive.

'What, Mistress Jenny? What should I do?'

'I think you should eat my panties!'

Oh good God!

'Turn it off!' I snap at Gerard. He doesn't hear me, so I'm treated to the sight of my grandmother seductively pulling her knickers down over the suspenders to reveal her naked bottom. 'Turn it off!' I more or less scream at the TV presenter, who is at last shaken out of his horrified reverie by the volume in my voice.

He lunges forward and flicks the off switch on the projector, mercifully ending the 1960s equivalent of *Fifty Shades of Grey* before I have to watch the woman who gave birth to my father stuffing her used underwear into the mouth of some random grey-haired sex pest.

I catch the look on Corporal Smith's face. He looks vaguely disappointed. I point a finger at him. 'You! Out!' I order.

'But—'

'I think you should do as she says,' Gerard tells him, noting my expression.

The soldier takes one last look at the now blank plastered wall before sloping off out of the living room. He doesn't seem too bothered by my outburst, but then he does spend most of his time around unexploded bombs of a different kind, I suppose.

I stare into space for a moment, trying to process the horrors I've just witnessed.

'Well,' Gerard begins carefully. 'That was unexpected.'

My eyes narrow. 'Getting a tax rebate is *unexpected*, Gerard,' I tell him. 'This . . . This is inconceivably horrid.'

He looks up in thought. 'At least we probably know who hid the stuff in the chimney now.'

I'm instantly incensed. 'Are you suggesting that the butt plug belonged to my grandmother? My elderly and lovely grandma, who used to buy me sweets, and always told me what a wonderful little girl I was? My elderly, *frail* grandma, who had trouble making it up the stairs in the last years of her life, but would always have the strength to give Danny and me a hug whenever we went to see her?!' My rage is absolute. 'Do you think a woman like that would own a gigantic butt plug, Gerard?'

He rocks one hand to and fro and looks at the projector.

'Out!' I scream. 'Get out!'

'But Hayley—'

'No, Gerard! No buts!' I realise what I've just said. 'Especially of the metal plug kind! Leave me alone!'

Gerard is quicker about his exit than Corporal Smith.

Once he's gone, the anger drains from my body, and is replaced by ice-cold shock.

All at once I realise that I have no idea who my Grandma actually was before her death – and more importantly, before my birth. To me she's always been the doting old woman in the armchair, ready to dole out kisses and bedtime stories whenever either was needed.

But now . . .

Now I see a whole different side to her. My grandmother actually had a *life* before I came along.

And what a bloody life it was!

Butt plugs, handcuffs, sex tapes . . .

What exactly went on in this house fifty years ago, and what part did my grandmother play in all of it?

This has gone quite, quite far enough! I have to find out, and I have to find out *now*!

DANNY
October
£138,321.17 spent

So it looks like I'm renovating a brothel.

At least that's what Hayley tells me.

This wouldn't bother me too much, if it weren't for the fact that it looks like the brothel could have been run by my *grand-mother*. This is an indescribably awful concept that I have decided to pretend doesn't exist so I can get on with my life. I know the saying goes that you shouldn't stick your head in the sand, but that saying obviously wasn't invented by someone who just found out that their deceased relative liked to whip people with a riding crop in their spare time. If I could permanently walk around with my head in a helmet full of half the contents of the Sahara, I would.

Things had been going pretty well before this recent revelation, as well.

Not only did I not make an idiot of myself on national TV, but I've also broken up an illegal drugs ring.

My self-confidence and sense of self-satisfaction have been at an all-time high, and I'm not going to let a little thing like having an ex-madam for a grandmother ruin my good mood. After all, she's the one responsible for leaving me this house and getting me off my arse to do something constructive with my life, so I'm not about to let a little thing like some light BDSM cloud my judgement of her.

I'll leave the hunt for the truth about Grandma Genevieve to my sister and concentrate on more immediate concerns instead.

Namely, the quest for Mischa.

My life took a turn for the unexpected when Mitchell and Mischa turned up at the farmhouse on a very auspicious day for the build. It was the day the kitchen was due to be completed. *Finally.* After several months of wrangling between very stubborn parties.

The design of the kitchen has proved a thorny issue, and there have been several . . . let's just call them 'heated discussions' between Hayley and Mitchell over what it should look like. Hayley has pretty much just accepted Mitchell's lead on all the big chunky architectural stuff, like the extension, en suite, new roof, and so on, but when it comes to the more aesthetic aspects of the farmhouse's new look, she's less willing to let him have free rein.

The main issue over the kitchen has been the colour. It was decided early on that the thing should be in keeping with the rest of the house, so a nice Shaker style design was agreed upon, with the main highlights being a large island, deep white butler sink and an enormous gas range. What was more contentious was the colour. I've never seen two full-grown human beings nearly come to blows over such a simple issue as colour before. It is truly a sight to behold.

Mitchell wanted to go with a deep green shade that was *a very bold statement of intent*, as he referred to it. Quite what the intent was, I don't know. Possibly to remind people of Kermit the Frog. Hayley on the other hand, wanted a more conventional cream colour. I have to say I agreed with her, but I stayed right out of it, as I am not a complete cretin. Besides, Mischa was in the room for most of the argument, which left me more or less struck dumb, as usual.

In the end, they compromised on a far lighter shade of creamy green that looked much more sensible. It goes particularly well with the white marble counter tops, I think. This is most certainly what I told the pair of them when they showed me the compromised design. In fact I made more of a big deal out of it than I needed to, just to shut the pair of them up.

It is with some relief then that we get to the day of the kitchen fitting. Given how important a part of the renovation it has become, it's not really surprising that everyone wants to be on hand to see its unveiling. Even Fred and the crew have got into the spirit of things, by putting a sheet across the patio doors and the archway between the kitchen and the lounge two days ago, so that none of us could see the thing until it was completely finished, and ready for its moment in the sun.

'I'm so excited!' Mitchell exclaims, clapping his hands together. Today, he's actually dressed quite conservatively for Mitchell. No hat on his head. No colourful corduroy trousers, no ridiculous cravat. Yes, I'll concede that the suit is yellow and the same style as Rupert the Boar's trousers, but at least the ensemble matches – what with the yellow Converse trainers and all.

Mischa is wearing a pair of blue jeans and a grey roll-neck jumper. This sounds completely unerotic, but you can't see the way her raven-black hair tumbles down over her shoulders, or how tight the jeans are stretched over her thighs. She's also wearing a pair of motorcycle boots, which basically makes her outfit sexier to me than a set of stockings and suspenders.

Look, I know this is sounding more and more pathetic, I'm fully aware of that fact. I'm in my late twenties for crying out loud, and have a few relationships behind me. It's not like I've never seen an attractive woman before. This one, though – she's something else. It's not just how pretty she is, it's everything else about her. The accent, the way she carries herself, the things she says. Mischa is the perfect package: incredibly good-looking and clever, to boot. She's the type of woman I've dreamt about meeting my entire life. Is it any wonder I get tongue-tied when I'm around her?

'It is exciting, isn't it, Danny?' she says to me.

'Mfmfn.'

'I'm sorry?'

'Yes. Exciting. Nice kitchen,' I tell her, like I'm a three-year-old boy pointing something out to his mother.

'I helped with the design, you know,' she says with a proud smile. 'The layout was mainly my idea.'

'Was it?' I say and look at my feet.

Oh come on, dickhead, you can do better than that, surely?

'Do you like kitchens?' I ask – because that'll impress her, won't it? 'I like kitchens,' I add, compounding the awkwardness.

She nods a little uncertainly. 'Yes, Danny. That is why I helped design it. Kitchens are very nice,' she responds. Now her tone of voice is one belonging to someone speaking to a person with special needs.

Let's just end this conversation and look back at the sheet covering the archway, shall we? It's probably best for all concerned.

'They're taking their sweet time,' Hayley remarks drily, looking at her watch. 'Are you lot ready yet?' she calls through.

'Nearly!' Baz exclaims from within.

'Gi's another minute!' Spider adds.

The two of them are responsible for all this ceremony. Both have worked long and hard getting everything right in the kitchen, so I can't really blame them. Who knew such big strapping lads could enjoy a bit of melodrama? They've been acting like an old married couple. It's all rather endearing, to be honest.

'We're just pulling off the last of the masking tape!' Baz tells us.

And so we wait for another five minutes. Hayley and Mitchell engage in a bit of light small talk, while Mischa and I remain silent and still as statues. It appears my awkwardness is contagious, as some of it has rubbed off onto the foreign beauty, and she stands there staring at the sheet alongside me, no doubt hoping and praying that it'll be ripped down soon so she can get away from me.

Excruciatingly, it takes the lads another five minutes to be ready. In that time I get to smell what Mischa's perfume is like and have a fantasy about running my hands through her hair while she kicks me lightly in the testicles with her boots.

Finally, though, we're ready for business.

'Okay, everyone!' Baz shouts.

'We're gonna do a countdown!' Spider adds.

Both of them start to count down from five together. 'Five! Four! Three! Two! One!'

The sheet is ripped aside with a flourish, revealing a rather startling transformation to the large extension. I've seen this area in every stage of its transformation. From hole in the ground to bare brickwork. From brickwork to plasterboard. From roofless to watertight. It's been a fascinating experience to see it come together the way it has, and this is the icing on the cake.

The kitchen is beautiful – and I'm saying this as a straight bloke who thinks that a wholesome dinner is making sure I eat an apple after my Domino's pizza. The cabinetry and work surfaces stretch along two sides of the room, with the island smack in the middle. To the far left-hand side is a dividing wall that leads to a utility area and downstairs cloakroom. On the right are those patio doors leading to what will eventually be a lovely garden, once we tackle that bit of the project properly. The whole room is light, airy and a very pleasant place to be.

'Gosh,' Hayley remarks.

'Fabulous, isn't it?' Mitchell cries. 'All of my hard work has come to its fruition *marvellously.*'

I see Fred roll his eyes from where he's standing next to the massive range cooker that we've had installed. This, as far as I'm aware, is the first time Mitchell has stepped foot in the kitchen area, so I can understand Fred's attitude. But he's as used to Mitchell's personality quirks as much as we are now, so he doesn't choose to make more of it, thankfully.

'It's lovely,' Hayley says, walking forward and running her hand over one of the gleaming marble work surfaces.

'You see how the sink is positioned just right to be bathed in a warm glow from the skylight?' Mitchell points out. I look up, and have to agree that the skylight in the middle of the raked ceiling does give the whole room a very atmospheric feel.

'Yes, yes. I can see,' Hayley says, still sounding a bit nonplussed. I'm impressed with the renovated kitchen, but she seems completely transported by it. Are those tears I can see forming at the corner of my sister's eyes?

She turns to look pointedly at Fred and the other members of the team who have been working on our farmhouse for the past few months. 'Thank you so much, all of you. This is the kind of kitchen everyone dreams about having. It's wonderful.'

All of them beam back at her with pride. Even Trey, the enormous Barbadian, looks a bit giddy, and as pleased as Punch – and this is a man who normally slouches around the place, exuding Caribbean coolness from every pore.

If he looks pleased, then Baz and Spider look like they're accepting Oscars.

'Glad you like it, girl,' Fred says in his typical matter of fact tone, but I can even see he is delighted by Hayley's reaction.

I step forward. 'Yeah, thanks guys. You've done us proud.'

'Thank yourself, china,' Fred tells me. 'You've been just as much a part of this as the rest of us.'

It's my turn to beam with pride.

Yes, this is indeed getting far too cloying and sentimental, isn't it?

Don't worry, Mitchell is about to bring us all down to earth with a bump.

'Oh good God, no!' he wails.

'What's the bleedin' matter with you?' Fred snaps.

Fred's relationship with Mitchell is what you'd have to describe as fractious. No surprise really, given that one is a flamboyant architect and designer, while the other is a roll-up smoking builder, who couldn't do flamboyant if you threatened to set fire to his flat cap. There's nothing guaranteed to ruin Fred Babidge's good mood more than a visit from Mitchell Hollingsbrooke, which largely consists of him examining every new addition to the house, and tutting loudly when he sees something he doesn't like. Given that Mitchell is actively wailing like a banshee rather than just tutting today, I think we can safely assume that something is very definitely wrong with the kitchen, as far as he's concerned.

'The handles!'

'What about 'em?' Fred asks.

Mitchell regards Fred with disgust. 'They are incongruous!'

'You fucking what?'

'Incongruous, man! They are inharmonious!'

Fred looks at Mischa imploringly. 'Can you translate, love?'

Mischa steps forward. This is usually her role in such circumstances. Mischa is as much Mitchell Hollingsbrooke's translator as she is his design assistant. 'Mr Hollingsbrooke means that the handles on the cabinet doors are wrong.'

'That's exactly what I said!' Mitchell yowls, propping himself up next to the large butler sink.

Fred looks quizzically down at the nearest handle. 'What's wrong with them?'

Mitchell is actually turning red now. 'The scallops, man! The dastardly scallops!'

'What about the bloody scallops?'

'They are too *obtuse*!'

'Eh?'

'Obtuse! Far too obtuse!'

Fred looks at Mischa.

'Mr Hollingsbrooke means the scallops are too flared. They should be smaller.'

And she got that from obtuse? I'm pretty sure obtuse doesn't even mean that. It's got something to do with angles. I've never heard it used in reference to kitchen door handles.

'They're fine, Mitchell,' Hayley butts in, trying to head things off at the pass. 'They look lovely and fit the kitchen perfectly.'

This time the scream that emanates from Mitchell Hollingsbrooke is loud enough to make your ears hurt. 'No! No! Philistines! You are all philistines!' And with that he's storming out of the room, back through into the lounge and towards the front door.

'Well, that went well,' I say, to no one in particular.

'I will go and speak to him,' Mischa says, moving to follow.

'Go with her, captain,' Fred tells me. 'Just in case he starts having a tantrum. I don't want him pulling any of the skirting boards off.'

'Me?' I reply.

He rolls his eyes again. 'Yes, you. Go on. Go help the poor girl.'

Not for a second does Fred Babidge's face betray any ulterior motive to his suggestion, but I know what he's trying to do here. I give him a highly suspicious look that he chooses to ignore completely, and set off in pursuit of Mischa and her boss.

I find them both in the front garden. Mischa is doing her best to calm her employer down, and it looks like it's having the desired effect. I'd feel pretty soothed as well if she used that honey-filled tone of voice with me, but then she could probably scream in my ear from an inch away and I'd enjoy it.

'Everything okay?' I ask.

Mischa smiles and nods. 'Yes indeed. Mr Hollingsbrooke is taking a . . . a more philosophical attitude now to the door-handle error.'

Mitchell regards me gravely. 'I cannot speak of it, though. It pains me too much. I shall retire to the car to collect my thoughts for a moment. You two please stand here and await my return!' He spins smartly on one foot, marching off towards his 2CV, leaving me standing alone with Misch—

Hang on a rosy fucking moment!

I've been stitched up like a kipper!

This entire thing has been for show. Designed to get me alone with the girl of my dreams. They've cooked up the entire thing between them, the sneaky bastards! I bet Hayley was in on it too!

Or am I being just a touch paranoid?

And does it really matter? Whichever way you cut it, I am now completely alone in the front garden with Mischa. What a horrible, horrible predicament.

Once again awkwardness descends. I should just turn and leave, but that wouldn't exactly be very gallant of me, would it? I can't leave her all alone out here in the garden while she waits for her maniacal employer to gather his wits.

'I'm sure he will be alright very soon,' Mischa says.

'Yeah,' I reply.

'He can be a little hard to handle, but his heart is always in the right place,' she adds, obviously feeling the need to defend him.

'Yeah,' I say again.

Mischa twirls a few strands of hair in her hand thoughtfully. 'Though, I cannot help but feel that this may be a little play designed for our benefit,' she says.

'Yeah.'

Oh good grief, I have turned into the Yeah Man – unable to say anything other than 'yeah' over and over again. From now on I will have to communicate with cue cards. Say yeah once for yes, Danny. Say yeah twice for no.

Mischa turns to face me properly. 'Do you like me, Danny?'

No, no, don't say fucking *yeah*!

'You're very nice, yes.'

Woo hoo!

'Then would you like to take me out sometime?'

'Whstfgl?'

'I'm sorry?'

What on earth is going on here? Has she just asked me if I want to go out on a date? That can't be right, can it? This isn't how this is supposed to be. I am meant to act awkwardly around Mischa, and she is meant to either ignore or rebuff me. Then at some point I will decide that she's not worth all the trouble (probably after some kind of embarrassing disaster on my part) and I will move on, having learned a valuable life lesson.

In no realistic scenario does she want to go out on a *date* with me.

I look around, checking to see where the wormhole is that has obviously spat me out into this strange and bizarre parallel universe.

Okay, now Mischa is starting to look worried. For all intents and purposes she's just asked a man out on a date, and he has responded by talking gibberish and staring into empty space. Not the response she was after, I'll warrant. I'd better say something quick before she calls for medical assistance.

'Yes. Yes, I would like to take you out, Mischa.'

Well done, Daniel. It was a slow delivery, but it made sense and you didn't mispronounce anything. We'll take that as a win.

'Great.' Mischa beams. 'You can buy me a drink in the village in a minute if you like.'

Whoa! Whoa!

This is all a little fast, isn't it? They may do things at a breakneck speed in Slovenia, but here in the UK we like to fumble about awkwardly and delay things for no apparent reason!

'Okay?' I hear myself say.

'Okay,' Mischa repeats and smiles, before walking past me and back into the house.

This can't be *actually* happening, surely? I can't have somehow gone from weird single part-time caretaker, to man with date with hot Slovenian girl in the space of a minute, can I?

I see Mitchell coming back down the driveway. He's whistling and looking very pleased with himself.

'I know what's going on here,' I say to him as he passes.

The feigned look of innocence is award-winning. 'I'm afraid I have absolutely no comprehension of what it is you are inferring, Daniel.'

I give him a sly look. 'Of course you don't.'

Back in the house I see the same look of mock innocence on everyone else's face other than Mischa's. This has all been planned, and by looking at my sister, I can see who the bloody ringleader was. It's frankly a surprise that she had time to manufacture a plan to get Mischa and me alone together, given how much time she's invested into finding out more about Grandma's shenanigans in the fifties.

'Alright, Dan?' Hayley says to me with a half-smile on her face.

'Ye-es,' I reply, not wanting to commit myself further.

Fred Babidge tries to suppress his own cheeky grin, and instead turns to Mitchell Hollingsbrooke. 'So, we're all good with the handles then?' he asks the architect.

'Oh my, yes,' Mitchell replies, continuing the charade for no apparent reason.

'So, that's the last big thing finished, then,' Hayley remarks. Unbelievably, I can almost hear a note of disappointment in her voice.

'Yep,' Fred agrees and looks around. 'This has been a tough one, sure enough.' He pats the marble kitchen top. 'But she's come up beautiful, I think.'

'Agreed!' Mitchell Hollingsbrooke exclaims happily.

Fred sniffs. 'Got a little something to celebrate,' he tells us. 'I know there's still a bit of painting left to do, and Sally's lot have to finish the back garden, but the boys and me are more or less finished here, so I reckon it's the appropriate moment for this.'

Fred opens a kitchen cupboard and produces a bottle of champagne and several glasses. I'm totally taken aback. Knowing Fred, I would have expected him to produce a six-pack of John Smith's and packet of pork scratchings. It just goes to show that people can always surprise you. I can't help but flick my eyes over to Mischa as she takes a glass from him.

Fred pours us all a glass of the bubbly. I have to smile as I watch Spider and the rest of the clan look a little uncertainly at their glasses. I have a feeling they would have preferred the six-pack and scratchings.

'To a bloody hard job, bloody well done!' Fred exclaims.

'And a huge thank you to all of you,' Hayley adds, addressing Fred's whole team. 'We really couldn't have done it without you.'

'Cheers, Hayley,' Baz responds, before draining his glass in one swift gulp.

The rest of us take more time over our champagne, savouring the moment a little more. It does feel very strange to be so close to the end of the renovation now. I've spent the last few months never actually believing we'd get to this point, so to arrive here feels almost surreal. Add to that the fact I'm about to take Mischa out for a drink in the little pub down in the village – is it any wonder I feel exceedingly strange right now?

Although, the bubbles in the champagne may have something to do with it.

With the kitchen reveal completed and the celebrations done with, Fred's crew go back to work painting the last of the plasterwork in the dining room and tidying their equipment away. I help them out while Hayley stands chatting with Mitchell and Mischa in the kitchen. It's almost like they can't draw themselves away from the centrepiece of the house. Not much of a surprise, considering how much blood, sweat and tears went into its design.

Eventually, though, it's time for everyone to make tracks, and time for my heart to start hammering out of its chest.

Mitchell drives himself away in the rickety 2CV, Hayley buggers off in her Golf, and Fred and crew speed away in a cloud of exhaust smoke. This leaves Mischa and I with a ten-minute walk down into the village, and that quaint pub.

'Er, shall we?' I ask tentatively and hold out my hand in the direction of the road. It seems that when I am nervous I become a butler.

'Okay.' Mischa smiles and starts to walk off, leaving me to catch up.

As we walk, we chat about the house. I remark on how lovely the kitchen looks, Mischa agrees and tells me all about how much she was a part of choosing the final design.

As we reach the pub we *continue* to chat about Daley Farmhouse. This time the subject is the bathroom, as we wait for the little old lady who runs the place to bring our drinks over.

Then we talk about the garden, and how Sally and her team are doing. Then we discuss the loft, and I scrupulously avoid any mention of shitting into a box. Then we talk about the new roof and how the choice of slates is entirely in keeping with the original aesthetic of the property. Then we talk about the—

Look, you can see a bloody pattern here, can't you?

Our only topic of conversation seems to be Daley *bloody* Farmhouse.

If it's *not* about the farmhouse specifically, it's about building work, interior design and architecture in general.

It's not my fault either; every time I try to steer the conversation to something other than the renovation Mischa steers it right the fuck back again.

'So, what kind of movies do you like?' I ask, taking a leaf out of the *Big Book of First Date Etiquette*.

'I loved *The Dark Knight*,' Mischa responds. 'The architecture of Gotham City was wonderful. It reminded me of a project I worked on with Mitchell last year; an office building in Hounslow.'

'Aha. And what hobbies do you have?'

'I love to draw.'

'Do you?'

'Yes. My architectural plans are getting very good. Did you see the one I did of the farmhouse?'

'I did, yes. Do you have any brothers or sisters?'

'Yes! Two brothers. Neither of them are in the trade, though. One is a lifeguard and the other is an insurance salesman. I am the only one who wants to be an architect. Have I told you about some of the work I did back in Slovenia before coming here?'

And so on, and so forth.

Three *hours* of this go by.

Three whole *hours*.

It doesn't seem to matter that I can't get a word in edgeways, because Mischa can talk for the both of us. That smoky, exotic accent is less appealing when you've heard it non-stop for what feels like a large portion of your natural life on earth. All I can do is sip another cup of coffee and try to think of a way to end the conversation, so I can go home and forget about bloody cornicing and architraves.

Now, were Mischa any less gorgeous, I have to confess that I would have been a bit more blunt about ending the lecture – sorry, *date* – a lot earlier. But we men are simple, crass creatures, and a perky pair of boobs and a dazzling smile will keep us in the game long after we should have thrown in the towel.

But after three and a *half* hours, I'm done. She could look like Wonder Woman in a pair of fishnets and I'd still want to get out of here.

I yawn theatrically as Mischa is regaling me with the story of how she designed the vaulted ceiling of her cousin's tanning salon back in Novo Mesto. 'Wow,' I say, looking at my watch. 'It's eight o'clock! I'm starving!' Then I remember the yawn. 'And also tired. Hungry and tired, that's me.'

'Oh,' Mischa replies. 'Would you like to order some food then?'

Bugger.

I have to head this one off at the pass, otherwise I'll be munching on cod and chips while Mischa tells me about her uncle's brand-new outside toilet with interlocking roof slates.

'Bit strapped for cash right now, Mischa,' I say. 'Maybe some other time?'

'Oh, okay,' she says, looking disappointed.

'I'll just call you a cab, shall I?' I say, trying my hardest to barrel through any awkwardness as quickly as I can.

I reach into my jacket pocket to grab my mobile . . . but no phone is in evidence. I check all my other pockets, but still no sign of the ruddy thing.

'Have you lost your phone?' Mischa asks.

'It looks like it.' Then I remember something. 'Bugger. I left it in the kitchen at the house.'

I'll have to go back to retrieve it, which will mean I'll have to spend more time with Mischa in the farmhouse. Who knows what kinds of mind-numbing information she'll want to impart once we get there?

Still, there's nothing for it. I have to get my phone back. If nothing else I'm on a very tricky level of *Plants vs. Zombies 2* and need to get home to have another go at it.

I pay the bar tab, and lead Mischa quickly away from the pub. Three hours ago the idea of wanting to get away from the beautiful European bombshell would have ludicrous – but now it's a must.

She still manages to tell me about how the roll-top bath is deliberately placed in the bathroom to accentuate the light coming in through the window, no matter how fast I'm walking. It's like being stuck with The Terminator of interior design. She absolutely will not stop until I am dead.

The house is pitch black when we reach it. I unlock the front door quietly. I have no idea why I'm doing it quietly, the place is deserted after all, but there's something about entering a darkened house that makes you move with trepidation for some reason.

Thankfully, it's a clear night, so I'm able to navigate the dining room and kitchen without much trouble thanks to the moonlight. Having said that, I'm so familiar with every nook and cranny of this place now, I could probably work my way around it blindfolded anyway.

Mischa follows me into the kitchen as I hunt for the phone. 'Aha!' I exclaim. 'There it is.' I grab the old iPhone from where it is by the sink and turn around.

Mischa is standing right in front of me. She has a look in her eyes. Yes, *that* look.

'Um . . .' I begin.

'You really like my kitchen, Danny?' Mischa says, running a finger down my chest.

Your kitchen, love? I'm pretty sure my sister and me paid for it, actually.

I don't voice this opinion though, as Mischa's hand is approaching my waistline, and her accent has suddenly become sexy again. 'Yes, it's lovely,' I say, mentally berating myself for my lack of willpower.

'Do you like its curves and shapes?' Mischa asks me.

'Er . . . I guess so?'

'And do you like *my* curves, Danny?'

On much firmer ground here . . .

'I do!' I blurt out.

Mischa leans in and kisses me lightly on the lips.

You know how I've just been saying how boring I found Mischa to be in conversation? How I couldn't wait to get away from her as quickly as possible, before I had to listen to her talk any longer?

Yeah . . . Fuck all that. Libido trumps common sense *every single time.*

I return the kiss and almost gasp in surprise when I feel her hand rub my crotch.

I think this evening is about to take a massive upswing!

Mischa kisses me harder, pushing me back against the marble kitchen top. 'I want you to take me on the island, Danny. I want to feel the cool Bianco Carrara under my body as you fuck me.'

'Come again?'

'The Bianco Carrara, Danny! It's beautiful, isn't it?' Mischa uses the hand that isn't massaging my penis to once again feel the surface of the countertop.

Great. Mischa doesn't so much want to have sex with me, as she does my bloody farmhouse kitchen. If I really want to impress her I should glue some taps to my nipples and install a dishwasher in my arsehole.

'This house used to be place for sex, yes?' Mischa says huskily. 'That's what your sister says.'

'Um, maybe, yeah,' I reply.

'Then have me here, Danny! Take me as the moonlight filters in through the central-pivoting VELUX!'

'You fucking what?'

'The skylight, Danny! Don't you think it's wonderful? I chose it from the broad selection on offer, because it best complemented the rake of the new extension.'

This is actually making her horny. Talking about extension rakes is a sexual thrill for this woman. From the one-sided conversation we've just had I understand how obsessed she is with house design, but this is another thing entirely.

I have no frame of reference here *whatsoever*.

I need a distraction – anything to get me away from Mischa, before she tries to wrap me in wallpaper and take me up the waste-disposal chute.

Luckily, I suddenly hear music wafting down from upstairs.

It's Marvin Gaye's 'Let's Get It On'.

Bloody hellfire! Has Mischa set this whole thing up? Does she intend to use Marvin Gaye's seminal hit as the background music to her seduction? If so, couldn't she think of something more appropriate, given her apparent sexual peccadillos? 'This Ole House' by Shakin' Stevens, for instance?

'What is that music?' Mischa remarks, breaking away from me.

Hmmmm. Looks like she's as clueless as I am.

'I don't know. It's coming from upstairs,' I mutter and walk back out of the kitchen, towards the sounds coming from above.

At the bottom of the stairs, we can both hear the music clearly, along with being able to see a crack of light coming from underneath the nearest bedroom door.

Squatters!

We've got bloody squatters!

'Who is it?' Mischa wonders, looking slightly nervous.

'I don't know,' I reply manfully, 'but they've picked the wrong house to set up shop in!'

I mount the staircase, and start to make my way up to the first floor with Mischa in tow, slightly hiding behind me. I'm pleased to have her along, as if the miscreants turn out to be dangerous, I can just have her bore them to death with the reasons why we chose cedar wood for the bedroom floorboards.

I grasp the master bedroom's door handle, a breath caught in my throat. Best to just fling it open and surprise the bastards. With any luck they'll just bolt as quickly as possible, and I can call the police while I watch them run up the garden path.

'You shouldn't be in my house!' I cry as I push the door open wide. 'This is private prop—'

I am stunned into sudden and complete silence.

On the floor of the bedroom is a large duvet. Beside the duvet are two portable lights casting the room with a soft yellow glow. An iPhone connected to a speaker blasts out the Marvin Gaye, and a small heater sits in the corner of the bedroom, warming the place up nicely.

This is just as well, as on the duvet are two naked people. Both of whom I recognise very easily.

As does Mischa. 'My God!' she exclaims, hand going to her mouth.

I can think of nothing to say myself.

The sight of Baz and Spider completely naked and locked in each other's arms is something guaranteed to steal away any coherent thought.

'Oh fuck!' they both exclaim in unison.

'I'm sorry!' I wail loudly, realising that I've just interrupted what is clearly a very intimate moment. I back away as fast as possible, nearly sending Mischa flying. The sound of the bedroom door slamming can probably be heard in the next county.

'I think we should get out of here!' I spit at Mischa, my face flaming.

The thought that keeps running through my head is that it must have hurt Spider a great deal to get that pirate skull tattooed on his left buttock.

That *glistening* pirate skull.

Oh good God.

I virtually push Mischa back down the stairs as I hear the bedroom door being flung open. Spider and Baz, both mercifully now dressed in boxer shorts, come hurrying down towards us, combined looks of horror and embarrassment on their faces.

'Danny! Hang on!' Spider calls.

No chance, mate. I've just seen you locked *in flagrante delicto* with Baz, and given that both of you could snap me like a fucking twig, I feel it's probably best for my continued health that I leg it away from here as fast as possible. I throw open the front door with a squeal, turning back to see how close our half-naked pursuers are to getting their hands around my throat.

'It ain't what you think!' Baz shouts, seeing my horrified expression. 'We're in love!' he bellows.

This brings me up short. 'Pardon?' I say, turning back from my hasty exit.

Baz looks totally dejected. 'We're in love, Dan. Me and Spider.'

'Are you going to beat me up?' I ask him. This elicits a look of horror from them both.

'Why would we want to do that, Dan?' Spider asks me, a hurt look on his heavily tattooed face. 'You're our mate.'

'Because, because I just saw you . . . saw you . . .' I can't say it. I just *can't*.

Now it's Baz's turn to look hurt. 'And you think we'd beat you up for that?'

I shrug. 'Well, you are both big and strong, and . . .'

Glistening?

'You're probably angry that we burst in on you,' I finish in a small voice.

This seems to remind Baz and Spider that I've just seen them in the early stages of having sex with one another. Baz flushes red in the face. Spider does the same, making his various tattoos look all the more terrifying.

'Are you going to tell anyone?' Baz asks me, looking less like a six-foot muscle-bound builder who's about to pummel me, and more like a small boy who's been caught with his hands in the cookie jar.

'Not . . . Not if you don't want me to, Baz,' I stumble.

'No, please don't,' Spider adds, sounding equally as distressed. 'The boys would hate us.'

I shake my head. 'No, they wouldn't! This is the twenty-first century, lads . . .'

'Doesn't matter, Dan,' Baz says glumly. 'They wouldn't have it, trust me.'

'Nah. Being gay and a builder? Hiding to nothing, that is,' Spider agrees.

I feel this is a good time to assure my two closeted friends that they have nothing to be ashamed of. 'Well, I think it's great,' I say in a strong tone. 'Good for you!'

'Danny, I'm going outside,' Mischa says in a much flatter, colder voice. I notice the way she's looking at Baz and Spider. It's not a look I approve of *at all*.

Mischa strides out of the doorway and marches off up the garden path. Poor Baz and Spider watch her go, looking miserable.

'You see, Dan?' Baz says. 'That's what we'd get from everyone if they knew.'

I open my mouth to argue, but I could see the look on Mischa's face just as well as they could. Slovenia is quite a religious country I believe, so maybe I shouldn't be too surprised by Mischa's reaction to finding out that Baz and Spider are gay.

Instead, I have to ask another question, one that's only just occurred to me now I'm over the shock a bit. 'Er, why are you both here, exactly? You've both got your own places, haven't you?'

'Well, it's romantic here, isn't it?' Spider tells me.

'Is it?'

'Yeah! The place looks beautiful.'

I'm stunned by Spider's choice of language. It seems there's a side to the heavily tattooed builder that only comes out once his deepest, darkest secret is revealed.

'Besides, people might notice if we saw each other where we live,' Baz adds. 'People would *talk.*'

The look of fear on his face actually breaks my heart.

'You're sure you're not going to say anything, aren't you?' Spider mumbles.

I shake my head hard. 'No, of course not. Not if you don't want me to.' I'm acutely aware that we're still standing in the now draughty hallway, with Spider and Baz wearing nothing other than their boxer shorts. 'Look, I'm going to leave, and make sure Mischa gets home. Why don't you guys go back upstairs? By all means stay as long as you want to. I will keep your secret safe.'

The combined looks of gratitude make me a bit uncomfortable. Neither of them should need to be grateful to me for keeping their homosexuality a secret. It shouldn't need to be a secret *at all.*

'Thanks, Dan,' Baz says. 'It is getting a bit cold down here.'

'Alright then, get yourselves back upstairs,' I repeat. 'I'll see you in the morning.'

I go out of the front door and close it carefully behind me, leaving my two friends to hopefully go back to their fun in the bedroom.

The kind of fun I shall resolutely *not* be getting now this evening.

For one thing, I don't think I could get Mischa's engine revving again unless I rubbed a couple of Ikea cabinets up and down against her, and for another, I really didn't like the way she looked at Baz and Spider just a minute ago. I guess she's entitled to her prejudices, but it doesn't mean I have to share them.

I join her at the front gate. We don't exchange many words. It doesn't really feel appropriate.

The both of us stand in uncomfortable silence until the taxi arrives, and I barely summon up enough enthusiasm to give her a peck on the cheek before watching the cab driver take her away.

What a very, very strange day this has been. And what lessons have I learned from it?

Whether it's Mitchell Hollingsbrooke and Fred Babidge scheming to get me and Mischa on a date, the girl in question turning out to be a pub bore, or stumbling on the most unlikely gay partnership in history, people always have the capacity to surprise and shock you.

I turn and look at Daley Farmhouse with a wry grin, thinking about Grandma and her secrets.

My sister and I thought all the shocks and surprises would come from the house itself during the renovation. That's what all the TV shows and websites tell you.

But in reality? A house is just bricks and mortar, and bricks and mortar are pretty predictable when you get right down to it.

It's the people inside you have to watch out for.

HAYLEY

December

£157,819.12 spent

Dear Grandma,

The last time I wrote you a letter like this I was ten, and you were still alive. I can't remember what I wrote, but it probably involved me asking you for sweets. Many, many sweets.

Given how much I've discovered about you in the past few weeks, I felt it best to sit down and put pen to paper once again, even though you are dead, and I stopped eating sweets about a decade ago because of the damage they were doing to my waistline.

If nothing else, I need to get all this down on paper so it's straight in my head. Also, at some point, I'm going to have to explain everything to Dad. Rather than stand there with a flaming-red face as I recount your colourful past to him, I'll just hand him this letter and run for the bloody hills as fast as my legs will carry me.

Oh my, Grandma, what a very colourful past you had!

I can see why you tried your hardest to cover it up. Especially when you married Granddad – a vicar, and man of quite high standing in the local community. Did he know about your previous life? I guess that's a question I can never have answered. At least I managed to uncover the truth about what went on here at Daley Farmhouse all those years ago, thanks to a bit of legwork, sifting through piles of old public documents, the Internet and the willingness of the local pensioners to talk once you've bought them a nice hot cup of tea.

We'll start with your first husband, shall we? He sounds like he was a nice man, by all accounts. James Antony Hayle. A man of means, it appears, given that he owned several properties in the local area, including the very farmhouse you left Danny and I in your will.

You married him in 1950 – and who can blame you? He was a man with a bright future, wasn't he?

Until he invested his money in that hat company, of course. Whatever possessed him to bury so much of his hard-earned cash into a venture like that? Did he have a thing for hats? I guess he must have done, given that most of his liquid assets went into the company he co-owned with Baron Leland Hanson, a man who turned out to be an unscrupulous cad.

Did you try to stop James, Grandma? I bet you did. You always came across as a very level-headed woman to me. I can't see you supporting your husband as he ploughed his money into such a strange venture.

I also know that you wouldn't have said 'I told you so' once when Hanson disappeared two years later with what was left of James's cash. No, I'm sure you would have continued to be supportive, even when James started to drink heavily.

His death must have come as such a massive blow, Grandma. I am so so sorry for everything you must have gone through.

There you were, a widow at the tender age of twenty-five, left with a mountain of debt and no support from anyone. What must that have been like? No money, no husband, no family to help you in your time of need.

The local community didn't seem to care either, did they? They just saw the widow of that madman who owned the silly hat company.

All you were left with was the farmhouse. The only thing to have survived James's folly.

I'd love to know how and why you decided to turn the place into a house of ill repute. Was it your *first* choice? Or was it your *last*? Did you try anything else beforehand? Why didn't you just sell the place and move on with your life?

Again, these are questions I will never have answers to. All I do know is that by 1957 the farmhouse was up and running as an establishment for discerning gentlemen's entertainment. A very successful one, by all accounts. I've spoken to men whose eyes light up when I talk about the farmhouse, and others who run a mile when I mention it.

Did you get on well with PC Chapman? He certainly remembers you and the farmhouse very well. A great source of information he was. All I had to do was keep supplying the garibaldis and smile sweetly at him.

It turns out that while your bordello was indeed illegal, the local constabulary turned a blind eye most of the time, providing you and your clients were very discreet. It came as no surprise when I found out that the area's chief inspector was a regular – sometimes coming over on a weekly basis. I wonder how many times you tied him to that bed and whipped him with that riding crop. It's a mental image I may never get out of my head, no matter how hard I might try.

Where did you find all the girls, Grandma? Did you advertise for them? If so, where? I can't see you sticking an ad in the local newsagent's! My best guess as to how many you had working for you at one time is seven. I couldn't find any of them to talk to – which came as no surprise at all. In fact, I only managed to track one of them down at all, and she slammed her front door in my face as soon as I mentioned your name. Genevieve Hayle is a name that conjures up all sorts of reactions when you mention it. Some of them good, some of them definitely *not* so good.

But there you have it. For a good three years, you kept your head above water running a brothel in the very same farmhouse I've just ploughed a hundred grand into.

I should be ashamed. I really should.

But you know what? I'm not. Not in the *slightest*.

I don't see a seedy woman of ill repute and no morals when I think of you as the madam of the local knocking shop. I may have done before I really started to look into your past, but once I uncovered more information, my impression of you changed for the better.

By all accounts you were a fair, even-handed woman, who treated the girls who worked for you with grace and dignity. You paid them well and gave them a roof over their heads. You seem to handle your clients with strength of character I don't think I could ever have. PC Chapman tells me that you neatly and comprehensively manipulated and controlled every single man with power in the local community to make sure that your business was allowed to thrive, and that your girls were well protected from harm.

You were, in short, something of a local legend. A woman to be respected. One who could make all your fantasies come true if you were nice, and make all your worst nightmares come true if you weren't.

I couldn't be more proud!

So, what happened, Grandma? What would make Genevieve Hayle – madam, businesswoman and local entrepreneur – give it all up for a kind, gracious man in a dog collar?

Again, this is one area of your past I have been unable to find out more about, so I'm just going to have to take a wild stab in the dark and guess that it all came down to *love*.

What else could make you shut the brothel down and leave the life that you had built for yourself so abruptly?

Was it *just* that you fell in love?

Or did things start to go wrong? Did some of those relationships you'd worked so long and hard to maintain begin to break down?

I notice that your favourite chief inspector retired in 1961, and was replaced by a much younger man from London. I'm willing to bet that he wasn't a weekly client of yours, like his predecessor. Without the tacit support of the local police, I can imagine life got very difficult for you and the girls pretty damn quickly.

This is all conjecture on my part, of course. But I'm the type of person who can make an educated guess if I have enough facts at hand – and I think I might just be right about all of this. The same way I was right about renovating the farmhouse. Sometimes you just have to go with your gut.

Any mentions of Genevieve Hayle and her brothel cease in 1961. From then on it was Genevieve Daley, through and through – vicar's wife and pillar of the community.

You reinvented yourself – again. And you buried any mention of your past as thoroughly as you did that trunk in the back garden.

Except you couldn't get rid of the farmhouse, could you? Couldn't let that last reminder of James go.

Maybe you couldn't let go of your exciting life as a madam either! Not completely.

Whatever the reason, you didn't sell the farmhouse. Nor did you try to rent it out to anybody, for reasons best known to yourself. You just left it behind. Left it to slowly rot into the ground, rather than hand it over to somebody else.

I can see you visiting the place over the years, once every so often. A lonely pilgrimage to your long-forgotten exploits in the late fifties. In my mind's eye I see you wandering around the deserted rooms that once held so many secrets, a tear forming at the corner of one eye as you think about your girls and your oldest, dearest clients.

The visits probably stopped as you grew older though, didn't they, Grandma? Time can be a harsh mistress – even if you weren't a harsh one yourself.

Okay, I'm probably being extremely fanciful about most of this, but without firm evidence I'm just going to fill in the blanks with what I *think* happened, no matter how whimsical it might sound.

And so, you fell into a life of domestic bliss with Granddad. Pregnant with my father a year after the marriage, it must have seemed such a lurch for you. Were you bored, at all? I bet you were! Maybe just a little bit? After all, I doubt caring for a baby and attending church every Sunday would compete with all that behind-closed-doors debauchery!

Whatever. I guess none of that is really important any more. What *is* important is that you are the kind of woman who can build not one, not two, but *three* lives for yourself – picking yourself up and 'getting on with it' each and every time. I hope and pray that I have some of that in me too.

Which leads me to my final unanswerable question: is that why you left Danny and me the farmhouse? Did you see your two grand-children lost and directionless, and decide that dropping a derelict ex-brothel on their heads would be the best way to shake them out of their respective ruts?

Because if it was, your plan has worked *spectacularly* well.

Before this project Danny was drifting through life, and was a lazy, stumbling mess. This house has given him purpose, a reason to get out of bed in the morning and go do some proper work.

Do you know what he said to me yesterday?

'Fred's offered me a job, sis. He wants me to come work for him on a build he's starting in the New Year. I'm going to pack it in at the museum and go for it!'

I've never seen him look so happy or so fulfilled. It's not like he's doing it for the money, either. Not if the house sells for what we hope it's going to. No, Danny is going to work for Fred because *it makes him happy*. I never thought I'd see the day!

And as for me?

Those last few months of your life must have been a *real* joy whenever my miserable little face turned up on your doorstep. Did you have to bite your tongue when I moaned and groaned about how Simon had treated me? How he went from the best man in the world to the worst in the space of five short years? I imagine you did, given that you appear to be the kind of woman who would never have taken that kind of rubbish from a man for more than a minute. Little did I know I was pouring my poor, pitiful heart out to a woman who was built of far stronger stuff than I was!

You left me this place to end all that self-pity, didn't you? To give me something constructive to think about, rather than wallowing in misery about the divorce.

I've always had an obsessive personality. You just turned that obsession away from a useless, pathetic little man, and towards a dilapidated house with no roof.

You crafty, clever old woman!

No wonder you ran a money-spinning brothel, and controlled the local police for three years!

(Oh God, I've just had a thought. What the hell is Dad going to say when I tell him that his eight-month cruise around the world was funded by his mother stuffing her knickers into the mouth of a senior police officer? I must remember to ask Gerard along, so he can set up a video camera to capture the look on my parents' faces when I tell them.)

* * *

And as for Gerard O'Keefe, you couldn't have seen *that* one coming, could you?

Maybe you hoped that the renovation would pull me up by my bootstraps, and that maybe I'd earn back enough self-confidence to one day meet another man and start a new relationship. I very much doubt you could have predicted a man like Gerard O'Keefe entering my life, though.

But *oh dear, Grandma*, I'm not sure I'm ready for that yet.

Stronger I may be, thanks to Daley Farmhouse, but I'm afraid that moping, sad little girl who visited you to complain about Simon is still there underneath it all and just waiting to rear her ugly head again.

I'm trying – really, *really* trying – to be as strong as you were, Grandma. To be as fearless as you. But it's hard. A little *too* hard, I think. I look at Gerard and see a kind, thoughtful man. But then Simon was the same when we first met, wasn't he?

It scares me.

Scares me as much as finding yourself alone in a rambling old farmhouse must have scared you.

Can I follow in your footsteps, though? Can I take the plunge and do something that scares me?

I'm deathly afraid that starting my own brothel would be a piece of cake compared to trusting my heart to another man again.

But anyway, the farmhouse is finished now, Grandma.

I did it!

Sorry – *we* did it.

From a ruined bunch of bricks sat in an overgrown field, we have restored Daley Farmhouse to its Victorian glory.

Actually, I'll go a step further than that – I think we've made it *better*. A grander, larger, prettier house than it ever was before. You would be proud if you could see it, I have no doubt.

You'd also want to immediately light some candles and jump in the bath. I know I do every time I walk past it.

It's kind of strange to see everything finished.

I have mixed feelings about it. On the one hand, I feel a tremendous sense of accomplishment, but on the other, I feel a strange sadness that the job is now done.

Maybe that's because we've gone twenty grand over budget and had to max out both our credit cards, but I also think it's because I really don't want to let the place go! I look at all the work we've done, all the beautiful things we've put into the place and I keep picturing myself living there, amongst all that finery. Every time I start to daydream about making breakfast in the kitchen, or drifting off to sleep looking at the stars through the enormous bedroom windows, I have to stop myself before it hurts too much.

Your story doesn't help either. Now I know how important the house was to you, the idea of selling it to a complete stranger fills me with a deep unease. There's so much *history* here. A majority of it X-rated I'll grant you, but it's our *family* history nonetheless.

But what choice do I have? We have to sell the place. There's that mortgage and credit cards to pay off, and I can't just turn down the prospect of dumping a huge lump sum into my bank account.

Why did you have to have such a colourful past, Grandma?

And why do I have to be the kind of person who gets attached to things that she really bloody *shouldn't*?

We had a meeting with our estate agent, Grant, the other day about the best way to sell the place. I thought we'd just sling it on Rightmove and wait for the offers to roll in, but he thinks it's better to sell the house at an auction.

'None of us have any real idea what this place is worth,' he told Danny and I over his large pink tie, as we sat in his office pretending to understand what he was on about. 'We know it'll go for about six hundred thousand, but for all we know it could be worth way more than that. The best way to sell the place is to let the market decide what it's worth. And I'd sell it on-site, rather than at an auction house. It doesn't happen much, but this is a unique property, so let's sell it in a unique way. We can really make it a grand event. Advertise the auction for about two months to build interest, I reckon. That way we should get plenty of potential players on the day.'

'Cost?' I replied. I've been at this game long enough now for that to always be the first thing out of my mouth.

Grant rocked his hand back and forth. 'The auctioneer will want two and a half per cent of the selling price, but you'll stand to make ten to fifteen per cent more on the house in total, I'd say.'

I don't think Danny and I were a hundred per cent sold on the idea, but after discussing it with Fred and Mitchell, we agreed to go ahead with it. It's funny how these two men have become so much more than people we've employed to help us renovate the farmhouse. I value their opinions as much as I value my own, and they both think the auction is a great idea.

'It's a *wondrous* way to encourage the more discerning, and aesthetically astute buyer,' Mitchell said. 'Grant's idea of a jubilant occasion fills me with delightful anticipation.'

'You'll make a fucking packet,' Fred said.

Good enough for me.

The auction date is set for – and I can hardly believe this – 14 February.

'People will remember when it is!' Grant told us. 'And it's a chocolate box kind of place. You never know, if romance is in the air, we might get an even higher price!'

Which is hard to argue with. It still makes me feel a bit uncomfortable though, for some reason.

Gerard was delighted with the date, of course. *Great Locations* wants to come back to film on the day of the auction, and you can just imagine how his eyes lit up when I told him it would be happening on Valentine's Day.

'What a perfect end to the story!' he said happily over the phone from his office in London. 'And with the whole fascinating history of the place, it'll make such great television.'

'Oh no, you're not mentioning my grandmother's past, thank you very much,' I told him.

'What? But it'll make great television!' Gerard repeated, in the tone of a small boy who's just been told he has to come in for his tea and can no longer play in the makeshift fort he's just built with his snotty compatriots.

'I don't care if it's BAFTA-worthy Gerard, I'm not having my grandma's past as a brothel madam revealed on live television! If nothing else, it might damage our chances of selling the bloody house!'

There was a moment of silence on the other end before Gerard reluctantly agreed with me. 'It could throw a spanner in the works, couldn't it?'

'You think so? I can just see Grant showing someone around the bedroom: "And this is the original mantelpiece. I believe they used to tie the clients up right here when they inserted the love beads." I don't think it'd go down too well, do you?'

'No, I guess not.'

Gerard and crew will still be out in force on the day of the auction, though. And he's promised to mention that it's happening in the shows running up to it. That should drum up even more potential business with any luck.

I am both hopeful of getting a good price, and terrified that no one will want to buy it.

Then again, I am terrified of getting a good price, and hopeful that no one will want to buy it.

My emotions are confused, to say the least.

So now the waiting begins.

This is likely to be *excruciating.*

I've spent virtually every minute of every day at Daley Farmhouse for the past few months. How the hell am I supposed to just go back to a normal life now the thing is finished, but knowing it won't be sold until early next year?

It'll be like ending a relationship knowing you still have to see them one more time to swap DVDs and get your clothes back.

I can go back to work a bit early, I guess. I'm sure the headmaster will be delighted to get me back in the classroom, given the horror stories I've had related to me by email about the poor substitute teacher they've had in for me. I just don't think I'm mentally prepared to take on that lot again, though. I now officially have until the start of March off, and I think I'm going to take every last day of it – even if it does mean feeling somewhat aimless until the auction comes around.

Maybe I'll download the Rightmove app to my iPad. There are bound to be some nice fixer-uppers in the local area. I might be able to find something more constructive to do with all that money I'm hopefully going to earn than just dump it in the bank account and watch what the interest rate does.

One way or the other though, Grandma, the story of Daley Farmhouse is going to take another turn come Valentine's Day. Someone else will get to sit in that bath, and look at those stars very soon.

I have to say I envy them so much it almost brings tears to my eyes. Maybe if you were still alive you'd feel much the same way.

That damn house has a way of working its way underneath your skin, doesn't it? That's why you couldn't let go of it all those years ago, and that's why it's going to kill me to have to do it now.

Thank you, Grandma.

Thank you for giving me the chance to rebuild your brothel, and my own life with it.

I think it speaks volumes about how odd my life has become that the last sentence doesn't sound weird to me in the slightest.

God bless,
Hayley

PROPERTY AUCTION NOTICE

Monday, 8 December

Whitlow & Cressida Auction House are pleased to announce a unique opportunity to purchase at auction a newly renovated Victorian cottage in the heart of the Hampshire countryside.

The Daley Farmhouse is a three-bedroom, two-bathroom detached property, sitting on over an acre of land. It has recently been completely modernised, and boasts a brand new extension, bespoke kitchen and bathroom facilities, and brand-new décor throughout.

The garden is landscaped to provide an idyllic backdrop to this wonderful, historic property – close to a tranquil English village, but within easy distance of major transport links.

Auction to take place during a very special event held at the farmhouse on Saturday, 14 February.

To register your interest, please contact Grant Evanshaw at Winters Estate Agents, or call into Whitlow & Cressida's offices.

DANNY

February – Auction Day
£173,765.97 spent

Valentine's Day is usually a day to be feared and dreaded – when you're single, anyway. But I can safely say that I have never been more nervous in the run up to 14 February than I am this year – even when I was eight and made Carla Peterson that card and had to give it to her at her birthday party.

I'm hoping the auction of Daley Farmhouse goes better than that did. Carla looked at the card for a few moments, before yakking up her fifth bowl of jelly and ice cream all over it. My timing was off that day, to say the least.

Thankfully, I won't actually have much to do today. The business of holding the auction is being handled by Grant, our bombastic estate agent and his auctioneer colleague, an equally bombastic woman called Camilla. If the two of them had a baby, the nursing staff would all need cochlea implants after the delivery.

No, all I have to do is turn up, try not to look stupid, and hope and pray that the house sells for the right money.

The right money is *more* money than I can comprehend to be honest. The reserve price on the farmhouse is a cool £600,000. This, to me, is an idiotic amount of money. I'm sure anyone living in London would laugh in my face if I were to tell them that, as it probably buys you a small cardboard box next to the fishmonger's there, but in the sleepy Hampshire countryside, it's a decent price for a three-bedroom detached, even a relatively small one like ours.

If it goes for that kind of cash, I will be rich. Like, proper, proper *well off*. Not rich enough to retire, but certainly rich enough to not have to worry about my finances for a good ten years if I'm careful with it.

The flip side is that if it doesn't sell, Hayley and I will be stuck with a renovated farmhouse, an unpaid mortgage and a load of credit card debt.

This is one of those boom or bust days. The type that can easily lead to a stomach ulcer.

As I peer out of my bedroom window at the overcast weather, I half contemplate rolling over and going back to sleep. Hayley could just text me when the whole ordeal is over, and let me know whether I have to sell one of my kidneys or not. That probably wouldn't go down too well, though. Not least because I would quite literally be the only person not there who has had any involvement in the renovation. Fred and the crew are coming along, as are Sally and her team. Gerard and the BBC are filming the entire debacle, and even my parents, fresh back from their ridiculously long cruise around the world, have decided to turn up to make everyone sick with how tanned they are.

Hayley promised not to tell Dad about his mother's morally grey past – right up until Dad told her he thought that the renovation had aged her a good five years. Then the gloves were off. The expression on Dad's face was priceless when he discovered that his suntan had been funded by extensive and well-managed prostitution. Mum, strangely enough, didn't seem all that surprised by the revelation. 'I always knew there was more to Genevieve than met the eye,' she said. 'She always used to terrify me when I first met your dad, and now I know why.'

Of course Mischa will be there too, right alongside her boss Mitchell.

I'm not quite sure how I feel about that, to be honest. I haven't seen her for the past few weeks. We've been on a few dates in the past two months, mostly consisting of her talking at me again. I took her ice skating because I thought that might end the endless stream of architectural-based anecdotes, but no, even when she's gliding around on ice, Mischa can quite easily bore you with her detailed description of the new health-centre entrance she's working on right now. Ice, you see, looks very similar to the brushed aluminium roof she and Mitchell are designing for the project. I would have skated over my own neck, if it weren't physically impossible.

I really should stop seeing her. I have nothing in common with the girl other than bricks and mortar. I'm also fairly dubious about her attitude to Baz and Spider's romantic involvement. That look on her face disturbs me.

But what can I say? She's the most incredible-looking woman I have ever met, and I am completely in thrall to those looks. I'm hoping that eventually she'll get bored of being boring, and we can move on from the architecture to any other subject of conversation. Next time I go out with her I'm going to ask her what she thinks of Brussel sprouts. If she says they remind her of the chicken coop she built for her Uncle Yuri back in Slovenia I'm walking out, gorgeous looks and perky breasts be damned.

When I arrive at Daley Farmhouse, the place is already alive with people. The auction isn't due to start until 11 a.m., but the house is swarming with prospective buyers as I look at my watch to find it's only 9 o'clock. Grant has certainly done his job in drumming up interest. There must be fifteen to twenty different groups of people here today.

My heart leaps. Surely one of these buggers is going to put a hand in their pocket?

I find Hayley standing with Gerard near where Pete the cameraman is busy filming some of those interested parties as they scour the outside of the house. I hope they're paying careful attention to the pointing.

'Morning,' I say to them both. 'Lovely day for it.'

'Not really.' Hayley looks decidedly unhappy. In fact, I'd go so far as to say she looks royally miserable.

'Cheer up, sis. You're about to become rich!'

'Yeah. Rich.' There is no enthusiasm in her voice whatsoever. I had hoped that as the big day came nearer she might lose some of the attachment she's built up for this place, but nothing could be further from the truth. After the morose conversation I had on the phone with her yesterday, and the expression on her face today, it looks like things have only gotten worse.

Hayley Daley is in love with Daley Farmhouse. This can only end badly.

I suddenly make the decision to stand very close to my sister as the auction starts. There's every chance she'll try to do something to sabotage proceedings, and I need to be there to rugby tackle her to the ground, before she jumps in front of the auctioneer and tells everyone that the house used to be a brothel, and is home to at least three chainsaw-wielding poltergeists.

I see Mum and Dad emerge from the front door, combined looks of admiration on their faces. This fills my heart with a warm glow. For years I've seen my parents look at me with a mixture of disappointment, pity and frustration. Not now, though. Not now they've seen how well I can lay floorboards and paint a ceiling rose.

'This really is a terrific house, kids,' Mum says to us, beaming with pride.

'Yeah, terrific.' Dad's expression is nearly as glum as Hayley's. While he's no doubt proud of our efforts, he's also coming to terms with his mother being a brothel madam. I can imagine he probably wishes he never got off the cruise liner when it docked at Southampton.

'Fred and the lads about?' I ask Hayley.

'Yep. They were in the kitchen last time I saw them. Trey and Weeble couldn't make it, though.'

'Oh, okay. I'll just go and say hi.'

Hayley's eyebrow arches. 'Don't you want to know where Mischa is? She's in the garden with Mitchell. They're both talking to Sally, I think.'

I grit my teeth. 'Thanks,' I tell her thinly. I haven't discussed my misgivings about Mischa with her as yet. It's a conversation I'll need to have shortly – to stop the knowing looks and smug grins, if nothing else.

I have to manoeuvre around about six or seven people as I walk through the house to find Fred. I remember to smile broadly at each and every one of them, as one of them could be the person who lines my pockets in a couple of hours.

Baz and Spider are standing in the kitchen together. When they see me, they unconsciously move slightly further apart. I have to suppress a sigh as I get closer to them.

'Morning, lads,' I say, trying to sound as jovial as possible. 'Where's the boss?'

'Gone for a piss,' Baz tells me. 'How are you doing?'

'Yeah, you nervous?' Spider asks.

'A bit. Big day for all of us. Big day.'

'Yeah. Big day,' Baz parrots.

There's a rather uncomfortable air to this conversation. An awkwardness that surely would not be present had I not stumbled upon them together upstairs. I feel as if I have to say something.

'Are you two . . . you know . . . *okay?*' I stage whisper.

Baz looks sheepish, Spider looks horrified. 'Dunno. Ask him,' Spider says in a frustrated tone, giving Baz a hard look.

'I just ain't sure we can make it work,' Baz attempts to whisper back to Spider out of the corner of his mouth. Baz is not the kind of man who takes naturally to whispering though, given that he is fucking enormous. The whisper carries quite easily across the room. 'If Fred found out, we'd be in real trouble.'

On the one hand, I think it's great that these two look up to Fred as much as they do; on the other, I'm horrified that Baz is so scared of him finding out they're gay that he's willing to end the relationship.

'If Fred found out what, lads?' I hear the head builder say from behind me.

Oh dear.

This could be bad.

'Nuthin', Fred!' Baz exclaims and moves even further away from Spider.

For a moment, for just a fleeting second, I see a look of extreme hurt on Spider's face, before he covers it up with what must be skill born of years of practise.

Fred's eyes narrow. 'Nah. There's something going on here. I can tell. You two have been well skittish around me for the past few weeks.' Fred looks at me. 'Usually when this one is around, as well. What's gone on between the three of you? Come on, I want to know. If Danny's gonna be working for me as well, I can't have any friction with you lads, now can I?'

Oh fuck me. This is my fault.

Baz and Spider have managed to successfully keep their relationship hidden all this time, and here I come, messing the whole thing up for them just with my mere presence. I feel awful.

Fred claps me on the shoulder. 'Is there something you want to say, Dan? It sure looks like it.'

Baz and Spider both look at me in fear. I shake my head emphatically. 'No, Fred. No problem here at all!'

'Bollocks.' He turns back to Baz and Spider. 'Is this something to do with you two being gay?'

Now, you've no doubt experienced stunned silence before. This is something of an entire order above that. This is struck by lightning silence. Hit with a thermo-global nuclear warhead silence. There are caves five miles underground that are noisier than this kitchen right at this moment.

Fred breaks the silence with a chuckle. 'Oh, come on, lads. You really think I don't know? You've both been working for me for seven years.'

Spider now looks like he wants to cry. This is a very disconcerting thing to see, given the tattoos. 'Are you gonna fire us?' he asks in a tiny voice.

'What?' Fred bellows. He then stands between the two of them and puts his arms around both their shoulders. 'Baz, you are the best bloody plasterer I've ever seen in my life, and you, Spider, I wouldn't want anyone else anywhere near my woodwork. I don't care if you're gay or straight. You're my lads, and that's all that matters.'

Oh god, that's *beautiful*. Really, really amazing.

Baz and Spider's expressions change from ones of worry and doubt, to beaming smiles in an instant. 'Cheers, boss,' Baz says gratefully.

'Yeah, you're a diamond,' Spider agrees, his voice tinged with relief.

'Danny?' Baz says, looking at me, his brow furrowed. 'Are you gonna bloody cry?'

'No!' I insist, trying to stop my bottom lip from trembling.

'He is!' Spider remarks. 'He's gonna cry!'

'You big poof!' Baz exclaims.

What?

What?!

Fred looks a tiny bit disgusted. 'Hold it together there, china. There's strangers about.'

I'm speechless.

These are the people I'm going to be *working* with from now on? I don't think my sanity will cope.

Baz moves towards me. 'Give us a hug, you big poofter!' he exclaims with an evil chuckle, and wraps both arms around me in the kind of bear hug you usually associate with professional wrestling. *Bad* professional wrestling.

A few minutes later I'm walking across the near back lawn, trying to get away from Baz's armpits as fast as my legs will carry me. I left the three of them in a highly amused state at my barely concealed emotional outburst. I'll just have to hope that I haven't earned a new nickname today. I don't think I could take being called 'Tiny Tears' for the next decade.

Still, I'm delighted at Fred's attitude towards Baz and Spider. I'll take a little ribbing about my emotions, over seeing two of my friends in distress any day.

I stop dead in my tracks. *My two friends.* That's how I see Baz and Spider now.

Blimey.

I *belong.*

Oh great, here come the waterworks again.

By the time I reach Mitchell and Mischa I've got the bottom lip back to a non-wobbly state. Just about.

'Ah! The man of the hour!' Mitchell cries in florid fashion as I near them.

'Good morning, Daniel,' Mischa says in a pleasant tone. 'The house looks lovely, doesn't it?'

I look back at the place. She's not wrong. Even with the dull grey skies, Daley Farmhouse looks picture perfect. I have to blink the pound signs away as I turn back to them both.

'An extremely good turnout, I'd say!' Mitchell says in a happy voice. He's already been paid for his services, so it's nice to see him come along today, even though he doesn't have anything invested in the house's sale. I guess professional pride must come into it. I'm sure he wants the place to fetch as much money as possible, just to prove how good he is at his job.

I spend the next ten minutes chatting with the architect and his raven-haired assistant. The topics of conversation are mostly about the house, of course. If Mischa's obsession with exterior and interior design is big, then Mitchell Hollingsbrooke's is *colossal*.

Mitchell is insisting I come with him to look at the chimney breasts from a more obtuse angle (he seems to love that word more than any other) when Sally Willingham butts into the conversation to ask the flamboyant architect what he thinks of the new veranda her team have erected over the repaired patio.

I throw her a grateful look as she neatly steers Mitchell around to look at her team's work.

This leaves me with Mischa and her tendency to bore my arse off with her talk of concrete columns and granite flooring. She is wearing a nice tight jumper today though, so maybe I can stave off brain death by staring at her boobs.

Thankfully, something then homes into my field of vision that will give me an excuse to steer the conversation away from building work.

'Look, Mischa!' I exclaim, pointing one finger down to the bottom of the garden. 'It's Pat The Cow!'

I have been extremely neglectful of my bovine friend so far today. Usually Pat The Cow is the first person I visit when I get to the house of a morning.

Yes, I described her as a *person*. Get over it.

Today is an odd day though, what with all the people crawling over the house for the auction and everything, so greeting my rescued milk-producing buddy has slipped my mind. Until now, that is.

'Shall we go down and say hello?' I ask Mischa.

Her face crumples, suggesting that she'd rather not. However, I am already walking off down towards my large, pasture-munching friend, so if she wants to continue telling me how good she is at her job, she's just going to have to follow me.

As I walk down to greet Pat The Cow, I have to marvel at what a good job Sally and her team have done to what was once such a shit tip of a garden. Okay, it won't win awards any time soon, but the grass is level, green and neatly trimmed. The few remaining apple trees have been trimmed so they look tidy and attractive, and all the tumbledown fencing has been replaced by stout, wooden panels that march in a dead straight line all the way down to the copse at the bottom of the huge expanse of garden.

Sally has also done right by Pat The Cow and the local wildlife. She's left a large patch of garden just in front of the copse as a natural wildflower haven. This not only provides Pat The Cow with all the cud she can chew, it also does a big favour to all the local insects and other small creatures that inhabit the area.

'Good morning, Pat The Cow!' I cry in happiness as my masticating chum looks up to see me coming towards her.

'Moo,' she exclaims, giving voice to her unutterable joy at once again clapping those big, watery eyes upon me.

I give Pat The Cow her customary pat on the head, and smile at Mischa. 'Isn't she great?'

Mischa looks like someone's just force-fed her a sweet made of boiled cow piss. 'Ye-es. Lovely.'

Pat The Cow, sensing some reluctance on the part of my stunningly attractive Slovenian date, moves forward to offer Mischa the chance to give her a pat on the head.

Wonderful stuff!

Pat The Cow obviously likes Mischa. And Pat The Cow's opinion is *very* important to me. Never have I met such an astute cheese-producing creature in my life. If Pat The Cow thinks Mischa is a worthy companion for young Daniel Daley, then so must I!

It matters not that the Slovenian is obsessed with her work, and I can even overlook her potential homophobia towards two of my best friends. Neither of these things is insurmountable, in my book. Pat The Cow obviously believes this as well, given how affectionately she approaches Mischa, head held high and ready for that all-important pat.

'Eugh!' Mischa screams. 'Get away from me, you stupid, ugly monster!' she wails, whacking Pat The Cow across the top of the head.

The sky darkens.

The temperature drops ten degrees.

In the trees, the birds sense what is happening, and take flight.

'What did you just do?' I hiss. 'What did you just do to Pat The Cow?'

'Moo,' Pat The Cow says.

You can almost taste the betrayal in her voice, can't you?

'It's so smelly!' Mischa screeches, waving one hand in front of her face. 'Get it away from me, Danny!'

I move next to my bovine companion. 'She is not an *it*,' I tell Mischa, voice dripping with disgust. 'This is Pat The Cow.' I place one hand on Pat The Cow's head, giving it a stroke. As I do, I make up my mind about something. 'And I don't think we should see each other any more, Mischa,' I tell her haughtily.

'What? Why not?' the girl asks, backing away from my cow and me. 'I don't think we have anything in common.'

Now Mischa looks like someone has replaced the boiled piss sweet with a mouthful of fresh cow dung. 'You go to hell!' she orders me. 'You and your stupid, smelly cow!'

'Moo,' Pat The Cow says, the menace dripping from every syllable.

Yes, I know *moo* has only one syllable, but Pat The Cow laughs in the face of your stupid grammatical rules.

'Moo,' Pat The Cow repeats, moving forward, this time with her head down.

'I suggest you go back to the house, Mischa,' I tell the Slovenian. 'Test not the patience of Pat The Cow.'

Mischa gives the cud-chewing heroine one last look of loathing before turning and striding back towards Daley Farmhouse.

I am surprised to find that I feel extremely relieved by this turn of events. Pat The Cow has set me free. She has shown me the error of my ways in continuing to pursue the wrong woman simply because she looks like a catwalk model.

There is no doubt a better woman for me somewhere down the road, but I will not be finding her this day.

Until then, I will just have to be happy as a single man. A single man, who in a few short minutes, may find himself richer and far, far better off.

Yes, someone is going to buy this house. They are going to buy it, move in and—

Oh God, no!

What about Pat The Cow?

Where will Pat The Cow go?!

She'll be *homeless*!

The new owners won't want her around any more, will they? She'll have no home. And we all know what happens to cows with no home, don't we?

I picture the McDonald's logo in my mind's eye, and I really start to panic.

Hayley, I must get to Hayley as quickly as possible!

We can't sell Daley Farmhouse! We must keep it! Pat The Cow needs somewhere to live!

Giving my yoghurt-producing ally a last, hurried pat between the ears, I leave her and rush back towards the house as fast as I can.

Mischa sees me coming, and misinterprets completely. She smiles at me as I come closer. 'Oh Danny, I knew you couldn't—'

'Get out of the way, Mischa!' I bellow at her, barrelling past her and nearly taking her off her feet. 'I must save Pat The Cow!'

Through the house I go, past Baz, Spider and Fred and all those prospective buyers. They don't get a cheery smile from me this time. They want to separate me from my cow goddammit, so they can all go fuck themselves!

Outside by the front door, Gerard is now speaking into a camera being held by Pete. He's obviously recording a piece for *Great Locations* – probably the introduction for the show.

This introduction does not need a full-grown man frantically bursting into shot to ask where his sister is, but it's going to get one anyway.

'She's upstairs, I think. In the bathroom,' Gerard says, looking pretty damn annoyed that he's been interrupted mid-flow. 'What the hell is the matter, Danny?'

'Pat The Cow, Gerard! I must save her!'

'What?'

'Never mind. Thanks!'

I turn and run back into the house, taking the stairs two at a time. I narrowly avoid crashing into a Middle Eastern couple as I reach the first-floor hallway. 'Sorry!' I apologise, swiftly moving past them to find myself in front of the bathroom door.

'Hayley!' I cry, knocking loudly. 'Are you in there?'

'Sod off, Danny!' I hear her say to me from the other side. She's been crying. I can tell from her tone of voice. You don't spend hours on the phone with your sister after she's been dumped by her piece-of-shit husband without getting to know the sound of her voice after she's been crying.

My demeanour and voice instantly soften. There's more afoot here today than my cow.

More ahoof, even.

'Hayles? Are you okay? Why don't you let me in and we can talk?'

There's silence for a moment, before I hear the lock being drawn. I open the door and go in to find my sister, red-faced and blotchy sat on the edge of the roll-top bath, looking miserable as hell.

She looks up at me. 'I want this bath, Danny!' she cries in misery. 'I don't want anyone else to have this bath!'

I don't know what to say.

Yes, I do.

'I have to save Pat The Cow,' I say to my sister, echoing her misery. 'If we sell this house, she'll be made into hamburgers!'

Hayley gets up, comes over to me and throws her arms around my neck. We both start to cry. It's a horrible, horrible scene.

Hayley is distraught at the idea of losing a roll-top bath, and I've just thrown away a potential relationship with a stunning Slovenian girl in favour of a cow.

You see? Property renovation. It's a piece of cake. And it has no effect on you psychologically *whatsoever*.

HAYLEY

February – Auction Day
£173,765.97 spent

I hate you.

Yes, *you*. The man in the expensive sunglasses. Standing over there by *my* living-room mantelpiece, sipping on that glass of champagne that *I've* paid for.

You want my lovely house don't you, you bastard? Yes. That's what you want. You want to take my precious, precious Daley Farmhouse away from me.

Grant says you work in the video-game industry, and you're looking for a place in the country as a retreat from the city. Well you can just piss off back there in your Aston Martin, you Ray-Ban wearing twat. This is my house!

And you can take that bloody Saudi couple with you.

Oh, they might be very friendly, and complimentary about all the work we've done, but Grant says that they're in the property development game, and that they hinted to him they only really want to buy the house for the land that comes with it. Grant says they may have plans to knock Daley Farmhouse down and build some kind of modernist monstrosity on the site.

Evil, evil *bastards*!

And oh look, what a surprise, you've found a friend to talk to, haven't you, Sunglasses Twat? Or should I say another rival? Yes. That's it. Laugh and joke with the nice couple from Essex who are looking to move closer to their eldest daughter. I hope you all choke on your champagne!

'Hayley? Are you alright?' I hear Gerard say to me. 'You've gone bright red, and I think you're about to break the stem of that champagne glass.'

'I'm fine,' I snap back at him, slamming the glass down onto the table beside me.

'I was thinking we could do a piece to camera with you and Danny? Set the scene for the auction?' Gerard asks.

I look at him daggers.

I'm irrationally angry with Gerard right now. If it weren't for his stupid TV show this auction probably wouldn't have anywhere near the attention it has. There would be no Sunglasses Twat or Saudi property murderers for me to hate from across the living room. The beautiful, beautiful living room that the bastards want to knock down and replace with a big stupid glass-and-steel shit palace!

Okay, okay . . .

I probably need to get out of the house for some fresh air. It'll do me the world of good. So far this morning I've gone from sitting on the edge of the bath crying my eyes out, to wishing a slow and painful death on anyone who wants to buy my farmhouse out from under me.

The living room feels very claustrophobic at the moment, which should be impossible, given how huge it is. But introduce an auctioneer's lectern and several rows of plastic seating, and the room fast becomes cloying and very, very hot with all the bodies gathered in it.

I look at my watch. The auction is due to start in just half an hour. My breath catches in my throat.

Definitely time for some fresh air.

'Alright, Gerard, let's go get it over with,' I say in a sullen voice to the TV presenter. I then make my way out of the room, and through the front door. The cold February morning air is extremely nice on my hot, flustered face.

I spot my brother leaning against the wall to my right, chewing on one of his remaining fingernails. While I can't entirely understand the bond he has with that stupid cow, I can fully and completely appreciate his new-found reluctance to sell the farmhouse.

'Danny? Gerard wants us to do a piece to camera,' I tell him, as Gerard goes over to where Pete is filming a few people milling around the window outside the living room.

'Do we have to?' my brother replies darkly.

'We did promise,' I say.

Yes, we did promise. Idiots that we are. We promised to let Gerard feature Daley Farmhouse as much as he liked on his TV show, because it'd help us make more money when we came to sell it.

Idiots!

Blithering, blistering idiots!

'Right,' Gerard says brightly, coming back over to us. 'Pete's setting up just here, so we can have a chat outside the front door. Don't worry, nothing too tricky. I just want your thoughts on the auction, and how, er, *excited* you are to be finally selling the farmhouse.'

'Excited?' I spit in disgust.

Gerard laughs nervously. 'Well, let's just say how *apprehensive* you are about it getting a good price, then.'

I manage to resist the urge to sneer. It's a close-run thing.

Gerard shifts Danny by the shoulders so he's stood in a suitable position, clears his throat a couple of times, and tells Pete to start filming.

'Hello, everyone! And welcome to a very special day!' Gerard tells his audience enthusiastically. 'It's finally arrived – the day of the Daley Farmhouse auction, and I'm sure you're all as eager as I am to know how much this lovely property will fetch today. I'm here with the property's current owners, the two people responsible for renovating it so delightfully. Good morning, Hayley and Danny. How are you feeling today?'

Two grunts.

'Aha, so nervous about what's going to happen at the auction?'

A couple more grunts. We sound and look like a pair of sullen teenagers.

Gerard makes a throat-cutting motion. 'Cut it for a moment, Pete.' He looks back at us both. Rather than being angry, he actually looks quite sympathetic. 'You two really don't want to sell this place, do you?'

I shake my head.

'Pat The Cow,' Danny says in a quiet voice.

Gerard looks to the heavens. 'I knew this would happen. I've seen you both get more and more attached as time has gone by. It happens a lot. Never easy to watch, I can tell you.'

There are tears forming at the corners of my eyes again. I start to feel quite, quite pathetic, but then I look at Danny and he looks like he's about to cry as well. This makes us both pathetic, but we're being pathetic together. I start to feel a fierce sense of sibling solidarity about the whole thing, and put one arm around Danny's shoulder. 'We're not happy, Gerard. We're not happy *at all*.'

Danny looks down the camera's lens and his mouth forms a thin line. 'I don't want to do this,' he says, and walks away, shrugging off my arm.

'Danny!' I call after him.

'Let him go,' Gerard tells me. He then turns to Pete. 'Forget about this, Pete. Go get more covering shots and set up in the living room for the auction.'

Pete, who can read a situation as well as his camera can film it, says nothing more and beetles away as fast as possible.

'Come and sit over on the garden wall with me,' Gerard tells me and makes off for the front left corner of the garden, away from the small groups of people currently wandering around us.

I follow him, knowing full well I'm about to get some kind of motivational speech that I could really do without.

As we near the wall I look down, remembering that this is the spot where they found the bomb. It disturbs me to realise that I'm thinking back on it with fond nostalgia. No one should ever think about the discovery of an explosive device with a sense of fond nostalgia, it's just not good for the soul.

Gerard sits on the wall and bids me join him.

'Do you want to talk about it?' he asks.

'Weren't we just doing that?'

'I mean properly. Without a camera shoved down your throat. Just me and you, away from everyone else. You can be as honest as you like.'

Oops, here come the tears again. 'I don't want to sell it, Gerard! In know I have to, but I want to keep it.'

'Yes, I know you do.'

'Why did I ever agree to get involved with this stupid project? If I'd have known it would end like this . . .'

'You would have done it anyway.'

'Really?'

'Yep. Because you're the type of woman who needs a challenge in life.'

I frown. 'No, I'm not. I'm the type of woman who needs a brand-new extension and roll-top bath in her life.' My brow furrows further. 'My brother is apparently the type of person who needs an unwholesomely intelligent cow in *his* life, but we'll try to gloss over that for the moment, I think.'

Gerard chuckles. 'He does seem very attached, doesn't he?'

'Oh, it's not just the cow. He loves this house too. It's changed him, for the better. He has new friends, a new job and a new life. I . . .'

I trail off. Danny has found a new purpose to life with Fred Babidge's building company, but *my* purpose is about to be wrenched away from me for ever. What the hell am I supposed to do when it's gone? Go back to work in my underpaid and undervalued teaching job? Blow all that money on a round-the-world cruise like Mum and Dad? Invest in the renovation of another property that will just remind me of this one?

I look at Gerard as a tear courses its way down my cheek. 'This place makes me happy, Gerard.'

'I know.'

'My grandma left it to me, because she knew I'd lost my way after Simon. And she was right to do it. This is the happiest I've been in years!' I wail miserably.

Gerard wraps his arms around me. Again, this is a very pleasant experience, despite the current circumstances. This time I can't smell paint thinner either, just the faint aroma of his aftershave. 'There, there,' he says, patting my back.

I pull away slightly. I might as well be completely honest with him. 'And it's maybe about you a little, as well.'

That takes him by surprise. 'What? What do you mean?'

'Well, I wouldn't have met you without this silly bloody house, would I?'

It's Gerard's turn to look a bit emotional. He does it with a lot more grace and style than I can muster. 'No, I suppose not. Do you think there could be something between us, then?' he says in a quiet voice.

Oh, this is very confusing and hard. My emotions are volatile enough at the moment with the impending loss of my farmhouse.

I just don't have enough room in my head for romance. I should never have said anything to him. Maybe, just maybe when all this is over, and I've recovered from the loss, then I can entertain the idea of starting a relationship with this kind, understanding man. Right now, though, I just can't deal with it.

Still, I've opened my big, stupid mouth now, haven't I?

'I don't know Gerard. I'd like to think so. I really do like you, but with all this going on . . .'

'You can't deal with any feelings you might have for me?' he finishes with a rueful smile.

I take his hand. 'Please don't take it the wrong way,' I tell him.

He shakes his head. 'Don't worry. I completely understand. There will be plenty of time for you and me later. Right now you have a house to sell.'

My face darkens again. 'Yes, I do.'

'Just one thing, then.'

'What?'

'Kiss me. Kiss me, then forget about us for the rest of the day.'

How can I refuse that?

I lean forward and finish the kiss that started months ago, just before I discovered my grandmother was a brothel madam.

It was very much worth the wait, I can tell you.

Astoundingly, the kiss also lifts my spirits. The black sense of doom and loss I felt beforehand has changed into one of philosophical grief. I'm about to lose what is obviously my dream house, but maybe I've just gained something equally as valuable in return.

'Thank you, Gerard. You've really helped,' I tell him, as my lips part company from his.

'My pleasure,' he replies with a smile. 'And hey, you never know how the day will end, do you?' He squeezes my shoulder gently. 'Things will be okay, Hayley, I promise.'

What Gerard can't promise is that none of these bastards will bid on the farmhouse once the auction starts.

I stand at the back of the room, Gerard on one side of me, Danny on the other. Our parents are sat in the back row of seats just in front of us, as are Mitchell and Mischa, and Sally Willingham. Fred, Baz and Spider are lolling against the mantelpiece. I can't help but notice that Spider is inspecting the mantel closely, and runs his hand over the top of it, checking for any signs of damage. I'm not the only one who will have problems letting go of this place.

Everyone is in attendance, then. About time we got this over with, don't you think?

'Ladies and gentleman, welcome to today's auction,' Camilla the auctioneer announces, from behind her lectern set just in front of the double doors that lead out onto the patio and Sally's brand-new veranda. 'I'm delighted you could all be here today for this very special occasion – the opportunity to buy this wonderful house. You've had plenty of time to look around, and you all have the detailed pack we've put together for it, so I'm sure you all know just how great a chance this is to own a slice of gorgeous rural England. I'm going to open the bidding at five hundred thousand, and we'll see where we go from there.'

So here it is, the moment of both glory and misery.

I hold my breath.

'Do I hear five hundred thousand from anyone?' Camilla asks the room.

There is silence in return. Sweet, glorious, potentially bankrupting silence.

No one is going to bid! No one wants to buy the house! My grandmother's legacy will be saf—

'Five hundred!'

Bastard!

He's not even taken his ruddy sunglasses off, the twat!

'Thank you, sir. That's five hundred thousand, then. Where should we go next? Can I hear five twenty-five from anyone?'

The male half of the Saudi couple raises his hand. My heart sinks. He's the last person I want to win!

'Excellent, that's five twenty-five to you, sir. Any more?'

'Five fifty.' Sunglasses again.

'Five seventy-five.' Back to the Saudi homewrecker.

Sunglasses doesn't respond. This is good. No, this is *great*. If he doesn't bid again, then the house hasn't reached its reserve and it won't sell today!

'That's five seventy-five with the gentleman in row three. Do I hear any more?'

Camilla once again scans the room.

Still no one puts in another bid.

'That's going once at five seventy-five . . . Going twice . . .'

My heart is singing!

'Six hundred,' says the wife from Essex who wants to be closer to her daughter.

No!

No *no no!*

That's it. The house is sold. It's gone from my clutches!

I hear Danny groan from beside me. I feel his hand take mine.

I will not cry. I will not cry. I will *not* cry.

Gerard's arm goes around my shoulder again. I wish I could say it gives me some comfort.

The bidding continues slowly. It's a very cagey game these potential buyers are playing now. If I was a bit more objective about the whole thing, I might find the psychology of it all fascinating, but I'm not objective in the *slightest*, and just want the whole thing over with as fast as possible.

A tiny voice pipes up to remind me that I have just made a good two hundred thousand pounds in profit before tax, but I frankly don't give a shit. I may do in a few days when I've come to terms with losing Daley Farmhouse, but at the moment I just couldn't care less.

The only other person who shares my worldview right now is my brother. He looks as miserable as I do. Everyone else seems delighted. Mitchell is clapping his hands together, Fred and the boys are beaming with pleasure, Mum and Dad are turning in their chairs and giving us the big thumbs up.

The bidding continues. The pace remains slow, with the price now going up in increments of just a thousand pounds. Sunglasses, Saudi and Close To Her Daughter are swapping bids in succession. No one else seems interested in getting into it with them. This begs the question of why they bothered to turn up in the first place. Grant did warn me that a lot of people just like to turn up to these things for a nose about and a bit of light drama. This would definitely appear to be the case for this auction, as only five people are actively involved in the bidding process, out of a total of twenty-five.

In about ten minutes we reach £633,000. A very nice amount, indeed. The renovation has been absolutely worth all the time, money and effort we've spent on it. Financially, anyway. Emotionally, though?

Yeah, maybe not so much.

'I want to leave,' I whisper to Gerard.

'Not yet,' he whispers back. 'Just see the whole thing out, eh?'

'But why?'

'Please? For me?'

What an extraordinarily strange thing to say. Why would Gerard want me to stay? The house has gone. He has been very kind to me today though, so I guess I can do what he asks. Maybe he wants me to stay because of the TV show. Pete is happily filming proceedings from one side of the lectern and I'm probably in shot. I can't blame Gerard for wanting the ex-owner of the farmhouse to remain in the picture until the auction is over.

Ex-owner.

That's what I am now.

Time for more waterworks.

The bidding stops at £640,000. It's with the Saudi couple. They are going to win, I just know it. The irony will be horrific. Months of work, all down the pan when they roll in their bulldozers. Will I come and watch it happen? Can I put myself through that living hell? Probably. I spent hours sitting at a line of police tape expecting the place to blow up at any minute, after all. I couldn't drag myself away from that, so I doubt I will be able to drag myself away from watching it get demolished.

'So that's six hundred and forty thousand pounds with the gentleman in the third row,' Camilla says. 'No more bids then?' she asks the room, to a completely silent response.

'No more bids?' she repeats.

Oh, just end this, you silly bitch. I need to go and get drunk somewhere.

'Six hundred forty going once . . . Six hundred forty going twice . . .'

The gavel rises. My heart drops. The end is nigh.

'Six hundred and fifty thousand pounds!' a strong voice calls out from right beside me.

I turn to look up at Gerard O'Keefe. He gives me a lopsided smile. 'I said you never know how the day will end, didn't I?' he tells me.

My jaw goes slack. I start to feel my legs shake.

'A new bidder at the back!' Camilla crows triumphantly. She would. She's getting two and a half per cent of whatever the house makes. She looks back at the Saudi man, who is looking quite disgruntled, it has to be said. 'Back with you, sir. Anything further?'

No, you bastard. Just leave it where it is!

He seems to think about it for a moment, then shakes his head. My legs start to shake even more.

'Okay then,' says Camilla, a bit breathless at all the excitement. 'So we're at six fifty. Anyone have any more than six fifty?'

Silence again.

'Very well, that's six fifty going once . . . Six fifty going twice . . .'

Time can be a strange thing, can't it?

The moments can stretch to hours, the hours can stretch to days, and the days to months.

The time it takes for small wooden gavel to fall can feel like an eternity.

The reverse is just as possible, of course . . .

You can spend months renovating an old house, and at the end feel like it's all gone past in the blink of an eye. One moment you're a sad divorcee with no hope for the future, the next you're an experienced property developer about to end your first auction with a successful sale.

Time. We never have enough, and we always have too much.

The only thing you can do is spend it wisely, either way.

BANG!

'Sold to the gentleman at the back of the room!'

A cheer erupts from Fred and the boys, closely followed by a shriek of delight from Mitchell.

Danny looks at Gerard with blank incomprehension for a second. 'Pat The Cow?' he says in a hopeful voice.

'Will always have a home here, Danny, I promise,' Gerard tells him with a smile.

Danny whoops with joy, gives Gerard an enormous hug and starts laughing his head off in sheer, unbridled relief. Once he's disentangled himself he goes over to Fred, Baz and Spider, who all proceed to squeeze the life out of him with a series of bear hugs.

I turn to look at Gerard, who has just finished shaking my father's hand. 'Why?' I ask him, voice flat.

He holds up his hands. 'Look, I'm sorry about this. I know you don't want to think too much about me and you right now, but I'm afraid I may have fallen in love with you, so I kind of had to buy this house, didn't I?'

Oh look. The room appears to be spinning, and I haven't even had anything to drink.

'You're . . . you're *in love* with me?'

'Yep. Have been for months. What can I say? I'm a sucker for a woman who knows her hardwood flooring.'

'You bought the house for *me*?' I ask him, dumbfounded. I'm rather hoping my wits will return to me shortly, but for now all I seem to able to do is make obvious statements in a high-pitched voice.

'I did. I would ask if you like it, but I'm pretty sure I know the answer to that already.'

I start to shake my head. 'I can't accept it, Gerard. It's too much. It's just too, too much.'

He takes my hand. 'You owe me nothing, Hayley,' he tells me, eyes fixed firmly on my tear-stained face. 'This house is yours whether you want me or not. I didn't buy it to win you over. I bought it to make you happy. If I make you happy as well, then that's great, but if you can't be with me because of everything you've been through, then I accept that too.'

My breath catches in my throat.

Slowly, I become aware of the audience that now surrounds

the both of us. Everyone I know and love is watching this little romantic drama unfold in front of their eyes. How utterly, utterly embarrassing.

Oh, what the hell am I saying? Pete is still filming all of this. It's all going to be broadcast on national TV at some stage, so why am I worrying about a few friends, relatives . . . and complete strangers seeing it?

I make a decision. It's quite a bold one for me. I've never been one for big, public displays of affection, but it might be about time to start trying them on for size. After all, I have a grandmother who probably didn't know the meaning of the word embarrassment. I need to start taking after her more.

I point a finger at Gerard. 'You. Outside. Now.' I tell him.

'Why?'

I look at Pete's camera. 'Because I want to give your show the climax it deserves.'

I take Gerard's hand and lead him out of the living room and through the front door. I then walk several paces up the garden path with him. As I do, I am reminded of the first time I stood in this very spot, looking up at the old derelict shell of the house that once stood here, wondering what the hell we were going to do with it.

A house I have now restored.

And a house that has also restored *me*.

Everyone files out of the front door behind us, Pete the cameraman in the lead. I look over to one side to see Pat The Cow amble around the corner from the back garden. She stops and regards me with a look of bovine comprehension that is quite disconcerting.

'Moo,' Pat The Cow says.

I couldn't have put it better myself.

Danny goes over and gives his friend a pat between the ears. Then he looks up at me, smiles and nods.

I look back at Gerard, snake one hand around his neck and stare deep into his eyes. 'You have my house, Gerard, and you have me as well. For better or for worse.'

'Really?' he says, choking up.

'Yep. Now smile for the camera and kiss me, you fool.'

He does, and we do.

It's all rather perfect, to be honest.

Actually, no. Not perfect *just* yet.

That will come later for Gerard and I – and it will involve candles, a fresh bottle of champagne . . . and a roll-top bath.

The End

ACKNOWLEDGEMENTS

A lot of people have helped me write this book. Okay, they haven't actually stood over me with a cattle prod, giving me a quick poke every time I make a spelling mistake, but without them, *Bricking It* would surely not exist. The following can therefore take a figurative bow, if they fancy.

My agent, Jon. The good folks at Amazon Publishing, including Emilie, Sana, Neil and Jenny. Whoever invented Google. My mother, Judy. My sister, Sharon (the real-life Hayley). My friend, Kaz. My consistently patient and beautiful fiancée, Gemma.

Thanks to all of them, for their help and support.

Oh, and you. Yes, *you*. The person sat there reading this list of acknowledgements. I'll probably get it in the neck from those listed above for saying this, but *you* are actually the most important person in this process. Thank you for buying *Bricking It*, and for supporting me. Words cannot express just how grateful I continue to be every time you put your hand in your pocket. You keep doing that, and I'll keep trying to write books like this – agreed?

Nick

ABOUT THE AUTHOR

Nick Spalding is the bestselling author of six novels, two novellas and two memoirs. Nick worked in media and marketing for most of his life before turning his energy to his genre-spanning humorous writing. He lives in the south of England with his fiancée.